Vegas
NERVE

Also by Susan Rogers Cooper

Vegas NERVE

Susan Rogers Cooper

THOMAS DUNNE BOOKS
ST. MARTIN'S MINOTAUR ⚜ NEW YORK

Cooper
Susan
Rogers

This is a work of fiction. All of the characters, organizations, and events portrayed in this novel are either products of the author's imagination or are used fictitiously.

THOMAS DUNNE BOOKS.
An imprint of St. Martin's Press.

www.thomasdunnebooks.com
www.stmartins.com

Design by Gregory Collins

            Library of Congress Cataloging-in-Publication Data
    Cooper, Susan Rogers.
        Vegas nerve/ Susan Rogers Cooper.—1st ed.
            p. cm.
        "Thomas Dunne books."
        "A Sheriff Milt Kovak mystery"—Cover.
        ISBN-13: 978-0-312-35603-3
        ISBN-10: 0-312-35603-X
        1. Kovak, Milton (Fictitious character)—Fiction. 2. Las Vegas (Nev.)—
    Fiction. 3. Sheriffs—Fiction. I. Title.

    PS3553.O6235V43 2007
    813'.54—dc22

                                                        2006052297

First Edition: March 2007

10 9 8 7 6 5 4 3 2 1

In loving memory of *Barbara Burnett Smith,* who could do 101 things in 30 minutes and still think she was slacking. She taught me to give a speech, pack luggage, and buy resale. We read each other's drafts, kept each other's secrets, and laughed together at our adventures.

Barbara Jo, you are sorely missed.

ACKNOWLEDGMENTS

I'd like to thank Rudolfo Alamia, M.D., and Detective Chris Knudson with the Lockhart Police Department. As always, my deepest appreciation to my agent and friend, Vicky Bijur; to the best editor in the business, Ruth Cavin; and to my friend, writer Jan Grape, who always gives a good read.

I'd also like to take this opportunity to thank a few guys I know who, all mashed up, became Milt Kovak: my late father, George Rogers; my late father-in-law, Allen Cooper; my late big brother, Frank Rogers; and my husband, Don Cooper. These are all men I love and respect and who, individually and together, provided me with laughs, tears, exasperation, and some really good Southern sayings. They are and were the best male role models anyone could have.

Vegas
NERVE

Okay," I said, more to myself than Emmett Hopkins, my second-in-command. "There's the monthly report, and there's the keys." I looked around my office, the office of the sheriff of Prophesy County, Oklahoma. "Maybe I should—"

"Milt," Emmett said. "You showed me everything. Now go."

I was on the verge of my first vacation since my honeymoon four years ago, and I was antsy. It wasn't Emmett; he used to be police chief of Longbranch, the county seat of Prophesy County, so he knew what he was doing. I guess I was just hoping he didn't do a better job than me and that, if he did, none of the voters would notice.

"Okay," I said again, taking a long, last look around. "You got everything you need? You know how to reach me?"

"I got your cell phone, Jean's e-mail address, the fax number at the hotel, and, if worse comes to worst, Milt, I can do it the old-fashioned way and just call you up at the hotel."

"Okay, then," I said and shook hands with Emmett, my best guy friend in the world, and hoped he wouldn't try to take my job while I was gone.

"Oh, Milt, wait," Emmett said, digging in his pocket and bringing out a ten. "On black fourteen," he said and grinned.

I was headed out, stopping at Gladys's desk—she's our civilian clerk—giving her some last-minute instructions, when she slipped me a quarter and said, "Any slot will do. I was gonna give it to Maida when her and Burl went, but I didn't get a chance to see her before they took off."

Maida Upshank was Gladys and my cousin-in-common. Me and Gladys were no blood relation, I'm happy to say. Maida was my third or whatever cousin on my mama's side, Maida's daddy's side, and Gladys was a first cousin on Maida's mama's side.

"When'd they go?" I asked.

"Couple a days ago. They're staying with Denise," she said, who I knew was Maida and Burl's youngest child and only daughter. "You got Denise's number?" she said, while jotting it down on a while-you-were-out slip. "You should call 'em while y'all are there."

I took the number offered with no intention of calling, since Maida and me had been only wedding-and-funeral cousins for the last decade, and was headed out the door when it slammed open, almost knocking me down. Harriet Barstow barged in, which was quite a feat considering she was using a walker. By my reckoning, Miz Barstow was in her early eighties. She was wearing a lime green polyester pantsuit, Nike running shoes that had seen better days, and carrying a purse that had to weigh at least ten pounds. She was hunched over her walker and scowling fit to beat the band. Seeing me, she yelled, "Sheriff! I want you to arrest my husband!"

"What seems to be the problem, Miz Barstow?" I asked, guiding her toward one of the benches.

She shoved my arm away and stood her ground. "He's been trying to crawl into my bed! And I just won't have it! You hear me, Sheriff? I won't have it! He's been running around with that Carson woman and I won't have him come climbing back into my bed!"

"Well, Miz Barstow, why don't you have a seat while I look into this?" I said, trying again to usher her toward the bench.

"See that you do, young man," she said, again brushing off my arm but at least taking a seat on the bench.

I left Miz Barstow under Gladys's watchful eye, and went back into my office, sat down, and picked up the phone for my last official call before my vacation. When the lady answered, I said, "Rochelle, this is Milt Kovak. Your mama's here."

"Oh, Lord," Rochelle said. "What now?"

"She wants me to arrest your daddy for crawling into her bed."

"Milt, my daddy's been dead for ten years."

"That I know, Rochelle. If you recall, I did the eulogy."

Rochelle sighed. "I'll come get her as soon as I get the grandkids off to school. Can you hold her for a few minutes?"

"Sure, but don't be too long."

"Or you could just lock her up," Rochelle suggested.

I laughed. "Don't think that would be exactly constitutional."

"Who'd she say he's been messing with this time?" Rochelle asked.

" 'That Carson woman' is the quote."

"The only Carson woman I know is that one on the local news."

"Don't think she's your daddy's type?" I asked.

"My daddy never looked cross-eyed at another woman in his whole married life, Milt."

"That I know, Rochelle."

"You know, Mama's gonna kill me one of these days. She's gonna blurt out something awful during church or something and I'll drop dead of a heart attack," Rochelle said.

"We all got our crosses to bear, Rochelle," I said.

"Well, Milt, there are crosses to bear—and then there's my mama."

"I see your point," I said.

Rochelle sighed. "I'll pick her up in a few minutes."

I left Miz Barstow sitting on the bench giving Gladys what-for, and headed home to my house on the mountain I share with my wife and son.

See, here's the deal. My wife, Jean McDonnell, Dr. Jean McDonnell, is a psychiatrist, and a good one to boot. She'd been asked to speak at this year's neuropsychiatric something-or-other convention, which was being held in Las Vegas, and had invited me to go with her. She invited me to go with her last year, too, but it was held in Houston, and that just wasn't much of a pull. I've been to Houston and the best thing about it was seeing it in the rearview mirror.

But Las Vegas? Sin City? Oh yeah, honey, I'd be happy to join you there.

We'd made arrangements weeks in advance with my sister Jewel Anne to take care of Johnny Mac for the three days we'd be gone, so that was all settled. We went to bed that night, Jean probably going over her speech in her head, me thinking about how much "mad" money I could blow.

First Thursday ◆ Prophesy County

Emmett Hopkins walked in the front door of his apartment that evening after work, and for some reason saw it for the first time. It was Jasmine made him notice it. He'd thought about inviting her over. But how could he do that? He looked at the place. He'd given away all his furniture when he'd moved out of the house he'd shared with Shirley Beth for so many years. With her dead, with her blood and brains all over the dining room, no way he'd ever go back there. No way he'd ever want anything out of that house. So here was the apartment, complete with rented furniture. A cheap Scandinavian knockoff sofa, a rickety coffee table, and an easy chair that wasn't very easy on his back—he could say that for sure. A pine dinette and matching chairs. And he wouldn't even think about the bedroom. A single bed, a press wood chest of drawers, and a living room end table doing duty as a bedside table. That was it. And he didn't own any of it. How could he ask a woman to come into this?

Jasmine had flirted with him some a while back, but he hadn't responded, didn't remember how. So he'd blown that opportunity. But this afternoon, after Milt left, she'd smiled at him. Jasmine didn't smile a lot, so he knew that she meant it. The smile was for him.

Jasmine came with a lot of baggage, he knew that. Just like he had baggage. They were the walking wounded, except maybe he was a little more wounded than she was. Hell, he was the walking dead.

Maybe he wouldn't invite her over, Emmett thought, but that didn't mean he couldn't invite her out. Take her to the Longbranch Inn for dinner. No, people would see them. Maybe to Bishop. They had that nice Mexican restaurant in Bishop. But Bishop was still in the county, and people would know them there. Maybe take her out of the county? Maybe to Tejas County? Surely they had restaurants there.

But so what if people saw them together? They were both single now, unattached. But the rumors. Oh, yeah, he thought, there'd be rumors. Prophesy County would have them married in two shakes of a lamb's tail.

He went into the kitchen and opened the refrigerator. Nothing much in there. Four beers left from a six-pack of Bud Lite, some cold cuts, and one of those bags of salad he bought last week on a whim. Why, he didn't know. Never could abide salad. He took out one of the beers and took it with him back into the living room. Turned on the TV. Maybe he should get a cat, he thought. Milt had a cat. Then Emmett remembered he didn't like cats. Maybe a dog, he thought. Then he thought a dog would be too much responsibility.

Hell, asking Jasmine out was too much responsibility. What if they hit it off? What then? He'd have to ask her out again. Then what if he slept with her? Shit, he couldn't imagine that happening. He tried to remember the last time he had sex, and couldn't. Shirley Beth had had her problem for so long, sex just wasn't a part of their life those last, long years.

He turned the TV to ESPN and found something that wasn't golf and wasn't soccer. That's all he really asked for out of life these days.

FIRST FRIDAY ✦ PROPHESY COUNTY

Emmett was standing at Gladys's desk when Jasmine walked in through the back door in her street clothes. He liked looking at her. She wasn't supermodel pretty, but she fit him. She had a big butt, and he liked that. She was shaped sort of like an avocado—big on the bottom, small on top. And she had freckles. He liked that, too. A good smile, when she used it, which wasn't often. Shiny brown hair, pulled back in one of those french braids.

He said "hi," and she said "hi." Now was the time to do it if he was going to, he thought. Gladys was in the ladies' room. So do it. Nobody around. Just do it.

Jasmine said, "Well, I better get in the locker room and change," and turned to do so.

"Hey, Jasmine," Emmett said.

She turned and looked at him, a small smile on her face. "Yeah, Emmett?"

"Ah, there's a new Chinese restaurant over in Tejas County. Thought about trying it out tonight." He'd looked that up—the Chinese restaurant. Wasn't really sure if it was new, but it was new to him. He swallowed. Way too much spit in his mouth. "Ah, you wanna come?" he finally got out.

She smiled big this time. Teeth and all. She had a little overbite, just like that actress he and his daddy had both liked—Gene Tierney. He liked that. "Sure," she said. "That sounds good. Haven't had Chinese in a long time."

"So, ah, meet you here after work? Take my truck. Bring you back here?"

She turned toward the locker room again, but over her shoulder she smiled at him and said, "Sounds like a plan."

FIRST FRIDAY ✦ LAS VEGAS

It was mid-September and the temperatures in our part of Oklahoma had finally begun to drop a little—mid-eighties during the day, mid-sixties at night, if it wasn't raining—cooler then if it was.

Leaving the airport in Las Vegas, though, it seemed we'd stepped back a couple of months. It was hotter than Hades. And dry. And when people say these desert areas are hot, but it's a dry heat (like that's a good thing), I'd like to mention that an oven is dry heat also. I could barely breathe between the doors of the airport and the air-conditioned mini-bus to our hotel.

I hadn't really paid much attention to where the convention was being held—I left all those details up to Jean; after all, it was her business. But I was a little taken aback when the taxi pulled up in front of the hotel—the Lonestar. In a city built on gaudy, this one stood out. There was a replica of the Texas State Fair's Big Tex, a huge guy in a cowboy hat and boots, in front of the portico. This Big Tex was about twice the size of the one in Dallas, and that one's pretty damn big. There was a huge star on the top of the hotel and hay bales lined the drive that circled up to the front door and back out to the street. I thought I might puke, but decided to keep that to myself.

"Oh, how cute," my wife said. It takes all kinds, I thought.

As we got out of the taxi and the driver handed our gear over to the attendant, the attendant said to me and Jean, "Howdy, pardners, welcome to Texas."

I didn't hit him. I think that showed what a mature and restrained fella I am.

Three things assaulted my senses when I walked in the front doors of the Lonestar: the overpowering smell of roses mixed with cigarette smoke, the sound of the bells and whistles of slot machines, and the sight of more Texas crap than I'd seen on any trip to that actual state.

Okay, I have a problem with Texas. They act like Oklahoma is their retarded third cousin. They make jokes about us, even when OU beats UT, repeatedly. Like they have something to joke about. Everything's bigger and better in Texas. Well, I beg to differ. And here I was stuck in a place that was gonna just plain rub Texas in my face.

Jean and I followed the bellhop to the check-in desk, which was designed to look like a Western bar, with a brass foot rail and brass spittoons at intervals. All the poor people working behind the counter were dressed in cowboy outfits, and looked just plain silly and some of 'em a little pissed off.

Our room was on the nineteenth floor and I unpacked

while Jean went down to the mezzanine to register for the convention.

After I'd unpacked, in my fashion (I opened the suitcases and hung up the dress Jean was gonna wear for her speech and put my Dop kit in the bathroom), I called Jean on her cell phone and left a message, saying I'd be in the casino, then went down to the slots. I took out the quarter Gladys had given me—I knew which one it was because she'd put her initials on it—and stuck it in a slot and got three cherries. Thinking she'd probably want to reinvest part of it, I took another quarter and stuck it in, but got nothing. So I figured Gladys did all right, getting fifty cents over her twenty-five-cent investment.

I wandered over to the roulette tables, but there was nothing much going on, so I took a walk around the hotel, seeing what kind of restaurants they had. The first one I found was called "Chicken Fried's" and they had the menu posted. And it lived up to its name: everything from chicken fried steak to chicken fried ice cream, with chicken fried vegetables thrown in for the health conscious, I suppose. The next restaurant I found was called "Maria's TexMex," and the posted menu lived up to its name, too. I hate to admit it but reading all this stuff was making me real hungry. Jean had had me on a low-carb, high-protein diet for about two years, which probably would have made me lose weight if I didn't eat my lunch every day at the Longbranch Inn, which has the best chicken fried steak in Oklahoma *or* Texas. But that's another story, and one we won't tell Jean about, okay?

I decided to head up to the mezzanine where I saw some shops, but when I got there I saw my wife talking to someone and just stopped and watched her. I like to do that, watch her when she doesn't know I am. I guess that would be stalkerish if I wasn't married to her, but I like looking at my wife, and that's not a bad thing.

She's as tall as me, about five-ten, and she's not skinny. She's not fat, either, just a nice, big woman. She's got dark brown hair peppered with silver—a lot more of the pepper since Johnny Mac entered our lives—and the greenest eyes you ever saw. She's got a scattering of freckles on her nose and cheeks, and a smile that'll make you catch your breath. She's got large breasts, a small waist, perfect hips, and she probably would have had real shapely legs if it hadn't been for the polio she contracted as a baby. Her mother had refused to get any of her kids vaccinated when the Salk vaccine came out; all of 'em made it okay except Jean. She's been on crutches and leg braces her whole life. But since she's been doing that since she could walk, the lady can move faster than most people. The only time she had a real problem was late in her pregnancy, when her belly got so big she lost her equilibrium and had to take to a wheelchair for the last two months.

She finished her conversation with the man and turned, seeing me. She smiled and I smiled back. When we got to each other, she said, "I don't have anything until the opening ceremonies tonight. They're serving dinner, you want to come?"

I thought about the rubber chicken and limp vegetables they usually serve at convention dinners, then thought about Chicken Fried's and Maria's TexMex. I thought about all the speeches that would come with dinner (Jean's not being one of them) and the lure of the slots and the roulette wheel. Then I put on my best hangdog expression.

"Honey, I'd really like to, but I didn't bring the right clothes."

"You brought something to wear when I give my speech, didn't you?"

"Well, of course, but you don't want me to wear that twice, do you?" I figured, being a woman, Jean could respect that.

She grinned. "Honey, you are so full of shit." She leaned over and kissed me. "Go ahead and ruin your diet, but don't lose too much money, okay?"

I grinned back and patted her cheek. "You're a good wife," I said.

Then we both headed downstairs to see what all the fuss was about Vegas.

What can I say? It was bright, it was loud, and, in the right frame of mind, I suppose it could be fun. Jean and me played the quarter slots and I got less enchanted with the place as my paper cup of quarters began to dwindle. Then Jean, who had moved down three stools from me, let out a very uncharacteristic whoop, and I ran to her side.

"I won three hundred dollars!" she cried, grabbing me by the lapels of my blue jean jacket. "Three hundred dollars!" she shouted.

"That's great, honey," I said. "We can pay a bill with it."

My ultra-practical wife said, "Are you out of your mind? Let's go shopping!"

I'm not much of a shopper, but it didn't take long to blow three hundred bucks in a Las Vegas hotel. She bought a Little Lord Fauntleroy-looking outfit for Johnny Mac—that I swear he'll never wear, not if I can help it—and a very small, very black, very see-through teddy for herself. That I swore she'd wear in about five minutes, if I had my way about it. Then she decided to buy something for me.

"Honey," I said, looking at the teddy, "you already did."

She had a few bucks left and insisted that I deserved a treat—I kept mentioning the elevator to our room as a way of getting my treat, but she ignored me. I ended up buying a Swiss Army knife I didn't need, spending about three times what I would have paid for it at my local army-navy store. Finally I got her on the elevator.

Just let me say that my wife looked real good in that teddy. We had three hours before her evening meeting/dinner was to start, and we put that teddy to real good use.

It had gone okay, the dinner. Emmett was surprised he talked so much. Didn't know he had that much to say. But she was a good listener, and when she talked she was funny. He liked that. And she had good table manners. Shirley Beth had always been real big on table manners, so his were pretty good, too.

They got back in his pickup and headed home to Longbranch. It would be okay. Since he was taking her back to her car at the sheriff's office, he didn't have to worry about her inviting him into her place, or having to invite her into his. This had been pretty easy, he thought. Hell, it was like riding a bicycle.

He pulled his pickup next to her little Mazda in the parking lot.

"Well, Jasmine, glad you went with me. I had a good time," he said.

"Thanks for inviting me," she said.

He took a deep breath. "Maybe we can do this again sometime," he said.

She nodded but didn't look at him. Emmett had his hand on the door handle, ready to get out of the pickup and walk around to let Jasmine out, when he realized she was kissing him. Her lips were on his and his body was reacting before his mind fully knew what was going on. He put his hands on her waist, kissing her back, hard, then harder. His hands found that great ass, kneading it like his mama used to knead bread dough. He wanted to touch her skin, but shied away from it. Too much, he thought. This is good. This is real good. But then Jasmine pulled away, but instead of saying something like, "We shouldn't be doing this," or something else similar, she was unbuttoning her blouse.

She took his hand, his left one he thought later, and touched it to the swelling of her breasts above the bra.

His voice was husky when he said to her, "It's been a real long time."

"For me, too," she said. Her hands went to his belt, and he forgot about saying anything else.

First Saturday ✦ Las Vegas

By the nightstand clock, it was 2:30 A.M. when the phone rang. I immediately wondered where the car wreck was before I realized I wasn't at home. I picked up and said, "Hello?"

"Milt?" came a female voice.

"Who's this?" I asked.

"It's Maida. Maida Upshank," she said.

Maida Upshank was my third or whatever cousin, and I vaguely remembered Gladys, my civilian clerk, saying that she and her husband Burl were in Las Vegas. But if this was a social call, it was a pretty damned unsociable hour.

"Yeah, Maida, hey, what's up?" I asked.

"I'm real sorry to bother you on vacation, Milt, but I called Gladys to tell her what's going on and she told me you were here. I really need your help." She sighed deep and long, then said, "Burl's been arrested," and started to cry.

Now *that* took me by surprise. Burl was Maida's husband and I'd known him most of my life and he was definitely the law-abiding type. Burl had been a few years ahead of me in high school and the best defensive lineman the school had ever seen. So good, in fact, that he got a full scholarship to OU and did real good up there. Would have made pro for sure if he hadn't blown his knee his senior year.

He graduated OU still on crutches, came home and married his high school sweetheart, my second or whatever cousin Maida Leroy, and settled down to run his father-in-law's insurance agency. After the old man died, Burl changed the name and expanded, and now there's an Upshank Insurance Agency in every small town in our part of Oklahoma.

The last time I'd seen Burl and Maida had been at their youngest daughter's wedding about two years ago. My boy Johnny Mac had been barely a year old then and made a real nuisance of himself, kicking the back of the pews during the ceremony, and trying to run wild at the reception, although he was real cute doing it.

I wondered if Burl had stiffed a casino or something. I figured they must take that pretty seriously.

I sat up in bed and put my feet on the floor. "Now try and calm down, Maida. Tell me, what's Burl been arrested for?"

"Assault and battery," she got out.

I figured if Burl wanted to assault somebody, they'd be pretty damned assaulted, what with Burl's size and all, even if he was well over sixty. The boy had kept in shape. I doubted he'd kicked anybody's teeth out with his right leg, but other than that, I figured he could do some damage. The only thing was, Burl Upshank was a teddy bear.

"Who's Burl supposed to've assaulted?" I asked.

"Our son-in-law, Larry," she said, gulping air and trying not to cry.

"And he's pressing charges?" I asked. Back in Prophesy County we tried to keep that kinda domestic squabble indoors. You know, mano-a-mano. Though when it came to mano-a-womano, I tended to get involved.

"Milt, can you come down here? I just don't know what to do!" Maida said, and started crying again.

Now that got me. Maida's the mother of six and a pretty down-to-earth woman. She and Burl live on a ranch, and I knew her to be able to diaper a baby, birth a calf, and have a full meal on the table, almost simultaneously. Having five boys before the birth of her last child, finally getting the little girl she wanted, I knew her to deal with bloody noses, broken bones, and drunken teenagers without a qualm. Crying just wasn't in Maida's makeup. But here she was, bawling her eyes out.

"Tell me where you are, Maida, and I'll be right there," I said.

"Just a minute. Talk to this man," she said, and handed the phone over.

"Ah, Sheriff?" a young male voice said, sounding pretty unsure of himself. "This is Detective Jimmy Broderick, Las Vegas PD. I'll have a squad car pick you up in front of your hotel, sir, if that's okay with you. Twenty minutes?"

"That's fine," I said. I told him where we were staying and hung up.

I got dressed, explaining to my wife where I was going and why, and went down to the front of the hotel. The lobby was still hopping, the bells and whistles of the slots still going strong, the smell of roses and cigarette smoke still hung in the air like a rain cloud about to explode, and the Texas crap didn't look any better at two in the morning than it had at three in the afternoon.

DETECTIVE JIMMY BRODERICK was down a long hall in a large room full of cubbyholes. He stood up to greet me and we introduced ourselves. He was sorta what I expected: looked a lot like Dalton Pettigrew, my stupidest (okay, least bright) deputy, except he wasn't quite so dull around the edges. He was dull, all right, just not as dull as Dalton. I'd always hoped Dalton was a one-of-a-kind; the world couldn't handle more than that.

Detective Broderick was at least six foot four, weighing in at about two-fifty to two-seventy-five, and his overly large head sported a bristly blond crew cut with military sides. He grinned when he introduced himself, showing a lopsided smile with crooked teeth that Jean woulda called "charming." I thought it just made him look stupider, but then what do I know?

"Hey, Sheriff," he said, shaking my hand until I figured I'd never play the violin again (which I never did before, either, but there you go). "You made good time from the hotel I see."

"Seeing as how it's three in the morning, I woulda expected better," I said.

Broderick grinned. "Yes, sir, but this is Las Vegas. We never sleep."

"Where's Mrs. Upshank?" I asked, having looked around and not seen my third or whatever cousin.

"She's in the ladies' room, sir, but she should be right out. You wanna have a seat, let me tell you what's going on?" Broderick said, indicating the chair next to his desk.

I sat and said, "I would like to know what's going on, yeah."

"Well, sir, seems Mr. Upshank assaulted his son-in-law."

I glared at the Dalton-like creature in front of me. "I got that much from Maida. Is the kid alive?"

"Oh, yes, sir," Broderick said.

"Then what's the problem?"

"Well, Larry Allen's daddy is Walter Allen," the kid said, saying it like I was supposed to know who that was. Then I remembered some wedding gossip about the groom's daddy being some bigwig in Las Vegas.

"And?" I asked, urging him on. It was after three in the morning, and I didn't care that it was Las Vegas, I needed my shut-eye.

"Well, Mr. Allen's pressing charges. Or having his son do it, I guess."

"Mr. Allen got a lawyer?"

"Oh, yes, of course. One of the best in Vegas."

"Well, I know Burl's got a lawyer, so why don't we get those two together, let 'em charge too much, and work this out? No reason for Burl to be locked up."

Broderick sighed long and hard. "Well, sir, Mr. Allen's definitely pressing charges. He keeps saying he wants Mr. Upshank hung, but we don't do that anymore."

Maida came back from the ladies' room, her eyes still red, but dry. I stood up and hugged her. "How you holding up?" I asked.

She smiled weakly. "By my fingernails," she said.

"Why don't we go into one of the interrogation rooms?" Broderick suggested. "More chairs in there."

We followed him down the hall and into a room that was far nastier than any we had in Prophesy County. There was a table, all scratched up with graffiti, three whole chairs and a fourth leaning up against a wall with one leg missing. There were marks on the wall, scratches in the faded paint, and scrubbed stains that looked like something had been removed. I was thinking blood.

As we came in the room, I asked the detective, "Do you mind if I talk to Mrs. Upshank alone for a minute?"

"No, sir, of course not," he said, heading back out the door.

"Detective," I called.

He turned around. "Yes, sir?"

I nodded at the two-way mirror against one wall, behind which I knew was an observation room with speakers plugged into the interrogation room. "I mean really alone," I said.

"No problem, sir," he said, flipping a switch on the wall that turned off the speaker.

Once Maida and I were seated in what I hoped was complete privacy, I said, "Tell me what happened."

Maida sighed and started her story. Seems she and Burl

came to Vegas the week before to visit their daughter and the casinos, not necessarily in that order. They'd been out last night and when they came home, they found their daughter Denise curled up on the couch crying and nursing a black eye and a busted lip. Her husband Larry stood over her, drunk as a hoot owl, shaking his fist. The fact that Denise was eight months pregnant only made Burl that much more incensed.

"Burl just went crazy, Milt. He grabbed Larry and threw him up against the wall and started hitting him. Denise was screaming, I was screaming . . ." The tears started again and she grabbed a Kleenex and blew her nose. She smiled slightly. "I'm sorry. This whole thing has been horrible."

I patted her hand. "I can only imagine, Maida. I'm so sorry. Is Denise okay?"

She shook her head, the tears starting up again. "She's in the hospital. He kicked her in the stomach, Milt!" She broke down in sobs. "I should be there with her, not here! That's why you had to come! It's God's own miracle you were here!"

She was sitting across from me, so I got up and walked around the table, knelt down beside her, and put my arms around her. She latched on and I let her bawl. Sometimes that's all you can do, and sometimes it even helps a little.

I WAS PISSED off. I got up from Maida and went to the door, outside of which Detective Broderick was hovering. "Detective," I said, "why don't you come back inside."

He came in and I said, "Is Larry Allen under arrest?"

"Ah, no, sir," the detective said, obviously embarrassed.

"Why not?"

"Ah, well, Mrs. Allen hasn't pressed charges."

That wasn't all that surprising. She probably had other

things on her mind, like trying to keep her baby alive. The bastard.

"Okay," I said, "two things are gonna happen. Right now. You're gonna get a patrolman to escort Mrs. Upshank to the hospital to be with her daughter, and then you're gonna get Burl, Mr. Upshank, in here pronto. I want him released under my recognizance."

"Ah, well, Sheriff, see, yeah, I can get Mrs. Upshank to the hospital, no problem, but releasing Mr. Upshank . . ."

"Get Mrs. Upshank out of here now, then get whoever's in charge in here to see me. And I want to see Burl immediately." I turned to Maida, who was still sitting in the chair, sobbing quietly. "Maida, honey, you go on to the hospital and be with Denise. I'll take care of everything here. And I'll have Jean get y'all a room at our hotel."

I helped her up and Broderick went for a patrolman, who turned out to be a patrolwoman, who guided Maida out of the bullpen.

"So?" I asked. "Who's in charge?"

"Ah, that would be my lieutenant," Broderick said.

"You gonna get him?"

"Ah, yeah, I mean yes, sir. Just wait here."

Broderick finally came back and escorted me down the hall to the glass-walled office of Lieutenant Mac Grayson. He was about my height, a few years younger, had a lot less hair, and a few more pounds. His handshake was firm without being painful, and his demeanor was friendly.

"Sorry about this mess, Sheriff," the lieutenant said. "I have a daughter Mrs. Allen's age, and I can't say I'd've done any different than Mr. Upshank."

"I'm glad you see it that way, Lieutenant," I said. "The thing is, I'd like Burl released under my recognizance. What with me being a law enforcement officer myself, I think I can be trusted to keep him in town."

"Well, now, Sheriff, I'd have to wake up a judge to do that right now. Think it can wait until morning?"

"I'd rather not. Burl isn't getting any younger, and he has

some health problems, you know." I had no idea if Burl had health problems or not, but I thought it couldn't hurt to say so. "Being locked up with the general population couldn't be healthy for him."

The lieutenant laughed. "Oh, he's not locked up with the general population, Sheriff. We were a little afraid for their safety. Mr. Upshank was swinging at everybody when we brought him in, so we put him in isolation."

"High blood pressure," I made up. "This whole thing can't be good on his blood pressure. I really need to get him released and to a doctor, Lieutenant."

Grayson turned to Jimmy Broderick who was standing at semi-attention by the closed door. "Jimmy, call Judge Maynard. He's an insomniac. Probably still up. If he is, get the paperwork over to him."

"Yes, sir," Broderick said and hightailed it out of the room.

I stood up. "Thanks, Lieutenant."

"Call me Mac," he said, standing to shake my hand.

"Where should I wait?"

He escorted me back to the empty interrogation room, handed me a catalog of police paraphernalia, said, "Should take about an hour," and left.

I called Jean, waking her up, told her what was going on, and asked her to get a double room for Burl and Maida, hopefully on the same floor as ours. Hanging up, I opened the catalog and checked the prices on handcuff-shaped tie tacks.

THE HOUR STRETCHED into two, and I was fast asleep when Detective Broderick brought Burl into the interrogation room. The opening of the door woke me, and I rubbed my face to get the sleep out and got unsteadily to my feet, holding out my hand to Burl Upshank.

Back in Prophesy County, Burl Upshank was a chinos and button-down-collar guy, occasionally a blue jeans and Western shirt kinda guy, but always clean-shaven and smelling like he just came from a barbershop. The vision in front of me looked more like a wino than an upstanding citizen of Prophesy County, Oklahoma. His face was thick with stubble, his eyes bloodshot, his shirt torn, and his pants dirty. And he smelled *bad*.

"Burl, how you doing, man?" I asked.

"Let's get the hell outta here," he said, his voice scratchy and tight.

I signed the papers Broderick had for me, and left, hoping Burl didn't put up a fight, 'cause I figured he could take me in a New York minute—especially the shape I was in right now.

Burl insisted we go to the hospital, so we took a cab straight there. Denise was in a room on the OB floor, all sorts of machines hooked up to her. I stayed outside while Burl went in to be with his family.

After a minute, Maida came out and shut the door behind her. She hugged me. "Thanks, cousin," she said. "What would we have done without you?"

"Gotten an expensive lawyer?" I suggested.

"Yeah, but you're so much cheaper," she said and grinned.

"How's she doing?" I asked, indicating the door to her daughter's hospital room with my head.

Maida sighed. "The baby's okay," she said. "There's a tear in the placenta so they're going to keep her here. They might have to do an early C-section, but since she's already over eight months, it should be all right."

"How's she holding up—emotionally?" I asked.

Maida shook her head. "She wants to see the bastard. Can you believe I'd give birth to a girl who'd want to stay with an abuser?" Tears sprang to her eyes. "He could have killed the baby,

Milt. And she wants to see him! Right now she's railing at her daddy for hurting her precious husband!"

"You know, Maida, it's a syndrome—battered women's syndrome. My wife's here with me—we came to a psychiatric convention here in town. Maybe she can talk to her?"

Maida nodded. "Burl has a problem with psychiatrists, but I'm willing to try anything. We gotta take her home."

"Maybe you two can go back as soon as they release her, but Burl's gonna have to stay here. You understand that?"

"About that, Milt." She sighed. "You're gonna have to keep an extra eye on him. Burl's got a problem." She took a deep breath and let it out. "With roulette. Last night? Whenever. The night we found Denise? He dropped twenty thousand dollars."

"Jesus," I said. Even for Burl Upshank, that wasn't chump change.

"Please keep an eye on him. Don't let him anywhere near a roulette table, okay?"

"Definitely," I said.

The door opened and Burl came out, his color high. "She wants you," he said to Maida.

She touched his arm. "You okay, honey?" she asked.

"She keeps calling for that SOB. But I'm telling you, Maida, he comes anywhere near her, he's gonna wish he hadn't."

I squeezed Burl's arm to shut him up and looked around for any official-looking types listening in. Thank God I didn't see any.

"Maida, I'm gonna take Burl back to the hotel." I jotted the number down on a piece of paper and handed it to her. "Call me if you need anything."

"I'll spend the night here—" she started.

"If he shows up, you call me, you understand?" Burl said.

Maida didn't answer and I pulled Burl toward the elevators. "Enough," I said.

Emmett drove the pickup to work Saturday morning with a smile on his face, but then thought about seeing Jasmine and the smile faded. How do you work with someone after a night like last night? he thought. Pretend it didn't happen? Act like they were good buddies? Shit, he thought. I don't know. Play it by ear? He decided that was the best thing to do. Take his lead from Jasmine.

She was a little late getting in, and he had to study on how to handle that. Would he normally chastise her for being late? Ignore it? What would Milt do? Calling him was out of the question. Lord howdy, but it was out of the question! Jeez, Milt would pick up on this in a New York minute.

When she finally came in, all of five minutes late, she was smiling. He smiled back. Funny thing, but the smile just wouldn't go away. Jasmine got changed in the locker room and went to her squad car. She gave him a little finger wave on the way out and he caught himself giving a finger wave back. Damn, he thought, I don't think I've ever in my life waved like that. He almost laughed out loud.

Jean had taken care of the room, across the hall from ours, and I got Burl settled, told him I'd send a patrolman over to Denise and Larry's house to get his and Maida's stuff, and left him to get some shut-eye. Back in our room, it took me about two minutes to fall back asleep, I was that tired.

The next morning, almost afternoon really, I got dressed and went across the hall for Burl. He didn't have a change of clothes with him, so I took some money from him and got his sizes and went to one of the shops on the mezzanine and bought him some skivvies, a T-shirt, a pair of jeans, some socks, and the cheapest shirt I could find; even so, the bill came to over two hundred dollars.

Jean had left early in the morning for her convention, so Burl and I went down to Chicken Fried's for some breakfast. I will say this about the place: there wasn't a drop of carrot juice or a bran muffin to be found. Burl and I dined on bacon, eggs, grits, pancakes, and, because we were both watching our weight, shared a plate of biscuits and gravy.

Around one o'clock, a patrolman showed up with Burl and Maida's stuff, and we followed a bellhop up to Burl's room and I helped him put the stuff away. I was doing Maida's stuff and Burl was doing his own, so it was God's own little miracle that I turned around to say something to Burl at about the same time he was slipping a Colt .45 1911 into the bedside table drawer.

"Whoa, now," I said, moving to the table and removing the gun. "You got any more of these?" I asked.

"Just leave it where you found it, Kovak," Burl said, his voice brooking no argument.

"Nope," I said. "You're under my supervision right now, Burl, and the last thing you need is a gun. You got ammo for this thing?"

"No," he said.

I laughed. "Burl, I'm not as big an idiot as you think." I broke the weapon down and found the thing was loaded, with a bullet in the chamber. "Damn, man, you shouldn't carry a weapon this way. Shoot your damn Johnson off."

"Not a Johnson I'd be aiming for," Burl said. "More like an Allen."

I unloaded the Colt and put the bullets in one pocket and the gun itself in another pocket. "Don't be talking like that, Burl. Anybody hears you, you'll end up back in the slammer. Now, you ready to behave?"

Burl was looking mean. "You know, Kovak, you were a bad ball player in high school, and now you're a bad sheriff."

I sighed. "Just finish unpacking, Burl. And shut up before I take you back where I found you."

He glowered and finished unpacking. I went to Jean and my room across the hall and stowed the gun and the ammo in my suitcase, then went back and got Burl.

We didn't speak until we were in the taxi, headed to the hospital. I told Burl about Jean and how I'd talked to her when I got back to the room. She said that if Denise wanted to see her, she'd be glad to do it.

"Psychiatrist, huh? I knew she was a doctor and all," Burl said, "but I didn't know she was a goddamn shrink."

"She's good, Burl, real good."

"Humph," he said. He looked out the window of the taxi as Las Vegas sped past. "Well, can't get any worse, I suppose." He shook his head. "I just can't understand it," he said. "The bastard beat the shit out of her, Milt, kicked the baby! How can she want to see him? Want to go back with him?"

"It's called battered women's syndrome—" I started.

"That's all bullshit!" He slammed his fist down on his knee. "This is my baby girl, Milt! My baby!"

I patted his other knee. "We'll work it out, Burl," I said, seeing visions of my vacation flitting away.

We spent the afternoon at the hospital, then I left Burl in Maida's care while I went back to the hotel to get ready for the big dinner and Jean's speech.

First Saturday ✦ Prophesy County

All things being equal, Jasmine was late getting back to the house. Emmett found himself watching for her, wondering if he should ask her out for dinner tonight, too. Would that be too obvious? Would she think he was just after sex? What *did* women think these days? He had no clue.

Anthony Dobbins was sitting at Gladys's desk. Gladys had gone home for the day, and Anthony was waiting for Jasmine to get back with the squad car they shared—hers days, his nights. Anthony was the only black deputy ever in the Prophesy County Sheriff's Department. Seemed like a nice enough guy, Emmett thought, though he didn't say much. For the first time, Emmett wondered if Anthony felt uncomfortable, being the only black man around. He got up out of Milt's chair and walked to the bullpen.

"Looks like Jasmine's running late," Emmett said.

"Uh huh," Anthony said. "Probably got her a speeder."

"So how you liking nights, Anthony?" Emmett asked.

Anthony looked up from his perusal of a catalog of useless things he'd found on Gladys's desk. "Fine, Emmett. Just fine. Been doing it since I got on with the department."

"You ever ask Milt for a transfer to days?"

"No, like I said, I like nights fine. Gives me the daylight hours to get things done."

Emmett laughed. "When do you sleep?" he asked.

Anthony showed him a slow grin. "Now and then. My wife works days, I work nights, this way we don't have to pay for child care."

Emmett felt lousy all of a sudden. He hadn't even known Anthony was married, much less that he had a child. "Got any pictures?" he asked.

Anthony pulled out his wallet and flashed a picture of a pretty black baby with a bow in her hair. "How old is she?" Emmett asked, glad for the bow.

"Well, in this picture she's three months, but she's close to a year now." He leafed through the wallet, coming to a more current picture. "This is her and my wife."

"What's her name? The baby, I mean."

"Chantelle Clarice," Anthony said, beaming with pride.

"Well, she sure is a pretty little thing," Emmett said.

Anthony said, "Thank you," but Emmett wasn't paying attention anymore. The side door to the back parking lot had opened, and he could hear Jasmine's footsteps coming down the hall. Anthony stood up. "Looks like my car's here. Talk to you later, Emmett."

"Sure thing, Anthony," he said, his eyes steady on the doorway to the hall.

Jasmine and Anthony met at the doorway, Jasmine holding the squad car keys up in the air, between her thumb and forefinger. "All yours," she said, dropping the keys in Anthony's hand.

"I'm out of here," Anthony said.

"Call in and let me know the radio's working," Henry Lopez, the night clerk, called to him as he came out of the break room.

Anthony waved at him and kept going.

"Ah, Jasmine," Emmett said, "see you a minute in my office?"

She followed him back and shut the door behind her. "Yes, sir?" she said, grinning from ear to ear.

"Well, I just wanted to say—" Whatever Emmett had been thinking of saying had to wait for a while. Jasmine had cleared off Milt's desk with one sweep of her hand, and the two were on it like bunny rabbits.

THEY WERE LYING on the desktop in the afterglow when the phone rang on Emmett's—Milt's—desk. Emmett almost fell off looking for it, found it on the floor next to the trash can. "Deputy Hopkins," he said into the phone.

"Everthin' okay back there?" Henry Lopez asked. "Heard some commotion."

"Just dropped something, Henry," Emmett said. "Everything's okay."

He hung up and looked at Jasmine and they both broke up laughing. It was good to see her laugh, holding her uniform blouse against her breasts, her ass bare as a newborn's, giggling fit to beat the band.

"We better get dressed 'fore Henry decides to come back here and check things out," Emmett said.

"Yeah, old Henry'd probably have a heart attack if he saw us." Jasmine giggled.

There was a bit too much reality to the statement for Emmett, and he got up and started putting his clothes on. Henry Lopez was a retired Bishop cop, doing the five to midnight to supplement his retirement pay and his social security, neither of which helped much when the last three of his eight children were still living at home. The vision of Henry having a heart attack was something he'd had before, looking at the older man's hands shake.

He wondered how come he knew so much about Henry, who'd only been with them for two years, when he didn't know diddly about Anthony Dobbins, who'd been with them almost five. Been there longer than Emmett.

He asked Jasmine, "Did you know Anthony's married and has a baby?"

She was still sitting naked on the desktop. "Yeah. His wife's a nurse at Dr. Purdy's office. He's my OB/GYN. Her name's Camille and she's real nice. And that Chantelle, their baby, is as cute as a button. You didn't come to the department picnic this summer, did you? Just like you didn't come the year before, or the year before that. If you ever came to anything, Emmett, you might know these things."

What could he say? No, he hadn't gone to the department

picnic, not ever. Those were family things, and he didn't have a family. Not anymore. But neither did Jasmine, he thought, and she musta went.

"Not much for socializing these days, I guess."

Jasmine hopped off the desk and came over to where he was sitting in the chair, tying his last shoelace. She leaned up against him, her uniform blouse on the floor, her naked breasts pressing against his chest. "Get over it, Emmett. Time you did."

He looked at her and for some reason, for the first time since this had started, she didn't turn him on. He pushed her gently away. "Get dressed, Jasmine," he said.

She backed away and stood before him for a moment, bare-ass naked. And then she covered herself, embarrassed. She got dressed while he picked up papers and office supplies from the floor.

"Maybe this wasn't such a good idea," Jasmine said.

First Saturday ✦ Las Vegas

I put on my navy blue suit with the red-and-blue-striped tie and a white button-down collared shirt, my shined-by-a-professional-downstairs brown Brogans, and looked pretty damn good. Then my wife came out of the bathroom and I forgot about how I looked.

She was wearing a midnight blue silk dress that made her eyes look turquoise. She looked almost as pretty as she had on our wedding day, and I gotta admit I was thinking of something other than her giving a speech. But she nixed that idea and we went down to the mezzanine for the dinner.

I sat at the podium table with Jean and some bigwigs I didn't know or care about. The food was just about what I expected: roast chicken that tasted like cardboard, green beans with almonds that had about as much taste as my son's crayons, a little mound of mashed potatoes with stuff in it (library paste, I think), followed by a bowl of chocolate mousse. I ate it all, of course, but groused about it the whole time. Jean ignored me.

After the dishes had been cleared, one of the bigwigs got up and introduced Jean. He said things about her I didn't know, like she was the president of such and such, the former chairperson of the whatever, and cocreator of the thing-a-kabob theory. I clapped along with everybody else, even more impressed with my wife than I had been twenty minutes earlier.

Her speech was a humdinger. I'd heard bits and pieces of it at the house when she'd practiced it, but I'd never heard it put all together. I didn't understand a lot of what she was talking about, but the audience sure seemed to. After the dinner was over, it took us a full hour to get out of the conference room because that many people came up to glad-hand her. I stood by, beaming, and if anybody looked my way, I said, "I'm the husband."

I guess I'm pretty secure in my masculinity, 'cause Jean being smarter than me and super-successful in her chosen profession doesn't make me feel less of a man. I know some guys have problems with that, but I don't. Now, if I don't win my next election, we may have to discuss this again, but right now, I'm just real proud of her—and that's a fact.

When we finally got out of there it was close to nine o'clock, but Denise had finally given her permission for Jean to see her at the hospital, so we went straight over there, all dressed up. Maida and Burl were in Denise's room, and the three of us left to get a cup of coffee in the cafeteria while Jean and Denise talked.

Afterward, Maida went back to stay in Denise's room, while Burl, Jean, and I took a taxi back to the hotel, with Burl peppering Jean with questions the whole trip.

"Burl, I can't discuss it with you," Jean said more than once. "Anything Denise said to me is confidential."

"But did you talk her out of seeing the bastard?" Burl insisted.

"It will be up to Denise to tell you anything we talked about, Burl. I'm sorry."

He finally shut up, pushed his big body farther into the corner of the taxi, and sulked all the way back to the hotel.

Once we got there he said, "By the way, did I mention this hotel here is the one owned by the bastard's daddy?"

"No shit?" I said. "We're staying in Walter Allen's hotel?"

Burl laughed. "Yeah, ain't that a hoot? I think I'll do like a rock star and trash the room."

FIRST SUNDAY ✦ PROPHESY COUNTY

It was his day off, and Emmett lay in his single bed, staring at the ceiling and thinking about his life. It had started out pretty good. His parents had been good people, a little strict, but his was mostly a happy childhood. Then he'd met Shirley Beth in high school, and they were engaged before he left for a three-year stint in the navy. He'd spent one of those years in the navy in Vietnam, but he'd come back okay. Not like a lot of guys he knew who never got over their year. He'd spent six months in Saigon, attached to an admiral who was so boring Emmett had longed for the front lines. He got his wish finally, but it was during a cease-fire, and all he did was play cards all day, drink, get stoned, and listen to the other guys tell horror stories. His last three months he'd spent back in Saigon, typing reports.

He and Shirley Beth had gotten married two months after his discharge, a week after he started with the Longbranch Police Department. The marriage had been good. Shirley Beth was a pretty girl, grew into a pretty woman who liked being a housewife. When she got pregnant, they were both real excited, but there were complications, and, when J.R. was born, they'd had to do a hysterectomy. But they had their boy and that was all that mattered. And Shirley Beth had taken to motherhood like a fish to water. J.R. became her whole life, sometimes so much so that Emmett got a little jealous. But, God, how he'd loved that boy. He'd been named Josiah Reynolds Hopkins after Shirley Beth's father who had died when she was three, but that seemed a mouthful for such a little guy, so they'd just called him J.R., and it seemed to fit him.

Then, when J.R. was nine, he started getting sick. They didn't know what it was, the doctors couldn't figure it out. Finally they took him to Oklahoma City, to a specialist there. When he said the word, leukemia, it was like a physical blow to Emmett's gut. A very long year later, J.R. died. And so did Shirley Beth, for all intents and purposes.

It started with the sedatives the doctors gave her. Then, months later, when they said she couldn't have any more, that she needed to start dealing, the drinking had started. That lasted eleven years, until the day she took Emmett's service revolver and blew her brains all over the dining room wall.

Those eleven years hadn't been easy for Emmett, either, but he had his job, working his way up to police chief of Longbranch, Oklahoma, and he took his work seriously. Maybe too seriously, he thought now. Or maybe he just used it as a crutch. A way to hide from the truth of his life, a way to try to forget about his son, and his drunken wife, and the dirty dishes that would be waiting for him when, and if, he ever went home.

He'd never talked about it. To anybody, not even Milt. He and Milt would even make plans sometimes to get together, especially after he and Jean got married, to go out to Milt's house and have a barbecue or something, but they never did, and Emmett knew that Milt knew that they never would. The second year, after Shirley Beth had tripped going down the aisle at church, they'd even stopped going there, and after that she never left the house. Emmett did the grocery shopping, took his uniforms to the dry cleaners, dealt with the house. He wouldn't hire someone to come in to clean, because then Shirley Beth's secret would be out, and he knew she wouldn't be able to abide that. Or maybe it was because he wouldn't be able to abide it.

Could he have done something different? Was he what they called an enabler? Should he have taken her to a doctor, thrown away the bottles, not bought the booze and brought it home the way he did? Did her having such a major problem keep him from having to deal with his own grief?

Emmett sat up in bed at that thought. Shit, he wondered, was that what I was doing? Could I have helped her? Stopped the whole thing years before?

Jasmine saying what she did, that he needed to "get over it," had pissed him off royally. How do you "get over" a life like he'd had? How do you "get over" losing a child and your wife? How do you "get over" being the walking dead?

Like comedy, he thought, his life had all to do with timing. If he'd gotten J.R. to the specialist sooner, could he have been saved? If he'd gotten help for Shirley Beth at any point, could she have been rescued from her demons?

He laid back down and stared at the ceiling some more. Was this to be his life now, then? To be wracked with guilt for his lousy timing, for his stupidity in enabling his wife to ruin her life? Would he push away Jasmine or any other woman to come his way simply because he was too guilty and too weak to deal with his guilt? The thought entered Emmett's head fleetingly that he might need to see somebody about all this, maybe a professional, but the only one he knew was Jean, Milt's wife. That would be awkward. That would be real awkward. And would she be able to keep confidentiality if Milt found out he was seeing her? Ah, hell,

Milt would be all over her. What'd he say? How's he doing? Is he certifiable? Should I fire him?

Shit. No way would he talk to Jean. No way he'd talk to anybody. He was a grown man, a Vietnam vet, the damned ex-police chief of Long Branch, Oklahoma, the chief deputy of Prophesy County. No way did he need to bare his soul to somebody and pay for the privilege.

First Sunday ✦ Las Vegas

The next morning Jean left early for the last day of the convention—a half-day, really. They had panels and meetings all morning, then the whole thing would end at noon with another dinner. I talked my way out of it, having to babysit Burl and all. I got dressed in a Hawaiian shirt I'd bought for the vacation and a pair of blue jeans, and headed across the hall to Burl's room. I knocked on the door but there was no answer. Thinking he might be in the shower, I went back to my room and watched TV for a while, then went back. Still no answer to my knock.

Considering the situation, I didn't waste any more time, but called the desk and said I needed to get in the room. After explaining who I was and the situation, a bellhop came up with a duplicate card key. The room, needless to say, was empty. I sat down on the bed and dialed Maida at the hospital.

"Hey, Maida," I said when she answered the phone. "How's Denise doing?"

She sighed. "Just a minute, Milt." A few seconds later she said, "I had to get where she couldn't hear me." She sighed again. "She's been crying nonstop since Jean left her."

Oh, I thought, that wasn't good.

"But she's decided she has to leave Larry," she said.

Oh, I thought, that *was* good.

"That's good news, Maida," I said, then added, "Burl there?"

There was a short silence, then she said, "No, Milt. He's with you, remember?"

"The thing is, Maida, I'm here in his room, and he's not."

"Where is he?" she demanded.

"Well, I don't know."

"Oh for crying out loud!" Maida said. Then sighed, "Better go check the roulette tables."

"Right," I said and hung up, heading down to the casino.

Burl wasn't at the roulette tables, the slots, the blackjack tables, any of the restaurants, bathrooms, or shops. I doubted he was in the conference rooms of the convention, but I peeked in each of them to see. They were pretty crowded, but Burl woulda stood out—but he didn't. He wasn't there.

I FIGURED I had two choices: I could go to the police station and tell the powers that be what happened, or I could go to the airport and hightail it back to Prophesy County. But I figured if I hightailed it, they could hightail it right behind me, and I'd be in even bigger trouble. I had to fess up. Since it was almost one o'clock, I figured I'd wait until Jean was out of her dinner, and tell her what was up.

"You what?" she said, wide-eyed.

"I lost Burl," I said for the second time.

"Did you look in his room?" she asked.

I gave her a look.

"The roulette tables? The restaurants? The bathrooms?"

"Honey, I've scoured the hotel. He's not here. And now I have to go report this to the police."

Jean sighed. "He's going to be in big trouble, isn't he, Milt?"

"Worse than a long-tailed cat in a room full of rocking

chairs. Worse than a one-legged man in an ass-kicking contest, worse than—"

"Okay," she said, her hands up in surrender. "I get it, I get it."

She put an arm around me and hugged me to her. "If they put you in jail, honey, call me, okay?"

I headed for the escalator. "You're seriously funny, woman. I ever tell you that?" I said, scowling. She grinned and waved bye.

I found Jimmy Broderick where I'd left him the day before. Without any preamble, I said, "I lost Upshank."

He stared at me. He didn't offer me a chair. Finally he said, "Sir?"

"I lost Burl Upshank," I said, slowly and distinctly.

His face turned about three shades of red, then he said, "And this guy is some kind of relative, right, Sheriff?"

I was pissed at Burl for doing this to me, and I was pissed at the kid for the implication. Burl wasn't handy. The kid was.

"Just a goddamn minute, *De*-tective," I said. "If you're insinuating I had anything to do with Burl being missing, well, we can just plain take this outside."

Broderick sighed. "I'm sorry if it sounded like that's what I was saying, Sheriff. I didn't mean to imply that." He shrugged his massive shoulders. "Hell, maybe I did. My apologies. But we're gonna have to go talk to my loo about this." He sighed again. "And I'd just as soon you take that heat than me, know what I mean?"

I sighed my own sigh and followed Broderick into his lieutenant's office.

Mac Grayson greeted me with a handshake and a big grin, both of which lasted until he heard that I'd lost Burl Upshank.

"Lost him?" he roared. "How in the hell did you do that?"

"I went to his room this morning and he was gone," I said.

"You left him in a room alone?"

"Well, his wife's in the hospital with his daughter, who your guy beat up—"

"He's not *my* guy—" Grayson started, getting even more heated up.

"And I'm on vacation. I'd rather sleep with my wife than Burl Upshank."

"Shit," Grayson said. "So you're playing tourist and a wanted felon skips."

I sighed. "Yes, sir, that's about the size of it."

Grayson stood up. "You know, when I hear 'small town Oklahoma sheriff' I automatically think hick, but I didn't know I should think stupid hick."

I headed for the door. "I made a mistake, Grayson. I admit that. But I'll find him and bring him in. And I don't need any shit from you."

"Well, Sheriff," he said, making the sheriff sound like he was saying "dog turd," "why don't you just leave that to us professionals?"

I didn't say another word, just turned with as much dignity as I could muster at that moment and left the office.

WHEN I GOT back to the room, Jean said she'd talked to the desk and we had the two rooms, ours and the one across the hall, until Wednesday. Just in case, she said. She'd also called my sister Jewel Anne and made arrangements for her to keep Johnny Mac a few extra days.

I didn't say a word, just went to the little refrigerator I'd seen in the room but hadn't opened, and perused the goodies. Jack Daniel's and macadamia nuts sounded like a nice little snack. I drank the whole bottle (it was one of those airline bottles so it wasn't all that much) and ate all the nuts, not even bothering to look at how much what I'd just consumed had cost.

Jean watched me silently—well, as long as she can stay silent—then said, "Milt, I hope you don't plan on drinking all the little bottles in that refrigerator."

"Maybe not all of 'em," I replied. "I'm not crazy about Kahlúa."

She sat down on the bed and looked at me. "We have to do something about Burl," she said.

"And what would you suggest we do?" I asked, keeping my back to her as I squatted in front of the refrigerator.

"Maida told you Burl has a problem with roulette, right?"

I ignored her. She went on.

"I think we should hit the strip, go to the different casinos. See if we can find him. If we split up we can cover more territory."

I turned on my haunches and glared at her. "And what are you gonna do if you find him?" I asked.

She wasn't quite prepared for the question, but it didn't take her more than a few seconds to say, "Call the police. Right? Or hotel security."

Which is probably exactly what I'd do. Sometimes being married to a smart woman can be a real curse. You never can one-up 'em.

We went downstairs and out onto the strip. It was so hot outside I could see little mirages of wetness on the street and sidewalk. The sun beat down on my head like it had a grudge against me. The Bellagio, New York New York, and Caesars Palace were on the same side of the street as the Lonestar; Aladdin's, the MGM Grand, and the Tropicana were across the strip.

"I'll take those," I said, pointing across the street. "You take the ones on this side. You got your cell phone?"

She nodded.

"If you find him, call me. If you don't, let's meet at that all-you-can-eat seafood place over there," I said, pointing a block down and across another street.

"Synchronize our watches?" she said, grinning at me.

"This isn't a game, Jean," I said.

My wife sighed. "For god's sake, Milt, lighten up." She kissed me and headed off down the sidewalk.

What can I say about the crazy hotels in Vegas? They all had a theme, a different theme, of course, yet they were all the same. From the Arabian Nights theme of Aladdin's to the giant Dorothy and the Tin Man at the MGM Grand, there was one solid connection: the smell and the noise. You walk in and you're assaulted by the mix of cigarette smoke and air freshener, the crazy buzzing and beeping of the slots, the din of voices, and the occasional scream when someone won something. I was beginning to feel a little autistic: too much input.

I wandered the casinos, checking out the roulette tables, but there wasn't much action in the middle of the day. Like in our hotel, the slots were buzzing, but the gaming tables were fairly quiet. No sign of Burl Upshank.

I'd just walked out the front door of the Tropicana when I saw my wife coming down the sidewalk toward me. She looked a little unsteady on her crutches and I felt guilty having her running around these huge hotels looking for the guy I lost. I hurried to her side and put my arm around her waist.

"Hey, honey," I said. "You holding up okay?"

She grinned. "Did you know they give drinks away free in those places?" she said. "Free, Milt! Anything you want! As long as you play a slot or two, they keep bringing you free booze!"

By the smell of her breath and the list of her body on her crutches, I got the feeling Jean had sampled a little at every hotel she went to. "Any sign of Burl?" I asked.

"Who?" she said. I gave her a look. "Oh, Burl! No, no. No sign of old Burl. I gotta say, though, Milt, he's got some Vegas nerve!" And then she laughed so hard I had to hold her steady.

When I didn't laugh in response, she said, "It's a joke, Milt! Vegas nerve! Get it?"

I shrugged. "Yeah, honey, really funny," I said, guiding her over to a bench near a bus stop.

"No, no, no!" she said. "Vegas nerve! Get it? Like vagus nerve? 'Cept I said Vegas nerve! Get it?"

"Yeah," I said, sitting her down on the bench, "vagus nerve."

She sighed heavily. "You don't even know what that is, do you, Milt?" she said, glaring at me.

I admitted my ignorance.

"The tenth cranial nerve!"

I must have looked blank because she sighed again, belched, and said, in her best teacher to student voice, her hands pointing to her head, "The tenth pair of cranial nerves that come from the medulla!" I nodded. She poked the side of her head with her index finger. "The medulla! It supplies the viscera with autonomic sensory and motor fibers—"

"Honey," I said, pulling her gently to her feet, "let's go back to the hotel. I could use a drink."

"Oh, I know a place—" she started, but by then I'd flagged down a taxi and was pouring her into the backseat.

FIRST SUNDAY ✦ PROPHESY COUNTY

Emmett brooded on it all day, wanting to see Jasmine, needing to see Jasmine, but thinking she just didn't know. "Get over it," she'd said. Maybe she didn't mean it that way, he thought. Or maybe she doesn't know. Oh, yeah, she did, he reminded himself. She was in the department then, when Shirley Beth killed herself. And if she knew about that, then she knew about J.R. "Get over it." You don't just *get over* something like that. Hell, it was his life! How was he supposed to "get over" his life? Huh?

He drank the rest of the six-pack in the fridge, three beers, and thought about going out to the store for more. He ordered a pizza, thought about having some of that bag of salad to go with it, then realized he didn't have any salad dressing. But he did have some Miracle Whip. So he poured some salad in a bowl, spooned on a couple of blobs of Miracle Whip, stirred it all up, and took a bite. Then he took it to the sink and tossed bowl and all into the trash. Decided his opinion on salad hadn't changed all that much.

Around four, on his third beer, he picked up the phone and dialed Jasmine's number, but he hung up after one ring. He'd barely sat back down when it rang again.

"Hello?" he said. His phone rarely rang, and when it did it was always Milt, something about work, or come out to the house for dinner, or you wanna go bowling, or something like that.

"You can't just call and hang up, Emmett," Jasmine said. "I have caller ID."

"Oh," he said. "Didn't think about that."

"Well, you need to get into the twenty-first century, old man." Her voice wasn't kindly.

"You mad at me?" he said, surprised. He was mad at her. He had reason. What reason did she have?

"Yes, I'm mad at you," she said, her voice hard.

"Why? What'd I do?"

"You treated me like a piece of meat, Emmett Hopkins! You have your way with me then you just act like it's no big thing!"

"Whoa, now! Who had whose way with who?" Emmett said. "I seem to remember you're the one who cleared off Milt's desk!"

"And now you're calling me a cheap whore!" Jasmine said, tears in her voice as she hung up the phone.

Emmett sat there in the easy chair that wasn't easy and

stared at the phone until the recorded voice told him to hang up. So he hung up and stared at the phone some more. Never in a million years, he thought, would he understand women.

He stood up and checked his pockets for his truck keys, then went outside and started the pickup, and drove the five miles to Jasmine's house.

He'd never been there, but he knew where she lived. He'd paid attention to it when he'd been reading her file, which he shouldn't have done, but did anyway. And he had driven by the street a couple of times, but never down it, never by the actual house. He stopped the pickup at the curb in front of her house and looked at it. Little yellow and white postwar cottage. Cute, like Jasmine. Geraniums in pots on the steps to the porch, nice mixture of Bermuda and St. Augustine, trimmed razor sharp along the sidewalk leading to the porch. Hanging baskets of impatiens on the porch rail. The front door was snowy white with a sparkling clean leaded glass window in a fan shape. She kept her house shipshape, just like he'd kept his, after J.R. died, and before Shirley Beth had.

He knocked on the door and waited. In a minute he saw her peeking at him through the fan window. Must be on her tiptoes, he thought. He said, "Jasmine, we need to talk."

"You better go away, Emmett, before somebody sees you and thinks we might be having sex or something."

"Just open the door."

"Now I wouldn't want the neighbors seeing you with me and putting you in a compromising position, Emmett Hopkins! You shouldn't be seen with a sleazy whore like myself!"

"Open the door or I'll break it down, Jasmine! It's a real pretty door, hate to do it but I will!"

She opened the door and he walked in. Nice sized living room with gleaming pine floors, a new suede-like sofa with older pieces mixed in. "Nice house," he said. "Can't image Lester Bodine buying a place like this," he said, mentioning Jasmine's former husband.

"He didn't," she said, arms crossed, voice tight. "This was my grandma's house. She gave it to me when she went to live in that senior place out on the highway."

"Well, it's real nice."

"What do you want?"

Emmett took a deep breath. "You said I should just get over it," he said.

"What?"

"That's what you said. And it was a mean thing to say."

"What are you talking about?" Jasmine asked, hands on hips.

"After we . . . you know, in Milt's office, and I said I didn't socialize, you said get over it."

"Yeah, Emmett, you should! Stop being so bashful! Try making friends! Stop pushing me away!"

Emmett looked at her for a moment. "Oh," he finally said. "Is that what you meant?"

"What did you think I meant?"

"Well," he scratched his chin, looked at the floor, anywhere but her. "Nothing," he finally said.

Jasmine walked up to him, took both his hands in hers. Her voice soft, she asked, "Emmett, what did you think I meant?"

He took a deep breath and looked into her eyes. "I thought you meant what happened to Shirley Beth and my boy."

Jasmine's eyes got big then filled with tears. "Oh, Christ, Emmett, I'd never say anything like that! I'm so sorry you thought that's what I meant!"

She put her arms around him and he put his arms around her, and they held each other for a while.

"I'm sorry," he said. "I guess, you know, us having sex and all, I've been thinking about all that maybe too much."

She pulled away and placed her hands on either side of his face. "Listen to me, Emmett Hopkins," she said. "You've been through the worst thing anybody could ever go through. Losing your boy, then your wife. It's taken me four years just to get over a no-good cheating rotten husband, who I never liked very much to begin with. I would never say that to you. I know it'll get easier for you, as you begin to fill your life back up—with me, I hope—but it'll never go away. And it shouldn't. They were your life, and they'll always be with you. Maybe someday we can talk about them, you can tell me about your boy. I'd like to hear it. But I know it's too soon. You haven't let yourself do any healing, honey, and that's where we should start."

"Did you just call me honey?" Emmett asked.

She put her hands around his neck and grinned at him. "Is that the only thing you heard?"

The door of our hotel room burst open around eight o'clock the next morning. Jean was in a bra and skirt and I had on my shorts and a T-shirt. I started to reach for the gun on my hip, but being as I was on vacation, there wasn't one there.

Jimmy Broderick was in the room, towering behind Lieutenant Mac Grayson, and a short, gray-haired guy I didn't recognize. The short guy seemed to be in charge, if screaming makes somebody in charge.

"Where is he, you son-of-a-bitch?" he yelled. He lunged for me and Grayson grabbed his arm. "Tell me where he is, now!"

"What the hell's going on here?" I demanded, looking at Grayson, not the short, gray-haired man.

"Kovak—" Grayson started but the older guy wasn't having any.

"Tell me where he is right now, or I'll gut you like a chicken, you Oklahoma trailer trash!"

Now I took exception to that. I've never lived in a trailer. I stood in front of Jean and, turning toward her slightly, but keeping my eyes on the old guy, I said, "Honey, go in the bathroom and lock the door, please."

For once she did as I asked with no third degree.

"Somebody wanna tell me what's going on?" I asked, trying to keep my voice calm.

"Kovak, this is Mr. Allen—"

The old man's face resolved into anguish as he wailed, "He killed my boy! The son-of-a-bitch killed my boy!"

Well, I was confused. "I didn't think his injuries were serious—" I started, but Mr. Allen broke away from Grayson and came for me. I lost my balance and landed butt first on the bed, which put me almost eye to eye with Allen.

"You tell me where he is right now or I'll have you killed, and if you think I'm kidding just ask Grayson."

Grayson turned to Broderick. "Jimmy, take Mr. Allen down to his office, get him a drink or something, okay? Mr. Allen, let me talk to Kovak. I'll find out what he knows, one way or the other," he said, the last words spoken with a lot more malice than I reckoned was called for.

Big as he was, it seemed to take a lot of strength on Jimmy Broderick's part to haul the little man out of the room, but he managed it, leaving me alone with Grayson. I stood up, thinking being in my underwear was enough of a disadvantage—I didn't want to be sitting down.

"Mind telling me what's going on?" I asked Grayson, matching my demeanor to his—that is to say, I was scowling just as bad as him.

To give him credit, Mac Grayson looked a little embarrassed.

"Larry Allen's dead," he said. "Shot. Sometime last night. By all appearances, he was passed out on the couch. Somebody," he said this sarcastically, "got close enough to him to leave powder burns on his temple. We know it wasn't suicide because there was no gun present. We came to the hotel to notify Mr. Allen and he went ballistic. He already knew you and Upshank were staying here—the guy seems to know everything that happens in this hotel—and he headed up here. We couldn't stop him. Best we could do was follow." He cleared his throat and went back on the offensive. "Anyway, we'd sure like to know the whereabouts of your buddy Upshank."

"Shit," I said. "And he's not my buddy. Look, I told you yesterday, I don't know where Burl is. If I did I'd tell you. I'm an officer of the law and it would be my sworn duty."

"You carried a piece with you on the plane?" Grayson asked.

"No, I'm on vacation. I don't usually carry while I'm not in my jurisdiction—" Then it dawned on me. "Oh, shit," I said, and headed for my suitcase where I'd stashed Burl's Colt. It and the ammo were gone.

First Monday ✦ Prophesy County

Emmett woke up disoriented. Had no idea where he was. Sun was shining through white ruffled curtains and bouncing off the rose-patterned wallpaper. He looked at the bedside clock, an old puppy dog with the analog clock in his belly, his tongue beating the time. And the time said six-thirty.

He knew where he was now, could feel her moving next to him. He turned and looked at her, her eyes still closed, her face open in sleep, a little drool marking the pillow. He used to watch Shirley Beth sleep sometimes, before J.R. died. After, they never shared a bedroom again. Shirley Beth had been all lady, even when she slept. Flannel nightgown in winter, nylon in summer, both up to the neck and down to the toes. When they made love, she'd take off her panties and he'd lift her nightgown, always under the covers. In twenty years of marriage, the only time he'd ever seen her naked was when he accidentally walked in on her in the bath. She'd been so embarrassed she hadn't talked to him for hours.

But here Jasmine was, naked as the day she was born, covers clamped around her breasts, bare arms and shoulders exposed. Freckles on her shoulders. Soft blond hair on her arms. He remembered her breasts from the night before. Small, but with big nipples. Something really sexy about that.

She stirred, turned over, and the covers moved, exposing her breasts. He leaned down and took one in his mouth, and she stirred again, moaned slightly, and her hands found his head, rubbing the blond buzz cut.

"Good morning," she whispered.

First Monday ✦ Las Vegas

Jean and I were finally dressed when the next knock on the door came. I opened it to a good-looking, if slightly cold looking, woman in a severe business suit. If they'd sent her from central casting she'd have had on horn-rimmed glasses and her hair in a bun, but this one had short blond hair and eyes so blue you knew she'd traded in the horn-rims for colored contacts.

"Mr. Kovak?" she said.

I agreed that I was.

"I'm Melissa Greevey, Mr. Allen's administrative assistant. And this is Mr. Sampson, the hotel's day manager."

That's when I noticed the man standing next to her. He was pretty much invisible; a beige kinda guy in a beige suit.

"What can I do for you?" I asked, not inviting them in.

"Under the circumstances, we thought it best if you and Dr. McDonnell, and the Upshanks—" she said their name like it hurt on her tongue—"leave this hotel. I've taken the liberty of getting you all accommodations at the Bellagio. For your inconvenience we've upgraded both rooms to suites." With an elegant arm, she pointed behind her to a bellhop and a girl in a maid's uniform. "Maria will pack up the Upshanks and help you in any way she can, and Tony will take everything down for you. We have a limo waiting to take you to the Bellagio."

Now, I hadn't noticed the maid or the bellhop, either, but I guess I need to mention here that Ms. Greevey's severe suit had a very short skirt, and the lady herself had some real killer legs. Hey, I'm married, but I'm not blind or dead, okay?

All in all, I thought the offer very generous. But it didn't seem the kind of thing the little man I'd met, namely Mr. Walter Allen, would do.

"Mr. Allen doesn't know about this, does he?" I asked.

"Mr. Allen is indisposed," Ms. Greevey said.

I nodded my head and accepted the offer. I'd seen the Bellagio, and it beat the hell out of the Lonestar.

It took about an hour to get everything packed up and moved over to the Bellagio. Now where the Lonestar is *HeeHaw*, the Bellagio is *Masterpiece Theatre*. It was some pretty, I can tell you that. Big old fountain at the front in this pretty big lake, a lobby you wouldn't believe with blown-glass flowers in all different colors hanging from the ceiling when you walked in. It was one of those places made you want to say "ooh" and "ah" a lot, but made you feel like a rube if you did.

While Jean was checking in (which I thought she should do since she did it at the Lonestar and did such a fine job of it), I wandered around looking at the menus at the different restaurants.

Well, I can tell you this: there wasn't any chicken fried anything—or any TexMex for that matter. What there was was something I couldn't pronounce with a reduction of something I'd never heard of. And the prices were so high they didn't even put 'em on the menu. I peeked in this one place that had a rug in it so weird I'da lost my dinner eating in there for sure; then I saw the discreet little sign: PICASSO'S. Well, that made sense.

The one thing the Bellagio had in common with the Lonestar, however, was the smell and the noise. The casino was a little farther off the main track than at the Lonestar, but the heavily perfumed air was still mixed with cigarette smoke, and the ping and plunk of the slots and the bells and whistles of the winners still raked the air.

Our suite was real nice, though. A nice sized living room with nice furniture and a balcony with a view of the fountain, and a bedroom with a king sized bed. I used the phone in our new suite to call Maida at the hospital. I told her where we were.

"A suite will be good, Milt. Can you see about getting about five more rooms, too?"

"For Denise and who else?" I asked.

"No, Denise will stay in the suite with me. The rooms are for the boys. I've called them and told them what these people are accusing their father of. They're all on their way here."

Oh, shit, I thought. "Maida, you think that was a good idea?"

Her voice stiffened. "Yes, Milt, obviously I thought it was a good idea—I did it, didn't I? This is family. Those boys know their father better than anyone. If he can be found, they'll find him."

I sighed. "When will they be getting here?"

"Various times, I'm sure. They're coming from all over. I'll give them your suite number and have them contact you, if that's convenient?"

I'd heard her use this tone of voice on the very boys she was talking about, over one transgression or the other. I wasn't sure I deserved the tone, but under the circumstances, I guess she needed to use it on someone.

"Of course it is, Maida. How's Denise?"

She sighed and her voice softened. "Doing better. She's stopped crying."

"Have you told her—"

"No, I haven't, and I'm not going to. Not as long as she's in the hospital. What's your plan for finding Burl?"

"Well, ma'am, now that I've got me some deputies coming, I'll be able to organize a better search."

There was a smile in her voice when she said, "That's a much better attitude, cousin." With that she said good-bye and hung up.

I asked Jean to find some more rooms and sat back to think about "the boys," and what I knew about them. John Bob was the oldest, in his mid-thirties by now, and a lawyer in Oklahoma City. I knew he was married and thought he had a couple of kids. He was a stuffed shirt who I remember was always being embarrassed by his loud but kindly father. Jason also lived in Oklahoma City, and was a district manager for a fast-food franchise. He'd flunked out of OU his sophomore year. He'd been married and had a couple of kids, but I heard a few years ago that he got divorced.

Taylor could probably be best explained by my wife: he was the middle child, or at least he had been before Denise came along, but he was definitely the middle boy. And he had all the earmarks of a middle child. He was married with a little girl, and was a vice president of a bank in Dallas. I'm sure he did okay there, away from his family, but get him with the other boys and all he wanted was peace—which he never got.

Now David Lee was another story altogether. I'd had to call

Burl a couple of times when David Lee was in high school to come get him at the sheriff's station. Underage drinking, marijuana, driving too fast under the influence of the drug of the week, getting in fights because some guy's girlfriend thought David Lee was too cute for words. I knew Burl and Maida had tried to send him to OU, but that hadn't worked out. As I remember it, he was running a craps game in his freshman dorm room and got caught and thrown out. I had no idea what David Lee was up to these days, but I doubted it was any good.

Michael was the youngest boy, just a year older than Denise, twenty-five maybe. He'd graduated from his father's alma mater, thought his daddy was a hoot, played varsity ball through high school and college, and now worked for an oil company in Houston, last I heard.

I wasn't sure how any of them could help in this situation, but I figured I was stuck with 'em, so I'd better come up with a plan.

Michael arrived first, towing a pretty girl behind him. Michael was as big as his father, with a short, blond buzz cut and wearing blue jeans and an OU football jersey. The girl came to just below his shoulder, had dark brown hair falling down her back, and wearing what in my day were called pedal pushers. Jean tells me they call 'em capris now. I figure if women were as smart as they think they are, they'd never throw anything away; someday it's gonna come back in style.

"Hey, Cousin Milt!" Michael said when I opened the door, then engulfed me in a bear hug that woulda broken the ribs of a lesser man. "This is my fiancé, Barbara Jo. Barbara Jo, this is my cousin Milt Kovak, sheriff of Prophesy County, Oklahoma. Milt, my dad didn't do this, you know. And even if he did, the prick deserved it. Beating up my sister! Hell, I'da castrated him first! So, what are we gonna do? Where do you want me to start searching? I'll do whatever you want—"

"Whoa, honey," Barbara Jo said with a smile. To me, she said, "He had a double espresso on the plane. He's wired."

"Y'all come on in," I said, opening the door to the living room of our suite.

I introduced them to Jean and we'd barely sat down and ordered room-service drinks before we heard another knock on the door. I went to open it and saw David Lee standing there.

As in true black sheep fashion, David Lee didn't look like the other Upshank boys; he took after Maida's side of the family. Actually, he was the spitting image of my grandfather, my mother's father. Tall and lean, he had dark brown hair and a Roman nose, and dark brown eyes that I'd heard more than one young lady describe as "bedroom eyes." He was wearing tight black denim jeans, a black T-shirt, and a black leather motorcycle jacket, which woulda killed me in this heat. He held up a fist, for me to shake I guess, then, with a sigh, opened his hand to shake properly.

"Hey, Milt," he said. "Daddy's stepped in it this time, huh?"

"David Lee," I said, ushering him into the room.

Michael jumped up and hugged his brother. "Man, are you a sight for sore eyes!" he said, grinning. "Haven't seen you in a month of Sundays!"

Introductions were made then another knock at the door. This time it was room service with our drinks, and I ordered another one for David Lee. We were all having sodas, but David Lee ordered a Dewar's on the rocks.

A half-hour later John Bob and Jason showed up. John Bob was a duplicate of his father, only in miniature. He was a short, stocky guy with thinning hair and a bit of a paunch. He was wearing Dockers and a button-down shirt. Jason was taller than his older brother, a little thinner, and his blond hair was longish and blown-dry. He was wearing golf clothes.

Before I had a chance, John Bob introduced himself to Jean, then started giving orders to his brothers. Jason, meanwhile, had found a brochure on the coffee table about the golf courses in Vegas and was busily perusing it.

Taylor arrived shortly after, apologizing for being late. His hair was darker than his blond brothers', but lighter than David Lee's. Like John Bob, he was wearing Dockers and a button-down shirt. Except for the hair, the height (he was the tallest next to Michael), and the weight (big but not fat), he looked like a slightly younger version of John Bob. The demeanor, though, was totally different. Where John Bob was a take-charge, run-the-show kinda guy, Taylor was big on making everybody happy and apologizing when he didn't.

So, these were "the boys," for what they were worth, and I was stuck with them.

IT WAS A circus. Jean took about half an hour of it, then suggested that she and Barbara Jo go see what kind of shops they had at the Bellagio. I didn't have the luxury of taking off. I was stuck with 'em. With John Bob telling everybody, including me, how this should be done; with Michael, still hopped up on the double espresso, breaking into everyone's conversations with tidbits that had nothing to do with anything; with Taylor trying to get everybody to "just get along." Jason spent the entire time on the phone trying to get a foursome together for that afternoon, and David Lee appeared to be sleeping through most of it.

By the time I got them out of our suite to go check into their own rooms, we'd accomplished exactly nothing. Zip. Nada. Not a damn thing. For all I knew, what with Jason being on the phone the entire time, Burl coulda been caught, shot, or in Mexico. I thought my best plan of action would be to have Jimmy Broderick arrest the bunch of 'em so I could get some work done. I just couldn't come up with an offense they'd committed more heinous than being pains in the butt. And I doubted that was considered a crime in Las Vegas. If it was, every casino would be empty.

"Are they gone?" Jean asked, sticking her head around the door to the suite.

"Gone but not forgotten," I said.

She came in on her crutches and sat down next to me on the couch. "Maida seems like such a rational woman," she said.

"How'd she breed that bunch, is that what you're asking?"

"Something like that," Jean said.

I shook my head. "The boys can be blamed on their daddy, I'd think. That or the devil." I asked, "So what was Barbara Jo like?"

"Typical girl in love. Couldn't stop talking about Michael. Seems like a nice enough girl," Jean said smiling, then sobered. "What are you going to do, Milt? I mean, do you have a plan?"

I just looked at her. When was the last time I recommended a diagnosis on one of her patients? Never, that's when.

"Oops," she said, smiling slightly. "Am I stepping on toes?"

I sighed and forgave her. "It's just that everybody's telling me what to do, and nobody has any earthly idea what they're talking about."

"Let me ask you a question, honey," Jean said.

"Shoot—" I started, then said, "bad choice of words. Go ahead."

"Do you think Burl shot Larry Allen?"

I shrugged. "Sure looks that way." When she gave me a look, I said, "He had a really good motive, he had opportunity, and since he stole his gun back, he certainly had means." Since she was still giving me that look, I said, "Honey, if it walks like a duck—"

"Sometimes it's a swan," she said.

"You don't think he did it?" I asked. "You saw how upset he was—"

"Yes, and I think given the chance, he would have gone back over there and given Larry Allen the beating of his life. But," she sighed, "I don't know, Milt, I know I don't know Burl well, but after spending a little time with him, I'd just say that he wasn't capable of cold-blooded murder. And that's what this was, right? Allen was passed out. He couldn't have put up a fight. Whoever did this, shot the man while he was down, and Burl strikes me as the type of man who would find that unfair. If Burl wanted to shoot the man, he'd make sure he was sober, give him a gun of his own, and duel it out."

I thought about what she said. And it made sense. Burl *wasn't* the type to shoot an unconscious man. He might have kicked him as a subtle way of waking him up, but he wouldn't have put a gun to his head and pulled the trigger. Although, as I've discovered in my years as a peace officer, you never know what people are capable of. Hell, we had a case one time where a bunch of ladies in their seventies and eighties were robbing convenience stores of all their canned peaches. Who'd've thought that was possible? Or what about little Cindy Montgomery, the sweetest little candy striper the hospital ever had, stealing the personal effects of sleeping patients? Or my own deputy, Jasmine Bodine, Eyeore personified, doing a Bobbit on her cheating husband? People were capable of anything, and I think I'd gotten jaded enough that nothing much surprised me anymore.

But Burl Upshank taking a gun and pressing it against the head of an unconscious man and pulling the trigger? I had to admit, that was a stretch even for me. But if Burl didn't do it, who did? 'Cause Larry Allen was certainly dead, and somebody shot him. Maybe that's what I should concentrate on, rather than finding Burl. 'Cause, God knows, the LVPD thought they had a sure thing with Burl and they wouldn't be looking for anybody else. I had me five half-assed deputies, and no rules of procedure out of my jurisdiction. This could get very interesting.

FIRST MONDAY ✦ PROPHESY COUNTY

They'd driven separately to work, him leaving first since he was always in before her. She arrived twenty minutes later, acting breathless, saying sorry, she just woke up. For Gladys's benefit, he supposed. He almost giggled out loud. Hell, he thought, I don't giggle. I don't smile at eight in the morning. I don't feel all gooey inside all the damned time. Well, he thought, maybe I didn't used to, but I sure as hell do now. And had to suppress another giggle.

She stuck her head in his office on her way out, after changing into her uniform. "Ah, Emmett, I'm heading out. I'll be on my radio," she said, loud enough for Gladys to hear.

"Okay, fine," he said, also loud. Then in a whisper, he said, "Lunch?"

She whispered back, "Where?"

"Longbranch Inn?"

She rolled her eyes. "Not a good idea."

"Meet me at your billboard," he whispered. "I'll bring something."

"To eat, you mean?" she said, giggled, and left.

Emmett never had been much for double entendre, mainly because he never understood them. But he laughed quietly at this one. He understood this one. Jeez, he thought, she's a hoot.

FIRST MONDAY ✦ LAS VEGAS

Since Maida was still at the hospital with Denise, who was going to be released the next day, I decided, for my wife's sake, to have the first official meeting with "the boys" in the living room of Maida's suite.

After everybody was seated with a drink in hand, I explained my reasoning: that Burl didn't do it, that somebody else had, and that our best bet was to try to find out who did, since the LVPD wouldn't even try. This statement was met with enthusiasm by Michael. Taylor, the peacemaker, nodded his head and said, "Well, that sounds like a plan." Jason, who was still pissed off that he had to cancel a golf game, looked at John Bob and they both snorted. David Lee laughed out loud.

"What's the problem with you guys?" I asked, addressing Jason, John Bob, and David Lee.

"What makes you so sure Daddy didn't do this?" John Bob

said. "He certainly had means, motive, and opportunity. Isn't that what you law-enforcement types go by?"

"Yeah," Jason said.

"Ah, hell," David Lee said, stretching his long legs out in front of him where he sat on the couch. "What does it matter if he did it or not? The point is, Milt, what do you think this bunch can do about it?" He waved a languid arm toward his brothers.

"We can question people," I said, a little piqued that Burl's own sons didn't seem that interested. Why were they here then? "We can find out who else had a grievance against Allen. A guy like that surely had enemies."

"Right!" Michael said, jumping up and glaring at his older brothers. "You know in your hearts Daddy didn't do this! What's wrong with you guys?"

"Mike," Taylor said, "everybody has a right to their own opinion—"

"Oh shut up, Taylor," four male voices said, almost in unison.

"I'm just saying—" Taylor started, but seeing the glaring eyes of his brothers, he stopped mid-sentence.

"Why'd you guys come here anyway?" I asked.

"To help Daddy!" Michael said emphatically.

"Because Mama called and she was upset," John Bob said. "I for one am here for my mother, and to help my baby sister. *And* to handle all the legal ramifications. It's just like my father to do something like this then run off leaving me to clean up his mess!"

"Ah, hell, that's true," David Lee drawled. "What *would* we do without old John Bob here to take care of everything?"

John Bob looked at David Lee and smirked. "Need any more bail money, Dave? I could write you another check."

"Guys, guys," Taylor started. "This is getting us nowhere—"

"Taylor's right about that," I said, standing up and trying to take charge. "There are things we can do, and I need to know now which of you will be around to help me. You others can explain to your mother why you decided not to help clear your father."

I threw that out there to see where it would land. Absolute silence. Then Jason said, "Well, of course I'll help. There was never any issue about that—"

John Bob said, "I'll do whatever I can. Being a lawyer—"

David Lee laughed. "Hell, Milt, you just got us all where we live. Not a one of us wants Mama mad at him, including me."

"I'm thinking of telling Mama that Milt had to threaten y'all to get you to cooperate!" Michael said, still standing up and still mad as a wet hen.

"Michael, son," David Lee drawled, "you're a big boy now, but the four of us can still whip your ass."

John Bob and Jason glared at Michael, and even Taylor said, "That's true, Michael."

"Well then you'd better shut up and help, that's all I can say!" Michael said, and sat back down. I think he believed the threat. I think I did, too.

"Okay then, if we're all in agreement, let's get started," I said, rubbing my hands together. "Who wants to take notes?" I asked. Taylor raised his hand and brought out a small notebook and a pen from his pocket. I nodded at him and continued. "Okay. We need to question people. Denise and Larry had neighbors, right? Neighbors are a good source of gossip, especially if there are any little old ladies around. They're great. Old men are, too. So we need to question the neighbors. Who else? Oh, that Greevey woman. Walter Allen's secretary—or administrative assistant, I think she called herself. She'll know something. Whether she'll tell it or not—"

"I'll take her," David Lee said, still stretched out on the couch. "I can always get a woman to talk."

"Talk?" John Bob smirked. "Is that what they're calling it nowadays?"

"I don't know," David Lee said, smiling at his older brother, "why don't you ask your wife?"

John Bob jumped up and almost knocked down Taylor, who was already standing in his brother's way, his arms outstretched.

"It was a joke, John Bob," Taylor said. "A really bad joke," he repeated, glaring at David Lee.

"Guys, you think you can cut the shit for just a little while?" I asked. "We've got serious business here."

John Bob sat back down, as did Taylor, and David Lee shrugged. "It was just a joke," he said.

"Okay," I said to Taylor, "write this down. David Lee's gonna talk to Melissa Greevey. Now, who else? Where did Larry Allen work?"

"At his father's casino," John Bob said. "He was assistant casino manager."

"Then we need to talk to some of the people who worked for him. Who wants to do that?"

"I will! I will!" Michael said, hand waving in the air.

I was a little worried about Michael's enthusiasm. I didn't think Walter Allen's casino was a place he should be.

"Mike, I need you on the neighbors. Taylor, can you handle talking to the casino people?"

Taylor looked up, his eyes huge. "Me? You want me to talk to them?"

"Yeah," I said, getting a little exasperated. "Can you handle that?"

"Ah, well, ah, I guess," Taylor said.

"Then write it down," I said.

He stared at me for a long moment, then wrote it down.

"What do you want me to do?" John Bob asked, somewhat reluctantly.

"You're a lawyer. Do some research. Find a computer or something and get what you can on Larry. Arrests, lawsuits, that kind of stuff."

John Bob nodded.

"Jason, I need you with Michael. It'll take two people to canvas the neighbors."

Jason nodded, looked like he was about to ask if there was a golf course in the area, thought better of it, and looked at the carpet.

"And what are you going to do?" John Bob asked me.

"Liaison with the LVPD," I said. I looked at my watch. "Look, it's getting late. Everybody needs to eat some dinner and I think y'all should probably make an appearance at the hospital. We'll meet here at eight in the morning and then start, okay?"

The reactions were as expected: Michael said, "You bet!" John Bob just glared at me, Jason got on the phone, Taylor shook my hand, and David Lee said, "There's an eight o'clock in the morning, too, huh?"

First Monday ✦ Prophesy County

Well, lunch hadn't gone so well. When he got to the KFC billboard, Jasmine and her squad car weren't there. He figured she had herself a speeder, and sat back in his seat, resting his head, windows down, feeling a slight cool breeze blowing in the September air. When he woke up and glanced at his watch, it was five minutes to the end of his lunch hour and Jasmine still wasn't back. Hell of a speeder, he thought.

Then he thought, maybe she's in trouble. A speeder who turned out to be a wanted felon. The felon had a gun and got the drop on her. He was holding her hostage. He started his squad car and headed down the highway, keeping an eye out for Jasmine's squad car. He found her by the turnoff to town. She had a car pulled over all right. A blue Volvo wagon. And she was leaning in the window. He stopped his car behind hers, got out, and walked up to the vehicle, right hand on the butt of his gun.

"Everything okay here, Officer?" he called.

Jasmine reared up and hit her head on the window frame of the Volvo, and he could hear the person inside laugh. "Shut up!" Jasmine said to the occupant, then reached in and appeared to hit the person.

Well, this was just all wrong, Emmett thought.

"Hey, Emmett. Just talking." She opened the driver's side door and another woman got out, one who looked a lot like Jasmine, a little heavier, a little shorter. "This is my sister, Lily," she said.

Emmett produced a smile and stuck out his hand. "Emmett Hopkins, acting sheriff," he said.

The woman giggled. "Oh, I know who *you* are!" she said, and punched her sister in the arm, who turned and punched her back, whispering, "Shut up!"

He'd left right after that, heading back to the house, fuming. Not only had she left him hanging at the billboard, she'd gone and told her sister about them! Damn, he thought, damn, damn!

He worried on it all afternoon, and when Jasmine wandered back in, late as usual, he called her into his office.

She strolled in and patted Milt's desk. "Honey, we can do better than this!"

"You knew I was waiting for you at the billboard," he said, his voice tight.

"Oh, Lord, I forgot! I hardly ever eat lunch, and just forgot about it after I spotted Lily. I'm sorry."

"And when you spotted Lily, you just had to tell her all about us, huh?" he said.

Jasmine pulled back from the desk, her hands on her hips. "Actually, no. I called Lily last night, after you were asleep, and told her. She's my sister and I won't apologize for letting her into my life!"

"I thought we weren't going to tell anybody about this?" he said.

"We never said that," she said.

"Hell we didn't!" he said. "We've been going out of our way not letting people know about this!"

"People, Emmett! And the guys here, and Gladys, of course. Not my sisters!"

Emmett blanched. "You got more than one sister?"

"I have three sisters and a brother. Lily, Rose, Iris, and Larry. And, yes, they all know. Except Larry. He wouldn't give a damn one way or the other."

"Well, how long before they tell everybody in town?"

Arms around her waist, hugging herself. "Are you that ashamed of being seen with me?"

"That's not what this is about and you know it!" Emmett said.

"Oh, I think it is," Jasmine said. "I think that is exactly what this is about. You've got yourself a little piece of ass on the side, and you want to keep that real private. Not embarrass yourself. Well, I'll tell you this, Emmett Hopkins, I am *nobody's* piece on the side!"

With that, she whirled and slammed out the door, almost knocking Henry down in the process. Henry looked after her and then at Emmett, grinned, and headed for the front desk.

"I think Maida expects a little bit too much from the boys," I said to Jean that evening. We'd finally made it to the all-you-can-eat seafood buffet on the strip and Jean had kept her mouth shut when I went back the third time. Vacation is still vacation, you know?

"They're her sons," Jean said. "She expects them to rally around their father. Sometimes it's hard for a mother to realize that each of her children has a different relationship with not only her, but their father as well. People often see shared experiences differently. What was a funny incident to one son could be a traumatic incident to another." She looked up at me. "Are you understanding this?"

I took umbrage to that remark. "Hey, I'm not Johnny Mac," I said. Then, thinking about my own sister, I said. "But I can relate to that. With the thirteen-year age difference between me and Jewel Anne, it's like we had different parents. I had the young ones, she had the old ones."

"And I'm sure they raised you quite differently. Not only because of the age difference, but because of the gender difference as well."

"Yeah, there's that," I agreed.

"Have you talked to Detective Broderick today?" she asked.

"One quick phone call. Just to see if the situation's changed at all." I shook my head. "No sign of Burl."

"Since you're handing out assignments, did you get any of the boys to check out the roulette tables at the various casinos?"

"No, I've got 'em all doing other stuff. I guess I can walk the strip again."

"Don't forget the old Las Vegas. The downtown area. There are still a lot of casinos down there. Why don't you let me handle that one?" she suggested.

I grinned. "Looking for that free booze again?" I asked.

Jean blushed. "I've seen that trap and now know how to circumnavigate it."

So we made a plan: after dinner she'd take a taxi downtown and check out those casinos, while I cruised the casinos on Las Vegas Blvd. I kissed her good-bye as the taxi pulled up, then started walking. Late as it was, with night falling hard and fast, I was still sweating. I figured all the food I'd been eating since I got here was gonna cancel out all the walking and the sweating. I hoped to stay my chubby self and not push over into fat.

It was nine o'clock at night and the casinos were hopping. All the gaming tables were in use and there was a crowd at the roulette table of the first hotel I went in. Luckily, as big and tall as Burl is, he woulda stood out in almost any crowd. Unluckily, he didn't. I took a quick turn around the slots and headed out the door to the next casino. Again, zip, zero, nada.

Funny thing about Vegas, you can see things there you just wouldn't see anyplace else. Like sixty-year-old men with young, scantily clad ladies hanging on their arms, and sixty-year-old women with young, scantily clad men hanging on *their* arms. The thought never even crossed my mind that these were affectionate grandchildren. Then there was the old lady Jean and I saw every time we left the Bellagio: diamonds dripping off her fingers, ears, and throat, wearing what Jean said were expensive designer clothes, sitting all day long playing the nickel slots.

In any crowd there you'd see middle-aged men in madras Bermuda shorts, older ladies in Spandex, girls walking down the street in string bikinis, and well-dressed drunks leaning against buildings at nine in the morning. Las Vegas was a smorgasbord of weird. Blue-haired punks waiting in line at the aquarium, blue-haired old ladies in house dresses waiting in line at a male burlesque.

When Jean and I had left the elevator at the hotel earlier, we'd been greeted by an Asian lady dressed in scrubs, saying she was a private duty nurse trying to get upstairs to her client, and could we use our code to let her get up there. Now, "client" was what gave her away to me. I think most private duty nurses woulda said "patient." We referred her to the front desk, then Jean talked nonstop all the way to the restaurant about the wonders of meeting her first hooker.

The fourth hotel I went in was the Lonestar, which was looking a lot less weird the more I saw of Vegas. I was hoping Walter Allen was still "indisposed," and I wouldn't get pounced on for walking in the front door. I checked the roulette table: no Burl. Walked around the slots and other gaming tables; still no Burl. I headed for the bathroom and that's when I saw her: Melissa Greevey in deep conversation with one of "the boys." Except it wasn't David Lee getting to his assignment early. It was John Bob. And the two of them were having words—as in neither was happy with the other and fingers were being pointed.

Interesting, I thought. I slipped into the men's room and peeked out the door, wishing I had some of that spy equipment that lets you listen in on conversations. Not only would it give me a heads up on what was going on here, but it would definitely be cool.

"Hey, buddy, you wanna move?"

I whirled around to stare into the blurry eyes of a man trying to get out the bathroom door. "Sorry about that," I said, moving back so he could leave. When I got back to my post, Melissa and John Bob were gone.

Getting back to the Bellagio, I took a quick turn around the casino, found nothing interesting, and headed back upstairs. Jean had beat me there, she said, by just a couple of minutes.

I told her what I'd seen at the Lonestar. "Well," she said,

smiling like the cat that ate the canary, "John Bob wasn't the only busy little bee tonight. I went into one of the sleazier casinos downtown and saw David Lee."

"Interesting," I said.

"Oh, it gets better. He was being hassled by this very sleazy guy, and ended up giving him money. A lot of money. I saw him counting it out. And it made me wonder, Milt: If David Lee just got into Vegas today, how does he know this man and why does he owe him money?"

She had a point. Seems like I was gonna be having some private conversations tomorrow with a couple of "the boys."

FIRST MONDAY ✦ PROPHESY COUNTY

Emmett lay in his own bed that night, thinking about Jasmine. Hell, in twenty years of marriage with Shirley Beth they'd never fought half as much as he and Jasmine had fought in just a few days. That should tell him something. This just wasn't gonna work. The woman made his blood boil. Yeah, well there was the good kind of blood boiling, and the bad kind of blood boiling, and she did both.

But she kept him on his toes. Nothing boring about Jasmine. Going and telling her sisters. Ye gods! What was she thinking? And accusing him of being ashamed to be seen with her! What kind of horse hockey was that? He wasn't ashamed of her. Just the opposite, he was damned proud to have a woman like that thinking he was hot stuff. He grinned to himself. And she did, too—think he was hot stuff.

He picked up the phone and dialed her number.

She answered a sleepy, "Hello?"

"Tomorrow I'm going to stand in the middle of the bull pen and tell everybody that I'm sleeping with Jasmine Bodine, and if they have anything to say about it we can just step outside."

She giggled. "Well, that's nice, but probably not a good idea."

"Okay," he said, "how's this? City council meets on Wednesday. I'll go there, in front of the mayor and everybody, and say, 'Jasmine Bodine thinks I'm hot stuff and she's right!' How's that?"

"Oh," she said. "I think you're hot stuff?"

"Yeah," he said. Then embarrassed, he said, "You do, don't you?"

She laughed. "Come on over here and I'll show you just how hot I think you are."

He didn't waste any time getting his pants on.

First Tuesday ◆ Las Vegas

The first thing on the agenda the next morning, however, was getting Denise out of the hospital and then she and Maida to their suite at the Bellagio. Denise was *really* pregnant. This was the first time I'd seen her standing up and it was amazing to me— what with the pouch sticking out in front the way it was—that Larry Allen's kick hadn't done more damage. The placenta had healed itself, and there was no more talk of an early C-section. Her doctor said she would probably carry to term and they would try a vaginal delivery. That was good news all around.

Maida had told her that Larry was dead earlier that morning, and the girl was some upset.

I know it's hard to understand how a woman who gets beat by a man can still love him, but it happens. I got pissed on pretty hard by a woman one time, nothing physical, but the psychological (as my wife would say) and emotional beating was pretty bad; and I kept on loving her for a time after. Even though I wasn't with her and *wouldn't* be with her.

Love's a funny puppy; nothing much you can do about it. Jean and other psychologists and psychiatrists who talk about the "battered wife syndrome" say that the batterer brings a woman down so far emotionally and psychologically that she becomes totally dependent on him, and begins to believe that the physical stuff is all her fault. If she hadn't overcooked his eggs, or if she had only mopped the floor earlier, or if she had had the kids in bed when he got home, whatever. They say the men, the batterers, all have real low self-esteem themselves, and that having control over "their woman" gets some of that back for 'em, or at least they think it does. And somehow all this gets interpreted as love, by both the woman and the man.

But all that psychobabble doesn't help a lot when you're looking at a real pregnant and battered young woman whose husband has just been murdered by, maybe, her own father.

"The boys" were all in attendance at the hospital while we checked Denise out. I noticed I hadn't seen Michael's girlfriend Barbara Jo since the first day. When I asked him where she was, he said, "Oh, shopping." He grimaced. "I sorta gave her my Visa." The other brothers hooted at their baby brother for his naiveté.

Jean was there, too, for moral and psychological support. Good thing too, since Denise asked if she could ride alone with Jean. I'd rented a van to cart everybody from the hotel, but David Lee had brought his own car, an old, beat up 280 Z. He told Jean it was an automatic and she could drive it and he'd ride in the van, which is what we all did.

It had been total chaos on the way over, what with "the boys" spouting off to each other, pushing buttons long left dormant, and more or less getting on each other's nerves—and mine— something fierce. But the ride back was a heap different. Maida's presence put the boys on their best behavior.

When we all pulled into the valet parking at the Bellagio and got out, I noticed a smile on Denise's face for the first time. Her eyes were red from crying, and the smile was kinda weak, but it was there just the same. We got Maida and Denise settled in their suite, and Jean stayed with them while I took the boys across the hall to the living room of our suite. I still needed to get John Bob and David Lee alone—separately—but there were other things needed doing, too.

"John Bob," I asked when we were all seated with coffee in front of us, "you get a chance to do any computer searches?"

"I called my paralegal back home and she was up half the night doing it, and she faxed me her results early this morning." I shoulda known he wouldn't—or couldn't—do it himself. He picked his briefcase up off the floor and opened it, pulling out a sheaf of paper stapled together. "This is everything she was able to get on Larry Allen, and on Walter Allen. Makes for interesting reading," he said.

"Just the highlights," I said. "I'll go over the whole thing later."

"Highlights, hum?" John Bob said. "Well, to start with Larry's got a record. Something in his youth, but of course, that's sealed, but at eighteen he was arrested for DWI and date rape. All charges dropped. At nineteen, public intoxication and failure to appear. All charges dropped. At twenty, possession of a controlled substance. Charges dropped. Y'all seeing a pattern here?"

"Yeah," David Lee drawled, "Larry was a regular asshole but Daddy got him out of it."

"Sound familiar?" John Bob asked, shooting daggers at his younger brother, David Lee.

"Is that it?" I asked, hoping to avoid the sniping that was surely to come if I kept my mouth shut.

"Oh, hell no," John Bob said. "Seems the other night wasn't the first time he's hit my baby sister. There are three calls on here for domestic disturbance at their address, and Betty—that's my paralegal—found hospital records on Denise for two occasions—one for a broken arm supposedly suffered after a fall, and one for internal injuries—another fall. Funny, my sister wasn't all that clumsy growing up."

"What about Walter Allen?" Michael asked. "You said there was something on him?"

"Yeah, he's been sued twenty-seven times. Most of 'em settled out of court," John Bob said, "which means he was probably guilty as sin and paid everybody off."

"What were the suits about?" I asked.

"The oldest one started out as a criminal case of negligent homicide. Some kid working for him during his oil days died in an accident on a rig. No details on that. Allen, of course, beat the criminal charges but the parents sued him and he settled out of court. Doesn't say for how much. Let's see," he said, scanning the papers in front of him. "Lots of ex-partners suing over this and that. Went bankrupt four times." John Bob looked up. "I didn't think you could do that in Texas." He looked back at his papers and said, "Oh, one bankruptcy was in Oklahoma and another in Alaska. Had a lot of investors suing to get their money back, but he won those suits." He shuffled the papers some more, then said, "Okay, here's a good one. Seems the late Mrs. Allen—that is, the third Mrs. Allen—had filed domestic abuse charges against him on two occasions; one she dropped, the other she didn't live to carry out."

"What happened to her?" I asked.

"Funny you should ask that," John Bob said, grinning. "Betty dug into that, too, and seems the late Mrs. Allen, Mrs. Andrea Allen, twenty-seven years old when she died—twenty-four when she married fifty-six-year-old Walter—died in a car wreck just days prior to going before a grand jury."

"You're not insinuating Walter Allen killed her, are you?" Jason asked. "I mean, with all his money and connections, he's been able to get his son and himself out of worse situations. Why would he kill her over a possible domestic abuse charge?"

John Bob glared at Jason. "I'm not *insinuating* jack shit," he said. "I'm just giving Milt here the facts. He's the expert. He can interpret them as he sees fit. And as for you, Jason, wouldn't you better serve this entire situation if you just went and played golf?"

"That's not fair, John Bob," Taylor said. "Jason was just asking—"

Simultaneously John Bob and Jason said, "Shut up, Taylor."

"Anything else?" I asked John Bob.

Still glaring at his two brothers, John Bob said, "No, that's about the gist of it."

"Okay, then the rest of you have your assignments for the day. Michael, you and Jason are interviewing Denise's neighbors; Taylor, you're doing Larry's staff; and David Lee, you're gonna talk to Melissa Greevey. John Bob, can you stay here with me a minute, go over these faxes?"

"Sure, Milt," John Bob said, puffing his chest out. Little did he know, I thought to myself. I also called myself a sly fox, but then I tend to do that sometimes.

The rest of the boys filed out to their assignments, which left me alone with John Bob. He handed me the fax and said, "Peruse it at your leisure. It makes for mighty interesting reading."

"I'm sure it does," I said, setting the faxed sheets next to me on the couch. "But that's not what I wanted to talk to you about."

The lawyer in him started peeking out big time. "Well, what is it?"

"Saw you last night at the Lonestar," I said. "I was there checking out the roulette tables, looking for your daddy—"

"So was I," John Bob said quickly. "Why didn't you say hello?"

"'Cause you seemed to be in deep conversation with Melissa Greevey."

"Who?" Oh, he was a lawyer all right. The lie came off his tongue like melted butter.

"Walter Allen's administrative assistant. The one David Lee's just gone to interview. The two of you seemed to be having words. There was finger pointing and everything."

"Oh, that woman!" John Bob said. "Didn't know who she was. I ran into an attorney I know from Santa Fe and he called me 'Upshank'. She heard it, and you know, Milt, it *is* an unusual last name. Anyway, she told me no Upshanks were allowed in that hotel. I took exception to that." He smiled, a shark-like smile. (You know why a shark won't eat a lawyer when he falls in the ocean? Professional courtesy!) "That's all that was, Milt." He stood up. "Well, if you don't have another assignment for me, I think I'll go check on Mama and Denise." And with that he was out the door.

The thing was, it was plausible. It really was. But somehow I still didn't believe it. Something else had been going on with John Bob and Melissa Greevey—I just didn't know what. But I figured, somehow, I was gonna find out.

Emmett was sitting at Milt's desk, thinking about Jasmine when Gladys paged him. "Got a holdup at Larry's Pawn Shop," she said. "Going down right now. Jasmine and Dalton both are responding."

"Silent alarm?" he asked.

"Yeah, somebody got close enough to the button to push it."

"Keep me posted," he said, going back to the paperwork spread out on Milt's desk, pretending he was studying it.

And that's when Dalton's voice came over the radio, loud enough for Emmett to hear it in Milt's office. "Officer down! Repeat! Officer down!"

Emmett jumped up and ran into the bull pen. Gladys was on the radio, trying to raise Dalton. Looking at Emmett with fear in her eyes, she said, "He won't answer!"

Emmett grabbed the mike and said, "Dalton! Dalton, come in! Anybody there!"

There was no response. Emmett's gut tightened into a fist. He ran out of the building and jumped in his squad car, peeling rubber as he exited the lot, siren blasting. It was a five-minute drive to the pawnshop, the new building they put up right outside the city limits. County jurisdiction. He made it in two minutes flat.

All he could think of was Jasmine. Officer down. Dalton had called it in, that meant the officer down was Jasmine. How bad was it? Was she alive? Was her life's blood pouring out of her as he drove? Did anybody call for an ambulance? Shit, he thought. Oh, shit.

People were standing around the entrance to the pawnshop as he brought the squad car to a screeching halt in the middle of the parking lot. He bailed out, running to the entrance. A Longbranch Memorial ambulance blocked his view of the carnage. Their flashers weren't on. That could only mean one thing: Jasmine was dead.

Emmett rounded the ambulance and stopped in his tracks. Jasmine was on the ground, bent over. He ran to her but stopped when he got close enough to see what was going on. She was bent over a suspect who was lying prone on the asphalt, arms behind his back as Jasmine cuffed him. The paramedics were several yards away, kneeling by Dalton, who sat with his back leaning against the bank building, his face a grimace of pain.

"What's going on?" Emmett finally got out.

"Hey, Emmett," Jasmine said, standing up and hauling her suspect to his feet. "Got us a real-life armed robber here. Clyde without his Bonnie. Baby Face Nelson with acne. John Dillinger without his tommy gun."

Emmett tried to ignore her, walked instead to Dalton. To the paramedics, he asked, "He shot?"

"Hell no," said one. "He tripped and broke his ankle we think. Could be a bad sprain, but more likely it's a break."

Emmett let out a gush of air. Nobody's dead, he told himself. Nobody's dead. Jasmine's okay. He turned to her. "How'd it go down?"

"Dumb ass here—" she said, poking the suspect in the back, "decides he can rob the shop with a poorly written note. Unfortunately, the clerk couldn't read it, and while he was deciphering it for her, another clerk hit the alarm. We come in the side door, asshole here—" she poked him again, "sees us and heads out the front. Dalton runs after him, the owner is trying to get the asshole, too—" again with the poke, "and he and Dalton bang into each other. Dalton goes down, but manages to grab this asshole—" poke, "while he's doing it. Dalton and the owner are all tangled up, and I think that's when he hurt his ankle." She looked over at Dalton and said loudly, "Dalton's a real hero, Emmett. Took this asshole—" poke, "all by himself."

Emmett glanced at Dalton, who was smiling through his pain. "And managed to call in his own 'officer down,'" Emmett said.

"Oh, that's how you got here so fast," Jasmine said, oblivious to the racing of Emmett's heart. She gave Dalton a thumb's up. "Way to go, man!"

Dalton beamed. Emmett sighed. "Take the perp back to the house. I'll ride in the ambulance with Dalton," he said. "Get somebody to take my squad car back to the house."

"Got it, boss," she said and grinned, then kneed the suspect in the butt and said, "Move it, asshole."

"You read him his rights?" Emmett called after her.

"Duh," she said, and kept going.

Emmett watched her walk away, manhandling the suspect as she went. He wondered if he'd live through this thing with her. Somehow, he sort of doubted it.

The assignment I'd given myself was to liaison with the LVPD. I hadn't been doing much of that, so I decided to take a taxi over to see what was going on in Lieutenant Grayson's bailiwick. It was cooler today, maybe in the high eighties, with a light wind blowing from the north. The sky was dark in that direction, but the sun still beat strong overhead. For some reason, the sun seemed closer to the ground here than it did in Oklahoma, so much so that I was thinking about buying a hat to protect my bald spot—or spots.

Lieutenant Grayson wasn't in, but Jimmy Broderick was.

"Hey, Sheriff," he said, standing up and smiling at me with his goofy grin. "Any sign of Mr. Upshank?"

"Not that I've noticed," I said. "I take it there's been no word around here?"

"No, sir," he said. "We've had lookouts at the airports, the bus and train stations, and the rental car places. Lot of those, though. Just had to leave a picture and hope somebody would call. No word though."

"I think he's still in town," I offered.

"Yes, sir, why's that?"

"I don't know," I answered. "Just a gut feeling."

"Well, sir, a cop's gotta go with his gut," Broderick said.

"I always thought so," I said.

"So you getting any vacationing in?" Broderick asked.

"Not so's you'd notice," I said.

"How big's your county, anyway, Sheriff?" he asked, looking goofy. Course, Broderick always looked a little goofy.

"Well, the county seat's a little over fourteen thousand souls, but I only know about thirteen thousand of 'em personally," I said with a grin. "But the whole county's about three hundred square miles."

"Wow, that's like Nevada. Big county, but not a lot of people, huh?"

"Lot of farm and ranch land, some small towns. All in all, the county's tax rolls show an additional three thousand."

"How many deputies you got?" he asked.

I tried to raise an eyebrow, but ended up, I'm sure, just looking stupid. "You looking to maybe transfer, Detective?"

Broderick laughed. "Oh, no, sir. Just asking."

"Well, I got four full-time deputies, a part-time jailer, and a civilian clerk."

"Boy, that's a lot of country for only four deputies."

"Tell me about it," I said.

Then we both just sat there for a minute, me checking my watch, Broderick looking slant-wise at his computer screen. I stood up. "Well, Detective, keep in touch," I said.

He shook my hand, rendering it useless for about ten seconds, and said, "Yes, sir, I sure will. You take care."

I gave him a half-hearted wave and left the office. If Broderick knew anything, I decided, he sure as hell wasn't going to tell me. Just like I didn't give him any information. Not that I had much, just that one of Burl Upshank's sons had an argument with Walter Allen's administrative assistant, and another seemed to owe some big money to a local. Neither of which might have anything to do with either Burl's disappearance or Larry Allen's murder. On the other hand, I think Grayson would jump on the information, if for no other reason than for something positive to do. Which was what I was doing, wasn't it?

I got back to our suite just in time to see my wife grabbing her purse and heading to the door. "What's up?" I asked.

"God, I'm glad you're here. I just got a call from hotel security. They've got Barbara Jo in lockup."

"Barbara Jo?" I asked, not sure who she was talking about.

"Michael's girlfriend," Jean reminded me.

"Lockup for what?" I demanded. She seemed like a real nice girl.

"Shoplifting," Jean said. "Are you coming with me?" she asked, her tone implying that if I didn't there wouldn't be a hell of a lot of dog food in my doghouse that night.

"Yeah, sure," I said, and turned and went with her down to the mezzanine where the security office was. The security chief was an ex-cop, which he didn't need to tell me—it was written all over him. He was a big guy in a nice suit, gold cuff links, a diamond stickpin in his silk tie, and Italian shoes that probably would've cost me a month's paycheck. I mentally toyed with the idea of getting one of these security gigs myself. Then I thought of my poor county with somebody like my deputy Dalton Pettigrew running the show, and I sort of let the fantasy go.

I introduced myself and Jean to the security chief, who said his name was Tom Dalrymple. We shook hands and I told him we were here to see about Barbara Jo.

"Don't know her last name. She's the girlfriend of a friend of mine," I said, "and he asked me to see what was going on."

"Barbara Jo Bailey, Sheriff," Dalrymple said. "And we got her for trying to walk out of one of the dress shops with two scarves, a nightie, and a pair of thong underwear."

"Hum," I said. "Maybe she was just too embarrassed to pay for them."

"This was after her Visa card denied the purchase."

"Oh," I said, hoping Michael had a low limit on the credit card. "Can we see her? My wife here is the girl's doctor," I lied.

"Yeah, sure." Turning, he called, "Charlie! Take these people back to see the detainee."

Detainee, I thought. Not prisoner. No, not in a fancy hotel like the Bellagio. We were taken down a long hall by Charlie, a black man in his twenties, dressed almost as well as Dalrymple, who unlocked a normal-looking door and led us down another corridor until we reached the right room.

Barbara Jo was sitting on the twin-sized bed in the room, which looked like a normal hotel room, except there were two twin beds, not queen or king-sized ones. She didn't look like the same girl I'd met the first day the boys got here—jeez, was that only two days ago? Her hair was mussed, she had a wild look in her eyes, and her face was flushed. She jumped up when she saw us and burst into tears.

"Oh, Sheriff Milt," she cried, "help me!" Then she threw her arms around me and started to sob. I just looked at Jean. I'm not much good around crying women.

"Barbara Jo, come sit down," Jean said, taking the girl's arms from around my neck and leading her back to the bed. "Tell us what happened."

"I don't know! This never happened to me before! I—I—spent all of Michael's money!" she wailed. "All of it! He just got that card and he was going to buy me an engagement ring with it, and now there's nothing left!"

"What in the hell did you buy?" I demanded, and lowered my head in mock shame as Jean glared at me.

"Everything! Anything! It didn't matter! I just bought it!" She looked at Jean with a scared look in her eyes. "I don't know what happened to me," she said, her voice like that of a little girl. "I've never been a big shopper. But I bought a set of golf clubs, for Christ's sake! Neither Michael nor I play golf!" she wailed. "I must have known I was doing something wrong because I hid all the purchases from Michael. Even though half of them are for him. I bought him three shirts he will just hate!" She burst into tears and leaned her head against Jean's shoulder.

"How much?" I asked. "What was the limit on the card?"

Barbara Jo shook her head. "I don't know," she said. Then lowering her head, she added, "but at least five thousand."

Now, I thought, this was a unique young lady: comes to the gambling capital of the world and gets a shopping jones. Just didn't seem right somehow.

"What about this shoplifting charge?" I asked.

She shook her head. "I—I—don't know. I—was just so shocked when the lady said the card wouldn't work, that I was over the limit, that I panicked. I just ran out of the store. I—I—didn't even realize I still had that stuff in my hands! I didn't mean to steal anything! Oh, God! Michael's going to hate me! It's all over! I can't believe I did this!" And then the crying started up again.

"Let me go talk to Dalrymple," I said to Jean. "See if I can straighten this out."

I knocked on the door and Charlie let me out and led me back to Dalrymple's office. He was on the phone and I waited politely right outside his door until he finished and motioned me in.

"Well, Sheriff, you see your girl?" Dalrymple asked.

"Yes, sir, and I appreciate the courtesy."

"No problem. I haven't called the LVPD yet to come pick her up, but that's the next order of business."

"I wonder if you might hold off on that," I asked. "See if we can't work something out."

Dalrymple shook his head. "We don't tolerate shoplifting around here any more than we tolerate card counting or chip stealing on the casino floor."

"I understand that, Chief," I said. "The thing is, the young lady didn't mean to steal anything. When she found out she was over the limit on the Visa, she just panicked." I smiled indulgently. "Seems she went on a shopping spree and ran up close to five thousand dollars on the card. And now she's gotta tell her boyfriend. It was his card."

Dalrymple shook his head. "You gotta wonder about a guy who'd give a woman a brand new card and let her loose in a place like this," he said.

"Ain't that the truth," I agreed. "The thing is, the girl's really distraught. She didn't mean to steal anything. She just panicked."

Dalrymple shook his head again. Finally he said, "Okay, listen. I see that girl in any shop in this hotel, she's a goner. I'm keeping this warrant open until she leaves the hotel. She can't go into any of the shops. Got that?"

"Yes, sir," I said.

"And she's gotta pay for the scarves, the nightie, and the panties."

"Can't she just return the merchandise?" I asked.

"They don't accept returns on intimate apparel," Dalrymple said, "which would be the nightie and the thong underwear. And just to keep everything real simple," he said, smiling at me, "why don't we just have her pay for everything?"

I took out my billfold. "That's no problem, I'll take care of that myself right now. How much did she owe?"

Dalrymple looked at the paperwork in front of him. "Six hundred and five dollars and seventy-seven cents."

"Six hundred dollars?" I exclaimed—okay, shouted. "For some undies?"

He showed me the paperwork. One scarf was ninety-seven dollars—"it was silk," Dalrymple explained, the other was one hundred and forty—"silk and designer." The nightie was two hundred and seventy-five and the thong underwear was sixty.

"Well, hell," I said, "it musta been a short shopping spree. Five grand'd go awful fast at these prices."

"We have very high quality shops at the Bellagio," Dalrymple said and grinned.

"Will you take an out-of-town check?" I asked, getting out

my checkbook and wondering who I was gonna get to reimburse me on this. Michael was probably dead broke now, and Burl—well, Burl wasn't exactly in a position to write me a check.

I paid off Dalrymple and he sent Charlie back to get Barbara Jo and Jean. In ten minutes we were back in our suite, me in the living room, Jean and Barbara Jo in the bedroom. I could hear the crying through the closed door and wondered if she was ever gonna stop.

After about an hour, the two came out. "Thank you for paying for that—that crap!" Barbara Jo said, hiccupping. "I'll pay you back every last penny."

"Don't worry about that," Jean said, while I was thinking, yeah, honey, worry about it! "Right now, we're going to your room and you're going to take a shower and then a nap. Right?"

Barbara Jo nodded. "Thank you, Jean, I don't know what I would have done—" She started crying again.

"Come on, sweetie," Jean said, leading her out.

Jean was barely gone before there was a knock on the door and I answered it to find Maida standing there. "What's wrong with Barbara Jo?" she demanded.

"Ah—" I started.

"I heard the crying, looked out my peephole and saw Jean and Barbara Jo walking down the hall toward Michael's room. What's going on?"

"Maida, you're gonna have to talk to Michael about that, but I'd wait a bit."

"Milt, when it comes to my children, I don't wait," she said firmly. "Where's Michael?"

"He's on a mission for me," I said.

"Doing what?" Maida demanded.

"All the boys are doing things to help clear their dad. I thought that's why you had them come down here?"

Maida was quiet for a moment. "Well, yes, I suppose it was. But what's going on with Barbara Jo?"

"Maida, I'm trying to help you here but I didn't sign on for all this shit. Now, you need to ask Michael tomorrow morning, okay?"

Well, that got her hackles up.

"If we're inconveniencing you, Milt, you can leave at any time. I would hate to think that me and mine have become a burden on you."

She had that tone again. My mama had that tone sometimes; always made me itch.

"Maida, I'm trying real hard here to clear your husband of murder charges. I don't think Burl did this, and I wanna prove it. Your boys are helping the best they can. All I'm saying is, talk to Michael. That's all I gotta say, and if you wanna make an issue out of it, then I guess you can do it to a closed door."

I was tired. Didn't get a lot of sleep the night before. That's my excuse for being rude to kin.

First Tuesday ✦ Prophesy County

Emmett sat at Milt's desk, the door to the office closed, and fretted. They'd set Dalton's foot at the hospital and sent him home. Luckily he lived with his mother, so that part was taken care of. Emmett wasn't fretting about Dalton. It was Jasmine. Why in the world would he get himself involved with a cop? Cops got hurt, they got shot, they got knifed, they got run into on the side of the road while stopping speeders. Cops had a high rate of alcoholism, divorce, and suicide. What in the hell was he thinking? But this was just a passing thing, he decided. They were both—what did they call it on TV?—in a transitional phase, yeah, that was it. He was her rebound guy and she was his rebound gal. When he thought about it, it really was all pretty casual. Ye gods, he was having casual sex! he thought. That was pretty damned twenty-first century, thank you very much, Miss Think You Know So Much Bodine.

He almost laughed out loud, then worried that Gladys would hear and worry that he was going nuts. Gladys worried about a lot of things. So, it was okay. He wasn't *involved* with a cop, he was having casual sex with a cop. And Jasmine was also having casual sex with a cop. She probably felt the same way about it as he did. Why would she want to get involved with a cop?

Emmett was relieved. This was no big deal. Casual. Nice and casual. Which meant he could go over to her house tonight with absolutely no worries.

First Tuesday ✦ Las Vegas

The boys started checking in around three o'clock that afternoon. The girls, as I will now call them—Maida, Jean, Denise, and Barbara Jo—had gone on a sightseeing tour and would be gone until around dinnertime. Which left me with plenty of time to grill the boys about their day.

David Lee was the first, and I was glad of that. I had some questions for him that didn't have anything to do with his interview with Melissa Greevey. He came in in his insolent way, a beer in one hand, a cigarette in the other. Although the smoke smelled real good to me, I knew it wouldn't to Jean, so I had to say, "Gotta put that out, bubba. This is a no-smoking room."

He looked around for a receptacle and didn't find one. I took the half-smoked cigarette from his hand and went into the bedroom and through to the bathroom. I held it in my hand, smelling it. It was a Marlboro. That's what I used to smoke. I felt the weight in my hand, breathed in the smoke, and thought about finishing it for David Lee. I let the devil and the angel, the two sitting on my shoulders, duke it out. The angel, bless him, won, and I tossed the cigarette in the toilet and flushed. Sighed real heavy, then went back out to the living room to talk to David Lee.

He was stretched out on the couch, eyes half-closed, the beer resting on his stomach.

"So how'd it go with Melissa Greevey?" I asked.

"Funny you should ask," David Lee said. The only thing moving was his lips. "Ms. Greevey is grieving. I'd say there was something either going on between her and Larry, used to go on, or she wished it had gone on. One of the three."

"Think she killed him?"

David Lee's eyes opened at the question. "Shit, Milt, how would I know? Women are capable of anything. Maybe they're having an affair, he promises to divorce Denise, doesn't, and Melissa loses it. Or she's been pining for him ever since they broke up, or if they never had an affair, she's been pining forever, and she just had enough and shot his ass. Hell if I know."

"Those are real nice theories, David Lee, but what I need are facts. You got any of those?"

"She worships Walter Allen, for some damn reason. She's a native of Las Vegas. Born and bred. Went to school here—University of Nevada at Las Vegas. Got her degree in business. Been working at the Lonestar since she was in high school, though. Doing this and that, she said. Old Walter took a fancy to her—not in a sexual way, she insisted—and sent her to college. When she got her degree, he made her his administrative assistant. She pretty much runs the hotel, according to her."

"So how long you been in Vegas, David Lee?" I asked out of the blue.

He straightened up on the couch. "What do you mean?" he asked.

"Something tells me you didn't drive that old Z all the way from Oklahoma," I said.

David Lee grinned. "You'd be surprised how much spunk that old girl's still got in her. And no, I didn't drive her here from Oklahoma. I drove her here from Dallas," he said, adding, "about six months ago."

"So you've been in Vegas for six months."

"Yeah," he said, stretching back out on the couch.

"Doing what?" I asked.

"This and that," he said.

"Denise know you were in town?" I asked.

He shook his head. "Never liked her husband much. Didn't see any reason to bother 'em. If I'd known he was smacking her around, though, I woulda made it my business to stop by."

"You ever see Larry while you were doing this and that?" I asked.

"Naw. I try to stay away from the new strip. Downtown's more my speed."

"Where'd you get the money you paid that shark the other night?"

David Lee opened one eye and peeked at me. "What you got, Milt? Spies? You got somebody stalking me?" he asked, grinning.

"Where'd you get the money?"

"From Mama. She's always been real nice to her baby boy."

I shook my head. David Lee was certainly living up to his black sheep reputation. "Maida gonna confirm that?" I asked.

David Lee laughed. "Well, first she'll read you the riot act for getting in her business, but, yeah, then she'll confirm it."

"How much?" I asked.

David Lee shook his head. "You know, Milt, I've been real agreeable, answering all these personal questions, when what

I was supposed to be doing was telling you what went on in my conversation with Melissa Greevey. But I think," he said, levering himself up from the couch, "I've had about as much of this interrogation as I'm gonna take. If you really want to know how much, ask Mama. And after you pick yourself up off the floor," he said, his hand on the doorknob, "please, ask her again. Just for grins." With that, he was out the door.

MICHAEL AND JASON were next. Michael was in good spirits, and since I knew Barbara Jo had gone on the sightseeing tour with Jean and them, I knew he had no idea how in debt he was at the moment. I, for one, had no intention of telling him. Barbara Jo was gonna have to do that all by her lonesome.

Instead, I asked, "Hey, fellas, how did it go? Find any good neighbors?"

"You bet!" said Michael, his enthusiasm apparent. "There's this little old lady who lives right next door to Denise, and just like you said, Milt, they love to talk and they know all their neighbors' business." He grabbed a notebook out of his back pocket and flipped it open. "This one's name was Mrs. Sherwood—didn't get a first name—and she's lived on that block since the forties. She told me all about Las Vegas back in its heyday. Said she even knew Bugsy Siegel—imagine that? She was a showgirl. Showed me a picture of herself back then. Real looker, not that you can tell that now. She's been married four—"

"Mike," I interrupted, "anything about your sister and her husband?"

"Well, sure, Milt, I'm coming to that," he said, a little irritated that I wasn't all that interested in Mrs. Sherwood's salad days. "She said Larry bought the house right before he and Denise got married, and then him and Denise moved in right after the honeymoon. And she said he started in on her that first week!" He looked from me to his brother. "Can you believe it? That asshole was beating on her from the very beginning and we didn't know diddly squat about it!"

I'd given Michael and Jason a list of questions to ask the neighbors, and it looked like I was gonna have to draw Michael out on each and every one of them. "She see anybody hanging around the night Larry got shot?"

"She was out of town that week, visiting her daughter in Fresno, she said. But she did say that there were a lot of comings and goings over there—all hours of the night, too. She said she saw Larry with a girl one night, real early in the morning, actually, and they were making out in the front seat of her car! Can you believe it? Right in front of Denise's house! The asshole!"

"I think we're all in agreement that Larry Allen was an asshole. What could she tell you about the girl Larry was with?"

"Huh? Oh, you mean like what she looked like and stuff." His expression went from enthusiastic to hangdog. "I didn't think to ask that."

Well, giving the boy a break, I hadn't written it down.

"I think that might be an interesting lead," I told him. "You wanna follow up with Mrs. Sherwood?"

"Sure, Milt! I'd get a hoot out of that!"

"Anything else?" I asked.

"Yeah," he said, consulting his notes. "Mrs. Sherwood said that there were cars going by at all hours. She thought maybe Larry was dealing drugs, but said the cars were all driven by women, far as she could tell, so she thought maybe he was running a string."

"Huh?" I said.

"Of hookers, Milt," Michael said, exasperated at my ignorance. I'd've bet a hundred bucks he'd had to ask Mrs. Sherwood what a string was himself!

"Well, prostitution's legal in Nevada," I offered, "so what would be the big deal?"

Jason and Michael looked at each other, then Jason said, "Mama and Daddy didn't raise their baby girl to be married to a pimp, Milt. Legal or not."

I nodded my head. I'm sure Denise would have taken exception to her husband "running a string," but what would complaining have gotten her other than a fat lip? If, and that was a big if, that was what Larry Allen had been up to.

"What about the other neighbors?" I asked.

"Well, there was nobody home on the other side of Denise's house," Jason said. "I thought I'd get in maybe nine holes this afternoon, then stop back by after suppertime. Somebody's bound to be in."

I noticed Jason was getting a tic in his left eye; the boy really needed to get on a golf course.

"Anybody else?" I asked. Two houses wasn't much of a canvass.

"The people directly across the street weren't home, either," Michael said, "but there was somebody home next door to them. A young mother with a baby. Real cute baby, too. Little girl. Had one of those bands on her head looks like they're trying to keep her brain from getting too big?" I nodded my head. I'd seen those things too and swore if me and Jean were ever to have a little girl (which we won't because we can't, but this isn't the time or place to get into that), I'd never put one of 'em on her head for anything.

"She have anything to say?" I asked. Then, seeing the look on Michael's face, I added, "The mother, not the baby."

"Oh, yeah. She said when she first moved in, like a year ago, she tried to get friendly with Denise because they were the same age, but every time she'd go over there, the phone would ring or the door would open and Denise would shoo her out. She said she never really met Larry, because Denise always got her out the back door when Larry was coming in the front. She said Denise acted like she was afraid of Larry. And I thought, 'no shit, Sherlock.'"

"I talked to somebody at number ten-fifteen, across the street from Denise in the other direction. A guy about my age. A real player. I think I woke him up. He wasn't very friendly. Said he was a friend of Larry's and that me and the rest of 'you crazy Upshanks,' as he put it, could go—well, let's just say it was graphic and physically improbable," Jason said.

"I tried three more houses on the block, Milt, and found only one person home, but she didn't know Larry or Denise or anything about them," Michael said.

"Yeah, same thing here. I got two other houses at home, but they didn't know 'em, either."

"Y'all write down the addresses where nobody was home?" I asked. Both boys nodded. "Then I think taking the afternoon off and trying again this evening is a good idea, Jason." I looked at Michael. "The ladies have all gone on a sightseeing tour, but they'll be back before dinner. We thought as many of us as possible could all get together at one of the places downstairs. You up for that, Michael?"

"Sure," he said, then laughed. "If I got any money left on my Visa!"

What could I do? I laughed with him, knowing he'd be crying in a couple of hours. Maybe Maida would pick up the tab for everybody.

MAIDA AND JEAN had conspired together and we ended up going to Le Cirque for dinner. I knew that was a fancy restaurant in

New York (I watch television!), but I didn't know they had one in Vegas. Well, they do and it was right there at the Bellagio. Like the name implies, it was circusy. Big tent-like thing over the dining tables, all kinds of colors, made of silk, Jean said. We were early by fancy-eating standards, it was only six-thirty, so we got a good table by the windows that overlooked the Bellagio lake and fountains.

Since I was the oldest male at the table, the waiter gave me the menu with the prices, but Maida gave him a look that shoulda curdled his stomach, and grabbed the priced menu out of my hand. I was quite happy with the menu she gave me. Lots of nice food, and, since there were no prices, it was all free. I had the braised rabbit in riesling with spaetzle (never did figure out what that was), and Jean had the lobster salad "Le Cirque" with black truffle dressing. We traded having bites off each other's plates. Can't say it was the Longbranch Inn's chicken fried steak and cream gravy, but it was mighty passable. Everybody ate heartily, except Michael and Barbara Jo. They were sitting across from each other at the other end of the long table, and I personally never saw them exchange a word. I figured Barbara Jo must have told him about his Visa card. I'd seen the boy eat, and I knew him to have a fine appetite, but that night he was barely picking at his food. I felt sorry for him, but I also felt sorry for Barbara Jo. She'd done something wrong for reasons even she couldn't explain, and now she was living with the consequences. I hoped the two could work it out. I didn't think I'd mention that six hundred dollars they owed me.

After dinner "the girls" went to see a show, and we fellas went back to our suite to discuss the situation. I still hadn't heard from Taylor on his interviews with Larry Allen's staff at the Lonestar. It was his turn in the spotlight. Taylor didn't do well in a spotlight.

"Well," he said, after we'd all raided the minibar and were sitting down with drinks in hand, "I went over to the Lonestar like you said, Milt." He was quiet for a minute. "Larry actually ran the bars on the casino floor, and all the waitresses who roam the casino handing out free drinks."

"Uh huh," I said by way of encouragement, also wondering if the waitresses could have been the women driving by Larry and Denise's house at all hours of the day and night. That would be a nice handy explanation.

"The way it's set up, Larry was in charge, and then there was the head bartender, who's in line to replace him, then the other bartenders, then the waitresses, then the cleaning staff. A real pecking order."

"Un huh," I said, getting antsy at the way he was telling the story.

"So I found out who was next in line and I was told it was this guy named Barber. Mickey Barber, but he wasn't in. By the way, all the bartenders are male, all the waitresses female, and all the cleaning people Mexican—both male and female."

"Pretty routine for a Texas boy," I said.

John Bob sighed loudly, then said, "Taylor, did you find out anything actually useful?"

"I'm getting there!" Taylor said, turning red. "Anyway," he turned to face me, excluding all his brothers, "I talked to this one lady, Lorraine, one of the waitresses—"

"Obviously!" John Bob interrupted.

"—and she said," Taylor continued, ignoring John Bob's interruption, "that Mickey Barber wanted the job real bad. He'd been in line for it two years before Larry lost his job at this bank where he worked and came to work for his dad. Mickey seemed to think Larry stole his job. Which I guess, when you think about it, he did."

"How bitter was he?" I asked.

"Lorraine seemed to think he was pretty damned bitter. She said he tried to get Larry in trouble all the time, but it never worked because Walter Allen, she said, and this is a quote, 'thinks his son's shit don't stink.'" He looked at all of us. "That's an expression," he said.

"You know, I mighta heard that once or twice," David Lee drawled, and Jason and Job Bob laughed.

Taylor's face turned red again. "Anyway, I thought that made him a viable candidate. What do you think, Milt?"

"Well, it's something anyway, Taylor. Our first actual suspect," I said, looking at the other boys as if daring them to come up with another one. "You talk to anybody but this Lorraine? Anybody confirm her story?"

"Ah, no. Everybody was pretty busy. Can't we just take her word? She seemed like a very sincere woman," Taylor said.

"Be that as it may," John Bob said, "she might have a grudge against Mickey Barber, he might have dumped her or shorted her check or something; you never know. You always need to get confirmation, Taylor."

What John Bob said was true, but I like to think I woulda said it a tad bit kinder than he did.

Taylor looked at me and his color was high. Either the boy was real embarrassed or about to stroke out. "I'll go back tomorrow," he said, "try to get confirmation."

I nodded. "That's a good idea. Maybe Mickey Barber will be back then and you can interview him. Feel him out."

"Yeah," Taylor said. "I'll do that. Maybe see how he felt about Larry. You know, sometimes you can tell these things by body language, not just words."

"Absolutely," I said and John Bob snorted.

Michael had been sitting in a corner and hadn't said a word

since we entered the room. Jason turned to him and said, "Well, Mike, you wanna head out to Denise's neighborhood again? See if we can't check out those houses where nobody was home this afternoon?"

Michael looked up. "Huh? Oh, sorry." He shook himself like a wet dog. "Ah, Jase, you think you can handle this? I'm not feeling so well. Thought I'd stay in tonight."

"Well, Mike, there are a lot of houses—"

"Get what you can," Michael said, standing and heading for the front door of the suite, "I'll get the rest tomorrow." With that, he was out the door and gone.

Jason looked from me to his brothers. "What the hell's wrong with him?" he demanded.

"He said he wasn't feeling well—" Taylor started, but shut up when he got the glares from his remaining brothers.

John Bob stood up. "Hell, Jason, I'll go with you. Might be interesting talking to Denise's neighbors."

I had my own thoughts about that, but decided to let it slide. I thought we'd gotten most of what we were going to get from the neighbors; I didn't think John Bob could do any real damage. That's what I get for thinking.

FIRST TUESDAY ✦ PROPHESY COUNTY

Emmett was sitting on the floor in front of a bookcase in Jasmine's living room. He'd seen her stereo and thought he'd play some music. She'd said there were CDs and stuff in the cabinet under the stereo. He opened the door and looked. There were CDs, tapes, and at least two hundred LPs. He hadn't seen that many LPs in years. He'd started going through them: Coltrane, Miles Davis, Charlie Parker, Stan Getz, Pete Horn, the Kingston Trio, the Limelighters, Peter, Paul & Mary, Joan Baez, early Dylan—all in their original jackets, all covered with plastic and in pristine condition.

"Jeez, you got some good stuff here," he called to Jasmine in the kitchen.

"The albums? They were my grandfather's. My grandmother left them with me, since she never liked that kind of music." She came in carrying a tray laden with two beers, cheese, crackers, and fruit. She set it down on the coffee table. "Grandma took her Bing Crosby and Perry Como with her."

"You ever listen to this stuff?" he asked.

"Oh, yeah, my grandpa used to play it for me all the time. Taught me to appreciate jazz and folk. Have you ever heard that Kingston Trio song about the guy riding around the streets of Boston?"

Emmett laughed. "Yeah, I loved that. I had a couple of their albums when I was a teenager." He grinned at the look on her face. "Yeah, honey, I'm that old. Actually, they belonged to my older brother, but he was the only one with a record player—no stereo in those days—and I'd sneak in his room and play the stuff. He had a bunch of Smothers Brothers, too."

She leaned across him and riffled through the albums. "Like this?" she asked, and handed him an LP.

Emmett looked at the list of songs on the back of the album, and, in an off-key baritone, sang, " 'Crabs walk sideways and lobsters walk straight—' "

Jasmine joined him on the line " 'So I can never take you for my mate,' " and they both laughed.

"Here, let's put it on," she said, and took the record out of its jacket and placed it on the turntable. They sat on the floor together, drinking beer and laughing at the Smothers Brothers. It was the best time Emmett could ever remember having.

First Tuesday ♦ Las Vegas

The call came while I was taking my shower. I usually take my shower in the morning, but something about all this made me want to take another one before bed. Besides, if I played my cards right, put on a little aftershave and my silk boxers, anything could happen. However, a little peaceful time with my wife was not to be. Jean knocked on the bathroom door, opened it and said, over the sound of the water, "Detective Broderick's on the phone for you."

"What's he want?" I shouted.

"I don't know," Jean said, using that fake patient voice she has, "why don't you ask him?"

I sighed, rinsed off, toweled dry, and went into the bedroom of the suite wearing the terry cloth robe the Bellagio so graciously provided. "Yeah?" I said into the phone, none too graciously.

"Hey, Sheriff," came Jimmy Broderick's chipper voice. "Hope you're not real busy."

"It's eleven o'clock at night, Broderick. I was going to bed. What do you want? You got word on Burl?"

"No, sir, it's not *that* Mr. Upshank."

The way he said it gave me chills all up and down my body. "What's going on?" I asked, sitting down on the side of the bed, ready for anything.

"Well, sir, we've got Mr. John Robert Upshank here in custody."

"For what?" I said, or shouted, or yelled, or whatever.

"Trespassing, for starters, then we got resisting arrest, assault on a police officer—that's verbal and physical, Sheriff—and to round out the evening we've got fleeing the scene of a crime."

"Oh, for God's sake," I said, shaking my head. "What about Jason? His brother?"

"The other Mr. Upshank. Well, he's not under arrest or anything. He *is* here, but mainly to try to keep his brother calm. That's not working so good though."

"I can only imagine," I said, sighing again. "Let me get my pants on and I'll be right down."

"Good, I'd hate to have to arrest you for indecent exposure!" At that, Broderick laughed like an idiot and hung up.

While getting dressed I had an idea: why not fight fire with fire? I decided to bring the whole contingent of brothers with me. I left our suite and headed down the hall to the boys' rooms. There was no answer at David Lee's door, which didn't surprise me much—he didn't seem like the in-bed-by-eleven type, at least not alone. Michael answered the knock on his door, but he looked so devastated that I hardly wanted to tell him what was going on. But I figured I had to.

"John Bob's been arrested," I said without preamble.

"Huh?" Michael said.

"John Bob's been arrested," I repeated.

"John Bob?"

"Yeah."

"What for?"

So I listed his offenses.

Michael shook his head and looked even more crestfallen than he had when he opened the door—if that's possible.

"It's all my fault," he said. "If I'd gone with Jason like I was supposed to, this wouldn't have happened."

"Ah, hell, boy," I said, "you've got enough on your plate. Don't be taking this on. Just get dressed and come with me. If Barbara Jo's all right?"

"She's packing," Michael said. "She's taking the first plane out in the morning." He straightened his shoulders. "Let me get dressed. I'll meet you in the lobby."

I nodded and headed to Taylor's room. He was up, but in his pajamas with a book in his hand. I noted the pajamas had clocks on 'em and the book was a romance novel. You just never know about people, I guess.

I explained what was going on and he said he'd get dressed and meet me in the lobby. I thought about going to get Maida, but decided that would be too cruel a thing to do to Detective Broderick. The brothers would be bad enough.

I went downstairs and wandered the casino for a bit, keeping an eye out for David Lee—and Burl while I was about it. I didn't find Burl, but I did find David Lee at the craps table. After I got his attention, I pulled him aside and told him about John Bob. He hooted with laughter. He was a little bit drunk, but I don't think it would have been different if he'd been stone-cold sober.

"You wanna come with us?" I asked.

David Lee laughed. "Ah, hell, Milt, I wouldn't miss this for the world. Let me get my chips." He had a pile of 'em and shoved them in his pockets and went to cash them in, saying he'd meet me in the lobby. I was hoping he planned on paying his mama back with some of those winnings, but somehow I doubted it.

It was 11:45 at night before we got the taxi that took us to the police station. It was well after midnight when we got there. As we walked up the steps of the station, David Lee stopped us and said, "If we can bail him out, let me do it." He grinned, and I could see how he was going to put his winnings to use. I could understand it. John Bob would be a hard person not to want to one-up.

Jason was sitting in a chair by the door of the detectives' bull pen when we got there. He jumped up on seeing us and said, "Thank God. Y'all gotta do something."

"How's John Bob?" I asked.

Jason rolled his eyes. "Not good," he said. "Seems these Las Vegas cops aren't that impressed by a corporate lawyer from Oklahoma City."

"Where is he?" I asked.

"Lockup, I think," Jason answered. "Detective Broderick won't tell me much."

"Where's Broderick?" I asked, looking around and not seeing him at his usual desk.

"In with his lieutenant," Jason said.

I wasn't looking forward to *that*. I turned to the boys. "Y'all come on. We're going to drown 'em in Upshanks."

Jason nodded, Taylor looked dubious, Michael didn't seem to be paying attention, and David Lee laughed outright. "Good one, Milt," he said, and was the first to follow as I led the contingent toward the lieutenant's office.

Broderick jumped up from his seat in front of Grayson's desk when he saw the five of us. "Sheriff," he said.

Grayson stood up. "Kovak," he said, leaving off the title—a pretty obvious sign that I was still out of favor.

"Hey, guys, y'all meet the rest of the Upshank boys yet?" I asked, and then introduced everybody.

David Lee moved forward. "I'm here to bail my brother out," he said, then turned and grinned at the rest of us.

"He hasn't been arraigned yet," Grayson said. "Won't happen until morning."

David Lee laughed. "John Bob's gonna spend the night in jail?"

"Oh, no, Lieutenant," Taylor said. "We can't let that happen!"

"Sure we can," David Lee said.

"We'd like to get him out earlier, Grayson," I said, leaving off his title; I mean, tit for tat, right?

"Don't see how that can happen, Kovak," Grayson said, staring daggers at me.

"Y'all have got it in for all of us, don't you?" Michael all but yelled. He charged forward, fists on Grayson's desk. "Well, let me tell you something! Upshank is a good, upstanding name in the state of Oklahoma, and y'all are biting off more'n you can chew, and that's for damn sure!"

I tried to pull Michael back, but he wasn't having any. I was guessing that he hadn't yelled at Barbara Jo any, and he needed like crazy to yell at somebody. Unfortunately, crazy was the operative word here.

"What did John Bob do? Walk on someone's yard? Anybody else in this city you'da slapped with a fine, but no, you got yourself another Upshank so you arrest him! You make me sick!"

David Lee helped me pull Michael back. "Calm down, bro," David Lee said.

"So looks like all these Upshanks have pretty bad tempers, huh, Kovak? You wanna reel this boy in before I have him arrested, too?" Grayson said.

"Now just a damn minute!" Taylor said, stepping forward. "That's uncalled for! Michael is upset. We're all upset. You've accused our father of something he's totally incapable of, arrested our oldest brother for total misdemeanors, and then ignored the fact, over and over, as far as I can tell, that Larry Allen was beating up our sister! Does Walter Allen own the police force as well as the Lonestar?" he demanded.

I started to clap; it was the best speech I'd heard from Taylor, but I thought it might be inappropriate to applaud.

"I'll pay any bail in the morning," David Lee said, "but in the meantime, I think it would be best if you released John Bob to Sheriff Kovak's custody."

"Oh, because that worked so well the last time we did that?" Grayson asked, sarcasm dripping.

"This is different—" I started, but Grayson interrupted.

"Nothing different about it. I let you take one prisoner on your recognizance, and the next day there was a dead body and your guy's missing."

"Oh, for God's sake!" Taylor said. "Who in the world would John Bob want to kill?"

"True," David Lee drawled. "He'll sue your ass, but he won't shoot it."

"He might be less likely to sue if he doesn't have to spend a night in jail," Jason said.

"Let my brother go!" Michael shouted, then looked at the others. David Lee grinned, and the two of them shouted, "Let my brother go!" Then Taylor and Jason joined in and the chant began. Everybody in the bull pen was looking. Broderick seemed to be trying to suppress a grin, but Grayson was turning bright red.

"I'm gonna have the bunch of you arrested if you don't stop it right now!"

The chanting kept on.

"Kovak!" Grayson shouted.

I shrugged my shoulders. "Kids," I said. "What you gonna do with 'em, huh?"

Grayson sighed and turned to Broderick. "Go get Upshank out of lockup." He turned to me as the chanting stopped. "If he does anything—I mean, spits on the sidewalk, anything—I'm arresting *your* ass! You got that, Kovak?"

I grinned. "At least I'll have me a good lawyer," I said. Grayson didn't find it amusing.

When John Bob was brought to us, he looked like he'd been rode hard and put up wet. His immaculate hair was every which way, his button-down shirt was torn, there was dirt on his face and his clothes, one shoe was missing, and his hand had a big bandage on it. He didn't say anything to anyone. He just glared, listened to Grayson tell him not to do anything, turned, and marched out of the detectives' bull pen. Me and the boys said our good-byes and followed John Bob. This was just getting more interesting by the minute.

I PULLED MICHAEL aside after we got everybody back at the Bellagio. I asked him to have a drink with me, and we went into one of the open bars in the lobby area and sat, both ordering beers.

"Michael, I need to tell you something," I said. "If you let Barbara Jo fly out in the morning, you'll probably never see her again. Son, she got caught up in the excitement of this place. You know that saying they got on TV about Vegas? 'What happens in Vegas stays in Vegas'? Well, that's because people tend to do stupid things in this city. They gamble away the mortgage on their house. A good, upstanding husband'll sleep with a hooker; a wife of forty years will buy thong underwear. Anything can happen. She's probably more upset about this than you are, son. Do you love her?"

Michael nodded his head. "I didn't ask her to leave, Milt. She's doing this on her own."

"Because she thinks you hate her. She's ashamed of her actions. Of all the things she'd coulda done in this city, she went on a shopping spree. A bad one, I'll grant you, but that's all it was. You gotta forgive her, make her know you forgive her, and, whatever you do, don't let her get on that plane in the morning. Not if you love her, not if you want her in your life." Me, Milt Kovak, giving advice to the lovelorn—can you imagine that?

Michael drank the last half of his beer in one long gulp. He shook his head and stood up. "You're right, Milt. I was screaming at that cop because I couldn't scream at Barbara Jo. Maybe if I yelled at her, she'd know I forgive her. You know?" he asked. "Women think that way sometimes."

I had to agree that sometimes they did.

I stood up and shook his hand. "Good luck, Michael," I said.

He nodded, shook my hand, squared his shoulders, and took off for the elevator. I followed a few minutes later. When I passed Michael's door, I could hear him yelling. "That was the stupidest thing—" "What did you think you were doing—" "How am I going to get you an engagement ring—" But then I heard Barbara Jo yelling back. "You were gone all the damn time—" "Your mother hates me—" "I don't need a stupid engagement ring—"

I left 'em to it. With any luck at all, there'd be some damn good sex going on in this hotel tonight.

FIRST TUESDAY ✦ PROPHESY COUNTY

Emmett and Jasmine lay in her bed, soft strains of Pete Horn's flute filtering in from the living room. He loved touching her, loved the feel of her skin. Her head was on his shoulder, her long brown, shiny hair tickling the side of his face, her fingers playing with the blond hair on his chest.

"Why'd you marry Lester Bodine?" he asked. He hadn't known that was coming out of his mouth; it just popped out.

She lifted her head and looked into his eyes. "Uh oh, personal question time?"

He touched her cheek. "You don't have to answer that if you don't want to. I don't really know why I asked."

She leaned her head back down on his shoulder, looking up at the ceiling. "Well, it's a question I've asked myself a million times. All I can say is I was very young, eighteen, and very stupid."

"Nothing stupid about you, lady," he said.

"I was stupid enough to think that because I slept with him I had to marry him," she said. She turned and looked at Emmett. "He was the first. You're the second."

He grinned. "I'm honored," he said.

"And well you should be," she said, slapping him on the arm. "It's not like I haven't had other offers."

"I bet you've had to beat 'em off with sticks," he said.

"Um, maybe not sticks. Just a very stern look and my badge."

He laughed. "How long were you married to him?"

"Ten years," she said. "The divorce was four years ago. If you can do the math, old man, that makes me thirty-two. Twenty-something years younger than you."

"Twenty-two, to be exact," he said. "I'm fifty-four."

She grinned at him. "Really?" she said. "I could have sworn you weren't a day older than fifty-three."

He rolled her over and tummy-gummed her stomach. "You're real funny," he said, doing it some more.

She was laughing and pushing at him, until the tummy-gums turned to kisses, and she wasn't pushing him away anymore.

FIRST WEDNESDAY ◆ LAS VEGAS

The next morning Jean and I got up bright and early to make a phone call. Although we'd been calling every day to check on Johnny Mac, he'd been asleep every time we called. It was always at night when we got around to it, so Jean and I made sure to call in the morning this time so we could talk to our son. Jean placed the call, spoke to Jewel Anne for a minute, then—I could tell by the look on her face and the sound in her voice—she had Johnny Mac on the line.

"John? Hi, honey, it's Mama," Jean said. I watched while my wife talked to our baby boy. Jean's a beautiful woman, but when she talks to or about Johnny Mac, she transforms into an angel. That's the only thing I can call it. Her face glows and her eyes shine, and her hair seems to shimmer. Her whole body changes when she talks to him.

I never knew my life could change the way it has. Having that little boy in it has made everything different—from the way I see myself to the way I see the world. Everything's more important now. Because I'm a peace officer, I see a lot of bad things, but I see even more now that Johnny Mac is with us. It scares the bejesus out of me. I have to protect him from so much. Shield him from the horrors out there. Keep him out of harm's way. That's my job, more a sworn duty than any sheriff's badge can make. But there's the other side of that coin, the side that sees things for the first time through my child's eyes. A bird flying through the air, a wildflower in the yard, *Sesame Street*, ice cream, first words, first steps, all of it such a miracle. Touching Johnny Mac's little hand is like touching God. You know there's more than just biology going on there. Something powerful blew life into this boy, and then gave this little miracle to Jean and me for safekeeping. It was such an awesome task, and such a joy.

After a real long few minutes, I gestured to Jean to hand over the phone. She did, and I said, "Hey, Johnny Mac!"

"Da? Dat you?" said his little voice.

"Yeah, buddy, it's me. How's it going?"

"Aun' Jewe' got lots of toys, Da. And I make cookies!"

"You did? You gonna save me some?"

"Uh uh," he said, "me and Unca Hawmon ate 'em all!" he said and giggled.

"Oh eee," I said, "little piglet."

"Oink, oink!" Johnny Mac said.

"I miss you, peach," I said, feeling tears behind my eyes.

"I know," he said. "It okay."

"See ya soon, cowboy. Let me talk to Aunt Jewel," I said.

"'K. Aun' Jewe'!" he screamed. "Da on da phone!"

I talked to Jewel Anne for a few minutes then hung up the phone. Jean and I looked at each other, both with tears in our eyes, then burst out laughing.

Jean wiped her eyes. "Oh, Lord, Milt, we need to get home."

I hugged her. "I know, honey. You wanna go on? Go home today. I gotta stay here until we find Burl. There's nothing I can do about it."

"I don't want to leave you here with all this," she said.

"I know you don't, honey. And I don't want you to. This has been a good time, in spite of everything. But you got a practice to get back to. And there's Johnny Mac."

"Well, the practice be damned. All I'm thinking about are those big blue eyes."

I batted my old, washed-out blues, even though I knew those weren't the ones she was talking about. "Wanna take 'em with you?"

Jean laughed and shook her head. "God, you're silly." She kissed me solidly on the lips. "That's one of the things I love about you—your sense of the ridiculous."

I figured she hadn't really called me ridiculous, that what she said was somehow a compliment, so I kissed her back. It was an hour later before we called the airline for her reservation.

WITH JEAN GONE I didn't figure I needed that big old suite so I traded with Michael and Barbara Jo. They were both smiling pretty big, even before I made the offer, but they jumped on it like snakes on a june bug. I moved my stuff that afternoon, but made sure Michael knew we'd still be using the living room of the suite for our meetings.

I got together with the boys around three-thirty, with Michael playing host. John Bob still looked pretty bad. He was clean and his hair was combed and his clothes pressed, but that just made the bruise on his cheek and the scratches on his face more apparent. The bandage was off his hand; there was a small gash, but it didn't look too deep. Today I could see the chafing on both wrists from handcuffs put on a bit too tight.

When we got all situated, I asked John Bob, "How are you feeling?"

He glared at me. "Don't ask."

David Lee grinned at his older brother. "So, John Bob, I took care of that bail problem for you this morning." He held up his hands as if shooing away words John Bob hadn't spoken. "No, no, don't thank me. I just thought it was my brotherly duty. Glad to be able to help out."

John Bob glared at David Lee. "If you don't shut up, I'm gonna fuckin' kill you."

David Lee shook his head. "Now, John Bob, what kind of attitude is that? Here I go out of my way to help you—"

John Bob leapt from his chair and pounced on David Lee. Jason, Taylor, and me tried to pull him off, but it took Michael to do it. And wouldn't you know, under all that weight, David Lee was laughing like the idiot he was.

Standing in the middle of the room, John Bob was breathing hard. Finally he calmed down and smiled at David Lee. It wasn't a friendly smile. "You're not getting the money back, asshole," he said. "I'm calling us even. You owed me every cent."

David Lee sobered. "I didn't expect you to pay me back."

John Bob grinned bigger. "Yeah you did. But I'm not going to."

"I don't want you to!" David Lee said, staring daggers at his brother.

John Bob kept grinning "Yeah you do. The only way you got that money was from Mama or from gambling. I'm hoping it took all your winnings to pay the bail. I'm hoping you're dead broke— again. But I'm gonna be guarding Mama. If you come sniffing after her for money, I'm gonna be there. I'm gonna make sure she doesn't give you any. I like seeing you broke. I'd like to see you under a fucking bridge!"

David Lee jumped up from his place on the couch and charged John Bob, grabbing him around the waist and wrestling him to the floor. John Bob kicked out, hitting David Lee in the head, but David Lee managed to get his hands around John Bob's throat. Things were going from real bad to just plain awful.

Michael again stepped in, picking David Lee up by the scruff of his pants and throwing him back at the couch. John Bob was coughing and choking, trying to catch his breath.

"You tried to kill me!" he screamed at David Lee.

"If I wanted to kill you, you son-of-a-bitch, you'd be dead!" David Lee yelled back.

"I'm gonna have you arrested for—"

That's when I lost it. I screamed, "Shut the hell up!" at the top of my lungs. Everybody stopped and stared at me. "Stop it! Just stop it! You guys are a piece of work, you know that?" I turned and looked at each one in turn. "All of you! You're family! Family's all we got!"

David Lee stood up. "I haven't been a member of this family for a very long time, Milt," he said quietly. The lazy drawl was gone, the eyes didn't sparkle with mischief. "John Bob's tried my entire life to get me out, and he succeeded a while back. I only came here because Mama asked me to." He shook his head. "Unfortunately, she didn't know what she was asking."

David Lee turned and walked out the door.

Taylor stood up. "Should I go after him?" he said, looking at me.

"Why?" John Bob said, slinking into a chair. "We don't need him. We never needed him."

Michael stared down at his oldest brother. "What is it with you and Dave, John Bob? I can't remember a time in my life when the two of you weren't at each other's throats."

"It's none of your business," John Bob said, taking out a handkerchief and wiping his face.

"Bullshit!" Michael roared. "It *is* my business! And Jason's.

And Taylor's! Hell, it's Mama's business and Daddy's business and Denise's business, too. Like Milt said, we're family. What goes on affects all of us. This sure as hell does. You just ran my brother off, and not for the first time. He's not yours, John Bob, he belongs to all of us. He's not yours to beat up or berate or run off. Don't you understand that?"

John Bob stood up. "You don't know what he did—"

"Then tell me! Tell me what he did!"

"No! It's none of your bus—"

Taylor stood up. "It was 4-H," he said. "We were all in it—"

Jason stood up. "Shut up, Taylor!"

Taylor turned on Jason. "How long are you gonna let this go on? We were kids, for Christ's sake! The statute of limitations has expired!"

"What are you talking about?" John Bob demanded.

"That money, Johnny, it wasn't Dave."

"God damn it, Taylor, I'm warning you—" Jason started.

"It was me. And Jason."

John Bob just stared at them. Michael looked confused. "What? Will somebody tell me what's going on?"

Taylor looked at Michael. "You were just a baby. The four of us were all in 4-H. You know what that is, Milt?"

I nodded my head. Every kid in a farm community belonged to 4-H at one time or another. It stands for "head, heart, hands, and health," and there have been more goats, sheep, pigs, chickens, turkeys, and even horses and cows raised for 4-H projects than you could shake a stick at.

"John Bob was the oldest in our group. We each raised a pig that year, and then John Bob was in charge of taking them to slaughter. And collecting the money. There was a lot of it."

"Three thousand, two hundred and seventy-five dollars," John Bob said.

Taylor continued. "John Bob brought it home and hid it under his mattress. Jason and I saw him do it. He had a date that evening, and while he was gone, Jason and I went in his room and took it."

John Bob sputtered. "But I saw David Lee in my room when I got home! He was in there!"

"Probably trying to read your *Playboys,* just like he said," Taylor said.

"Jesus," Michael said. "Y'all stole all that money? What did you do with it?"

"Nothing much," Taylor said. "We were too young—I was nine and Jason was eleven—to do much with it. We'd take out a five or ten occasionally when we went to the store with Mama, buy chewing gum and comic books."

"I got thrown out of 4-H," John Bob said. "That followed me all through high school. And into college. I almost didn't get into law school because of it."

Taylor nodded his head. "I know. And we knew you blamed David Lee. But we still kept on spending it. Remember that Chevy Jason bought when he was sixteen? He didn't get a deal on it. He spent the rest of the money. I never got much more than comic books with it."

I looked at Jason. He was sitting in his chair with his head down. He hadn't said a word.

"Jase?" John Bob said. "Is this true?"

Jason finally looked up. "It was a hundred years ago, Johnny."

"I've hated David Lee all this time because of what you did."

"It wasn't just me!" Jason said, standing up. "Taylor was in on it."

"Taylor never had an original idea in his life!" John Bob said. "It was you!"

I stood up. "Stop it! Y'all are doing it again! Just stop it. David Lee's down in his room right now, packing. You think you got something you need to say to him, John Bob?"

John Bob shook his head. "Too late now. The damage is done."

"Oh, for Christ's sake!" Michael spat out. "You guys are the biggest bunch of cowards I ever saw in my life! And to think I used to look up to you guys! I swear to God if somebody doesn't go down there and straighten this out with Dave, I'm gonna go tell Mama!"

The magic words. John Bob walked slowly to the door, opened it, and silently went out, not looking back at his brothers. Not saying a word.

The room was deathly still after John Bob left; Michael paced, Taylor sat, and Jason had his head in his hands, not looking at anybody or anything. Finally, I said, "Taylor, you were gonna try to find confirmation for what that waitress told you. How'd that go?"

Taylor looked up at me as if I'd spoken a foreign language. "What?"

"The confirmation," I said.

"Oh," he said. "Oh." He straightened up, shifting gears it seemed, and said, "Yes. Of course. I talked to one of the cleaning crew, guy named Roy Lopez. He's sorta the head guy in the cleaning crew, and he confirmed what Lorraine said. Then Mickey Barber showed up and I tried to talk to him. But he'd gotten the word not to talk to any Upshanks and had me thrown out."

"What did Roy Lopez say exactly?"

"Basically the same as Lorraine. That Mickey Barber had been in line for Larry's job, had actually started it, when Larry showed up. He said Mickey got demoted after a week on the job, and he was really pissed. Roy seemed to be on Mickey's side in the whole deal, said he didn't blame him, he woulda been pissed too. Said Walter Allen really stiffed Mickey. He also said Larry didn't know his ass from a hole in the ground. All he seemed to want to do was hit on the waitresses."

"That's real good, Taylor," I said. "We got the confirmation we needed about Mickey Barber, and that also confirmed something I've been thinking."

"What's that, Milt?" Michael asked.

"All those women your Mrs. Sherwood said she saw driving by Denise and Larry's house: I'm thinking he wasn't running a string so much as entertaining the waitresses."

"Yeah," said Michael, not all that sure I was right, "but why would they all want to do Larry? He was okay looking, but he wasn't all that great."

"He was Walter Allen's son," said Jason, looking up for the first time since John Bob had left the room. "I doubt if all of 'em would fall for Larry's line of crap, but I'm sure some of 'em did. I can hear him now, 'Hey, stick with me, girl, and my daddy'll make you a pit boss,' or a chorus girl, or head chef, or whatever it is the waitress aspired to."

"Good point, Jase," I said. Since he was talking, I thought I'd take the opportunity and find out what had happened the night before. "So what did you find out last night?"

Jason shook his head. "The neighbors on the other side, the opposite side from Mrs. Sherwood, are a black couple who've only lived there for a few weeks. The wife said she'd met Denise and they talked about her pregnancy and stuff because she, the wife, just had a baby. You know how women are: love to talk bodily fluids."

I had to smile at that. How many times had me and Harmon left a room when Jean and Jewel Anne had started talking bodily fluids? Can't even count the times.

"Oh, yeah," I said.

"So I went across the street to the one that hadn't been home, and they still weren't home. I peeked in the window and noticed there wasn't any furniture, so I guess no one lives there. Didn't see a FOR SALE sign, but maybe they haven't put it on the market yet."

"What happened with John Bob?" Michael asked. I'da been more subtle about it, but, hey, at least he got it out there.

"He got the wrong house, went to the one where that guy told us he was a friend of Larry's and wouldn't talk to any Up-shank. Remember, Michael?"

"Oh, yeah," Michael confirmed. "Couldn't forget *that* dude."

"Soon as John Bob introduced himself, the guy started yelling that he was trespassing and he was gonna call the police. Well, you know John Bob, he took exception to that, started doing his lawyer pontificating, and the guy pushed him off his porch, then called the cops. They got a really good response time in that neighborhood. Took about three minutes for a patrol car to show up. John Bob had just gotten up off the grass and was yelling at that guy when the two patrolmen came up, asked him what was going on." Jason shook his head. "So John Bob told them the guy had pushed him. He said *he* wanted to press charges for assault. But, you know, it was the guy's property. The guy was yelling trespass."

"Where were you?" Michael asked.

"Standing on the sidewalk—public domain—watching. Any-way, the patrolman, nice as you please, tells John Bob he needs to exit the property, but that stubborn streak comes out, and he in-sists they arrest the other guy. When one of the patrolmen grabbed his arm, John Bob jerked it away and accidentally hit the other cop in the face."

"That was the assault on a police officer?" I asked.

"The only one I saw," Jason said.

"Well, we'll get him off that one."

"Then they try to cuff him and John Bob goes ballistic—pulling away, pushing at the cops, then starts running down the street."

"Oh, shit," Michael said.

"Oh, yeah," Jason said. "They tackle him, throw him to the ground, cuff him, and then throw him in the squad car. And this whole time that asshole guy is laughing his ass off. If the cops hadn't been there, I'da gone up there and knocked his lights out."

I sighed. "I think we can get most of this thrown out, or at least get John Bob probation. What'll this do to his license to practice law in Oklahoma?"

"Well, you know what they say, Milt," Taylor said, grinning for the first time, "what happens in Vegas stays in Vegas."

"From your lips to God's ears," I said.

At this point, the front door of the suite opened and John Bob and David Lee came in. Nobody said a word. David Lee walked over to Taylor, who was sitting on one end of the couch, and held out his hand. Taylor took it, expecting, I believe, for his younger brother to shake his hand. Instead, David Lee pulled him to a standing position and sucker punched him in the gut. Taylor made an "oof" sound and fell back on the couch.

David Lee walked over to Jason. "You gonna take it like a man, Jase?" he asked.

Jason nodded his head and stood up. David Lee inflicted another gut punch, knocking Jason back in his chair, then turned to the assemblage. "Okay," he said, "that's over. Let's get serious about who killed that asshole Larry, okay, guys?"

Michael lumbered over and hugged David Lee. "Welcome to the family, bro," he said.

David Lee hugged him back. "You start crying, you little dick, and I'll punch you, too."

Taylor stood up and looked at John Bob. "You want a shot?" he asked. A pretty brave thing to do, for Taylor, I thought.

John Bob shook his head. "You know me, Taylor, I don't get physical. But I hope you never need a lawyer on the cheap." He turned to Jason. "And, Jase, I'll be calling in that loan you owe me."

"Ah, jeez, John Bob—" Jason whined.

"Thirty days notice." He turned to the rest of us. "Other than that, I agree with Dave, let's find Daddy and whoever killed that asshole Allen."

FIRST WEDNESDAY ✦ PROPHESY COUNTY

Emmett had never seen so much paperwork. Seemed to be at least double what he'd had on the city force. Must be because the county has more state forms to fill out, he thought. Whatever the reason, he was sick and tired of it. All he wanted to do was sit back and reflect on the night before. Twice in one night, he thought and grinned to himself. You old dog, he thought. And he was getting real good at it. Shirley Beth had never been one for foreplay. To her, sex was her wifely duty and she just wanted to get it over with. Jasmine treated sex more like an adventure or a thrill ride. And he was getting real good at the thrill part. He knew where to touch her to get her to moan, where to touch her to make her suck in her breath, when the touching stopped and the real stuff began.

Thinking about the night before, he found himself getting a woody, and decided maybe he should concentrate on the paperwork. That's all he would need, get an all-call to go out to the bull pen, and step up to Gladys with a stiffy. He almost laughed out loud at the thought, but put his head down and went back to shuffling the papers. God, he hated this part of police work.

FIRST WEDNESDAY ✦ LAS VEGAS

We had a little excitement that evening, as if we hadn't been having enough of that. We were at dinner, me and Maida, Denise, John Bob, and David Lee, when Denise started having contractions. We were at the one restaurant I'd feared, Picasso's, and I can't help wondering if the crazy rug wasn't the thing that set the girl off.

"Mama," she said, gripping her stomach, "I think it's time!"

"Oh, shit!" David Lee said, totally losing his cool, jumping up and knocking over his chair. The whole restaurant stared at us. "Want me to get the car?"

"We're not taking the girl to the hospital in that heap of rust of yours, David Lee," Maida said. "John Bob, go get a taxi!"

"Yes, ma'am," John Bob said. He had two kids of his own, and was a lot calmer than the childless David Lee.

Turning to Denise, Maida said, "How close together are your contractions?"

Breathing hard, Denise said, "I'm having one now, and I had one a few minutes ago."

Maida turned to me. I glanced at my watch. "Seven-twelve," I said. We watched Denise through the contraction. It lasted until seven-fifteen. "Three minutes," I said. I got my little notebook out of my back pocket and wrote down the times. To Denise I said, "Honey, let me know when the next one starts."

" 'K, Cousin Milt," she said, leaning back against her mother.

"What can I do?" David Lee demanded. "Want me to get some boiled water? I can ask a waiter. Hey, you—"

"No, honey," Maida said, touching her son's arm. "Just go see if John Bob has the taxi yet, then come let us know."

"Okay!" David Lee said and sprinted out of Picasso's.

A guy in a suit came over to the table. "Is everything all right here?" he asked.

"We may be having a baby," I said, grinning at him. "You know how to deliver one?"

The guy's face turned red and he said, "Your dinner is compliments of Picasso's, sir. Let me get some help escorting you and your party out."

I grinned at Maida who grinned back. "Why, that's mighty neighborly of you, sir," I said, drawling big time.

We let the wait staff show us the door, then headed for the lobby. David Lee was coming our way, waving his arms and shouting, "We got a taxi! Hurry up! We got a taxi!"

"Calm down, David," Maida said. "We're coming. Help me with your sister."

David Lee ran up to Denise. "You want me to carry you?" he asked.

"Lay one hand on me and I'll kill you," Denise growled. To me, she said, "They're starting again."

The black clouds that had been hovering for two days decided now would be the perfect time to drop their load. There was a strike of lightning so bright you could read a newspaper by it— if you were a speed-reader. Then came the clap of thunder that rattled the chandelier in the lobby. Followed by a couple of really big drops, then the deluge. We got Denise in the taxi, but me and Maida and David Lee got drenched before we could get in.

We got to the emergency room in less than ten minutes, being whizzed there by a taxi driver who had six kids and knew the drill. I tipped him a ten and we all piled out under the awning. After two hours waiting and watching the street float by, Denise and Maida came out of the ER.

"Braxton-Hicks," Maida said.

Denise was crying. "I don't want to do this again, Mama!" she said.

David Lee looked at me. "Who's Braxton-Hicks?"

John Bob, of course, answered. "False labor, basically," he said.

David Lee stared at all of us in turn. "You mean we're gonna have to do this all over again?"

"For real next time," Maida said, smiling bravely at her sons and daughter. "Now, let's get back to the hotel. Denise, we'll call room service for some dessert and rent a movie. How does that sound?"

"I won't be able to see the TV over my big, fat stomach!" she said.

"We'll rig something up, honey," Maida said.

"That's right," I agreed. "Don't you worry, Denise."

"I'll worry if I damn well feel like it!" she snapped, then started crying again. "I'm sorry," she said.

We took a taxi back to the hotel. The city sparkled after the rain; everything looked refreshed and new. The neon was somehow brighter, the streets cleaner, the people happier, if a bit wet. The temperature had dropped to the seventies, and a cool breeze blew when we stepped out of the taxi at the Bellagio.

We got Denise back to their suite and into the bedroom, and David Lee and I propped up pillows on her bed while John Bob supervised and Maida called room service. The "death by chocolate" she ordered got me hungry, so I went back to my room and ordered the same. And a light beer to go with it.

Around ten that evening there came a knock on my door. I went to answer it, hoping Denise wasn't having more labor pains, but it was Taylor.

"Hey," I said, "come on in."

"Milt, I've been thinking," he said, taking a seat in a chair by the little desk. "Mickey Barber seems like a good candidate to me. He won't talk to me, but he might talk to you."

"Yeah, I've been thinking along those same lines," I told him, because I had. "I'll go by the Lonestar tomorrow and see about that."

"And maybe we can have John Bob's paralegal run a check on him?"

I nodded. "That's good thinking. Let's go down to John Bob's room and talk to him."

So we did that. John Bob was getting ready for bed. He was shirtless and had on royal purple silk pajama bottoms. His chest was hairier than any human I'd ever seen, giving him an apelike appearance. It was actually a little scary.

"Can you get Betty to run a check on Mickey Barber?" I asked, standing in the doorway. John Bob didn't invite us in. "Under 'Mickey' and 'Michael,' just in case 'Mickey' is a nickname."

"Yeah, I'll call her first thing in the morning." He grabbed a hotel stationery pad off the desk and wrote down the two names. "While I've got her, I think maybe I'll have her run some other stuff. See if there were any accomplices in Larry's little crime spree. If there were, we might be able to interview them and get some more ideas about Larry."

"That's a good idea," I said, thinking mostly it was busywork, but busywork's okay when you got nothing much to go on—which is what we had: nothing.

I said good night to the boys and headed back to my room. Jean had called earlier, leaving a message saying she'd gotten home okay. I thought I'd call her back now, see what was going on. Maybe tell her I missed her. You know, mushy stuff.

FIRST WEDNESDAY ✦ PROPHESY COUNTY

Emmett decided maybe they were spending too much time in bed; what they needed, he decided, was a real live date. So after work he asked Jasmine if she'd like to go to dinner and a movie. There was a four-plex in Tejas County that he'd seen when they'd gone to the Chinese restaurant that first night, and he'd noticed a Mexican restaurant in the same shopping center.

The Mexican restaurant was okay, a little expensive for what you got, but passable, but of the four movies playing at the theater, there was only one they could agree upon. After half an hour, they decided it wasn't worth the time, and left. Coming out of the screening room, they passed the arcade so many theaters have nowadays.

"I bet I can beat you at 'Star Wars Invasion,'" Jasmine said.

"These are video games, right?" Emmett asked.

"You've never played a video game?" Jasmine asked, wide-eyed.

"Never saw the need."

She pulled him by his arm into the arcade. "It's not a need,

Emmett," Jasmine said, "it's a want. And I *want* to play 'Star Wars Invasion.'"

Well, all I can say is that I doubt John Bob is paying his paralegal Betty enough money. The woman is a whiz. By nine-thirty the next morning, John Bob called a meeting in Michael and Barbara Jo's living room to give us results.

"Michael 'Mickey' Barber: born in Pharr, Nevada, in 1968, graduated eleventh in a class of fifteen at Pharr High School, moved to Las Vegas in 1986. No job of record until 1991, when he went to work as a bartender at Caesars Palace. Went to work for the Lonestar in 1997 as a bartender, became head bartender in 2000. Was arrested in his teens; records sealed. Speeding ticket in 1992, going fifty-five in a thirty-five; took defensive driving in lieu of paying the ticket. Never married, no children of record. That's the sum of it."

"Wonder what he was doing between graduating high school and going to work at Caesars Palace?" I asked. "That's a pretty big gap—five years."

"Yeah, Betty mentioned that. Said she couldn't find anything on him during that five-year period, except an address. DMV had him living at an address on Piedmont," John Bob said.

"Piedmont, huh?" David Lee said. "That's a pretty skuzzy part of town."

John Bob started with "You should know—" but David Lee held up a finger and John Bob grinned. "Sorry, habit," he said.

"Break it," David Lee said. To me, he said, "It's a pretty transient neighborhood, doubt anybody would remember him, but I can give it a try."

"Excellent," I said. "Anything else?" I asked John Bob.

"Yeah. Betty's been checking into Larry Allen's arrests on

her own. Found some good stuff. Said she was just about to call me with it."

"Hope you're paying her well," Jason said.

"Not what she's worth," John Bob admitted. "I couldn't afford that. Anyway, she ran lawsuits on him and guess what? He had a paternity suit against him. Dates figure out to be right for the date rape in college. Before the results came in, Walter Allen paid the girl off—for an undisclosed amount, of course."

"Did you get a name of the girl?" I asked.

"Yeah. Belinda Norwalk. But Betty couldn't find anything on her. She's probably gotten married and changed her name."

"But wouldn't there be a marriage license?" I asked.

John Bob frowned. "Yeah, there would be. If she got married in Nevada. If Betty was only checking Nevada. Hum." He picked up the phone and dialed lots of numbers, then said, "Hey, Betty. Yeah, hot here, too. Look, that girl, Belinda Norwalk. How deep a search did you make on her? Um hum. Yeah. Well, there should be something. Um hum. Okay." There was a small silence, which is golden when it comes to John Bob, then he said, "Yeah. Okay, call me back." He hung up the phone. To the rest of us, he said, "She's gonna do a more extensive search. Said she checked marriage licenses in Nevada, California, Arizona, and New Mexico. But she'll do a national search."

"The date rape was on campus, right?" I asked John Bob. He nodded his head. "Why don't you go to UNLV and see what you can dig up? You know, mention you're a lawyer," I said and grinned. I looked around at the other boys. "Somebody needs to go with him. Michael, you game?" I asked.

"I don't need a babysitter!" John Bob said.

"Yeah, you do," everyone else in the room said.

Michael said, "I'll keep him in line," and grinned at his oldest brother.

"Okay," I said, "I'm going to go talk to Mickey Barber, Michael and John Bob are going to UNLV, and David Lee's checking out Mickey Barber's old address on Piedmont." I looked at Jason and Taylor. "What about you guys?"

"I've got a noon tee time," Jason said. There was much rolling of eyes. "Hey!" Jason said, indignant, "I can ask questions while I'm there! You know, this is really a small town and everybody knows everybody. I'll see what I can find out about Walter and Larry Allen. At least one of the foursome works for the casinos, I know that. I'll get some gossip. A golf course is the guy's version of a beauty shop, ya know."

Taylor said, "Well, if David Lee doesn't mind, I'll go with him."

David Lee shrugged. "I don't mind, bro, but I'm telling you, Piedmont is not a tourist area."

Taylor said, "Hey, I've been in bad parts of towns before, Dave. I'm not a chicken."

David Lee grinned. "We'll see about that."

MICKEY BARBER WAS not hard to find. When I walked into the main bar area of the Lonestar, I saw a guy chewing out one of the waitresses, and I figured it had to be Mickey. He was about five foot, six inches, stocky, a fireplug kinda guy, with sandy brown hair growing thin on top, and oversized hands and feet. I mean big hands and feet. Huge even. The woman he was chewing out was about three inches taller than him, built like a brick shithouse, had improbable black hair, and was chewing gum. When she took the gum out of her mouth and handed it, spit and all, to Barber, I got the feeling that might be what the chewing out had been about. Excuse the pun. She was one of those women that I woulda said— back in my single days, and in spite of the improbable black hair and chewing gum—I wouldn't throw out of bed. She was some kind of looker, let me tell you. Too much makeup, too much hair, boobs probably paid for, but still and even . . .

As she flounced away from Barber, I walked up to him. "Mickey Barber?" I asked, sticking my hand out to shake. Luckily the chewing gum was in his left hand.

Barber nonchalantly stuck the gum in his pocket and shook my hand, saying, "You got him, sir, what can I do for you?"

"I'm looking into the Larry Allen murder, Mr. Barber. I wonder if I could have a minute of your time?"

"Sure, Detective," he said, pointing to a booth in a far corner. I followed him over there, thinking I never told him I was a detective, never said I was with LVPD. I couldn't help it if the man assumed such things. Wasn't my fault.

We sat down in the booth and he said, "Coffee, soft drink, something harder?"

"Coffee's fine," I said.

He motioned a waitress over—and I gotta say I wouldn't'ta thrown this one outta bed, either—I mean, back in my single days. Legs clear to the ground, an ass on her you could strike matches on, blond hair, blue eyes, big tits. Jeez, Larry Allen sure knew how to hire 'em.

"Yolanda, two coffees," he said, barely looking at her. The lady looked at him, though, and if looks could kill, old Mickey Barber would be a bloody mess on the floor.

"So what can I do for you, Detective?" he asked, once the waitress had gone.

"As I understand it," I said, "you worked closer than anyone with Larry Allen. I just wanted to get your impression of him, find out if he had any enemies, that sort of thing."

He looked puzzled. "You guys thinking his father-in-law didn't off him after all?" he asked.

I shrugged. "We like to cover all the bases," I said.

He nodded. "Sure," he said. "That makes sense. Well." He stared off into space. "I can't say I worked with him any closer than anybody else. Actually, Larry was closer to the waitresses than he was to me or any of my bartenders." He laughed. "I mean, real close to the waitresses, if you get my drift."

We both looked up at that point and saw the blond, blue-eyed waitress was there with our coffee. She'd obviously heard what Mickey had said. Looking at her, Mickey smirked and said, "Ain't that true, Yolanda?"

Glaring, Yolanda said, "Whatever you say, Mickey, you're the boss."

The smirk left his face and a scowl replaced it. "Yeah, and don't you go forgetting it again, Angel."

I couldn't help thinking that if I talked to one of my employees like that, or called one of my female employees "Angel," I'd be up on charges in about two minutes flat. Even if I had to press the charges my own self. I was getting to where I didn't like old Mickey Barber much.

Yolanda stomped off, which did wonderful things to that really fine ass she had, covered only in a little micro-mini buckskin skirt that matched the buckskin string-bikini top. You had to hand it to whoever came up with those uniforms.

"As far as enemies," Mickey Barber said, and shrugged, "I'd say Larry had his share. Like any husband or boyfriend of any waitress in the joint."

"Are you insinuating that Mr. Allen had, um, physical relations with some of the waitresses?" I asked.

Barber barked a laugh. "Hell, no, I'm not insinuating that," he said. "I'm flat-out saying it. And not some of the waitresses—all of 'em. Larry's idea of a job interview included seeing how the girls worked on their knees, if you get my drift. So there might be a few, a very few, women out there who are holding a grudge because they *didn't* take that particular part of the exam—and didn't get a job. Couldn't give you any names on those, though. But the rest of 'em—the hires—have at 'em."

"Are you saying every waitress in here had sexual relations with Larry Allen?"

Barber looked around the room. "Well, no," he said, then pointed to an older woman, about forty, working the casino floor. "See that lady? Rita McReynolds. She was already here when Larry came on. The only one he didn't fire when he started his own harem."

"How come?" I asked.

"Well," Barber said, grinning, "she was hired by Walter Allen, some time ago. Old as she is, she still visits him pretty regular up in his suite."

The lady in question wasn't old; like I said, she could only have been in her early forties, but age works differently in places like Las Vegas and Hollywood, especially for women. Anything over thirty is ancient. The lady in question, Rita McReynolds, had the only natural-looking breasts I'd seen in the waitstaff. Her hair was red and probably dyed, but her skin and her eyes said that at one time she was a natural redhead. She was busty, didn't have any cellulite on those really fine legs, and carried herself with a lot more class than any of the other women around. Okay, bed, wouldn't throw out. You knew I was gonna say it.

I got permission to interview the waitresses and started with Rita McReynolds, which was a big mistake. Since she hadn't had a sexual relationship, as far as Barber knew, with Larry Allen, my thinking was she'd be more inclined to talk. That's what I get for thinking.

I got her between customers, and said, "Ms. McReynolds, mind if I speak with you for a moment?"

Up close the lady had pearly white skin, so sheer you could see the blue veins underneath. Her eyes were huge and bluer than a robin's egg. Fine wrinkles were visible around her eyes, but that didn't mar this woman's natural beauty. I had to say, Walter Allen had a lot better taste than his son.

She smiled at me and my knees got weak. "Yes, sir," she said. "May I help you?"

"Yes, ma'am," I managed to stumble out, "I'm looking into Larry Allen's death, and I've got permission from Mickey Barber to ask you a few questions."

The smile disappeared as soon as I said Larry Allen's name. "Are you with LVPD?" she asked.

Uh oh, I thought. This one's smarter than Barber—course, that wouldn't be hard.

"No, ma'am," I said. "This is a private investigation."

"On whose behalf?" she asked.

"I'm not at liberty to say, ma'am," I said, which was a flat-out lie.

Her huge, blue eyes narrowed. "You're working for the Up-shanks, right? What did you say your name was?"

"I didn't," I said.

"What *is* your name then?" she asked.

I sighed. "Milt Kovak, ma'am," I said.

"The sheriff from Oklahoma who let that murdering SOB Upshank escape. Is that correct?"

"Now, I didn't *let* him escape. He just did it."

"Um hum," she said, adding, "Does Wal—does Mr. Allen know you're out here harassing the waitstaff?"

"Ma'am, I'm not harassing anybo—"

"Butch!" she called, and a large, black security guard came over and stood in front of her, hands clasped in front of him.

Remember that movie *The Green Mile*? Remember that

great big black man who was at the crux of the whole thing? The one with the gentle smile who saved the mouse? Well, this guy looked just like him—except for the gentle smile and the mouse.

"Hey, Rita," he said, his deep voice reverberating off the rafters.

"This man here was just leaving. And he won't be coming back—ever."

Butch looked at me. "Sir, are you going soft or are you going hard?"

I was thinking hard would probably kill me so I opted for soft. "I'll be leaving now," I said, nodding my head at Rita McReynolds. "But you and the other ladies will be interviewed, ma'am. If not by me, then by the LVPD."

"The LVPD already knows who killed Larry. I think you should pay attention to them, Sheriff. And I think you should leave."

Butch took one step closer to me and I turned and headed for the front door. I could feel him behind me the whole way, breathing down my neck. When I stepped out the front doors of the Lonestar I felt like I'd just escaped from some level of Dante's inferno. Maybe the tenth or eleventh.

After that experience, I felt I deserved a little R&R. Wishing Jean was still with me, I went over to NewYorkNewYork and rode their roller-coaster. I've always been a big fan of roller-coasters. They get your adrenaline pumping without having to take out your piece, arrest anybody, or look at dead bodies. I rode it three times then went over to the all-you-can-eat seafood restaurant and spent seven dollars making myself sick on fried catfish, fried oysters, fried shrimp, and a shrimp salad—so I could tell Jean later on the phone that I ate good.

Afterward I noticed I wasn't too far away from the Mirage, which is where Siegfried & Roy's Secret Garden is. I tramped around with a hundred other tourists, all going ooh and ah over the beautiful big cats, then I took the monorail back to the Bellagio. Since I hadn't really seen that much of the hotel, I walked around, spent some time in their atrium garden, looking at plants I'd never seen or heard of, wishing I had the kinda green thumb that could grow that stuff—I'm good with turf, got a good two-inch growth of solid St. Augustine—but I'm not much good with flowering stuff. I walked by the shops where Barbara Jo had fallen from grace, and couldn't help stopping outside Armani, staring at the suits. I'm certainly not an Armani kinda guy, but I figured if I ever had the extra money to burn, and ever had a reason to really dress up, well, I'd certainly think about trying on one of those suits.

I went out to the pool area for a little while, and watched the bikini-clad women walk around. There were some that were fun to watch, and some that weren't so much fun. What my daddy used to call mutton dressed as lamb. Then there were the guys— Lord almighty, I thought, seeing all the Speedos, put the socks on your feet, boys, not there!

I gotta admit, the Bellagio is a beautiful hotel, but I'd rather have been on my mountain, in my house, with my wife and my son. Right now I could be out back, grilling steaks on my new gas grill, or playing with Johnny Mac in his blow-up pool, or sitting upstairs in Johnny Mac's playroom, looking out all the windows at Oklahoma mountains covered with Oklahoma trees, watching *Aladdin* with my boy for the forty-second time, and hoping I'd live to see him graduate high school. I could be playing footsie with my wife under the dining room table while we watched our son smear his dinner all over his face, or I could be watching while she read him a book, seeing the shine in her eyes, the smile on her beautiful face.

Okay, I was getting homesick. I decided to head upstairs and call Jean.

I was waiting for the elevator when the doors opened and Maida came out with Denise leaning on her arm.

"Thank God, Milt! Her water broke! I've called the hospital and her doctor. She's going to meet us there. Can you get a taxi?"

"Yeah," I said, and headed fast out the front doors. The taxis were already lined up and I had the door open when the two women got there. I helped get Denise in the backseat, slid myself in next to the driver as Maida ran around and got in the back with her daughter, gave the driver the address of the hospital, and told him it was an emergency. It mighta worked if this one spoke English, but he didn't and my hand gestures didn't impress him. Maida, however, grabbed him by both shoulders and said, "Hospital now or you'll regret it the rest of your life!" This he understood. We got there in less than fifteen minutes.

A nurse was there to meet us with a wheelchair and Maida sent me back to the hotel to gather up her boys. "And if you can find my asshole husband, Milt, now would be a good time to do it."

Well, from her mouth to God's ear, I thought, but knew God didn't have much to do with Burl right now. I figured I was on my own when it came to finding him.

The boys and I were supposed to meet back at Michael's suite by five o'clock. That would give Jason at least nine holes, and we figured that was enough for his jones today. It was five-fifteen when the taxi pulled up in front of the Bellagio. The boys were all in the suite, arguing the merits of baseball vs. football, with Taylor saying he preferred hockey—I had to agree with the majority on that one—hockey's a Yankee game.

"Y'all come on, we gotta get to the hospital," I told them, "Denise's water broke."

David Lee jumped up. "That means it's real, right, Milt? Not those Braxton-Hicks things?"

"That's right, Dave. This time the show's on for sure."

Michael jumped up and ran to the bedroom, throwing the door open. "Barbara Jo, come on! Denise is having the baby!"

Barbara Jo came shooting out of the bedroom, remembered she was barefoot, ran back in and got her shoes, remembered she needed her purse, ran back in to get that, then, with all the boys yelling at her to hurry up, we crowded into an elevator and headed out of the hotel.

There wasn't a taxi van available. Not waiting outside the hotel, and not available when the attendant called for one. David Lee said, "Let's take my car!"

"How in the hell are we gonna all get in your car?" I asked, but realized I was talking to the wind. All five boys and Barbara Jo were headed at a run to the parking lot and David Lee's Z. Now let me tell you, seven people in a 280 Z, even with the top down, is not doable. But we did it. There were a lot of laps being sat on, mine being one, and I'm not sure whose butt was resting on me, but by the heft of it I think it mighta been John Bob. All I know is that by the time we got to the hospital, ten minutes later, both my legs were asleep and my back was cramping up. It took Michael and John Bob both to pry me out of that damn car. I figured I'd walk home before I got in that Z again.

Denise was in active labor when we got there. They'd only let two people in at a time, so me and Barbara Jo just sat down to wait it out. We weren't immediate family and we figured Maida and the boys needed to be in there with her more than we did.

SECOND THURSDAY ◆ PROPHESY COUNTY

Experimentation is a wonderful thing, Emmett thought, except I'm going to break something.

"Ah, Jasmine," he said, "I hate to be a stick in the mud—"

She cocked her head and looked at him. "You're not comfortable?"

"No, not really."

She crawled off. "I'm sorry, baby. I read it in a book, thought we could try it."

He straightened out his body and lay down on the bed. He grinned at her. "What kind of book you reading there, girl?"

"Oh, it's a good book," she said, straddling him. "Pictures and everything."

He touched her breasts, playing with her large nipples, making them smaller. "I don't think I need pictures, honey, I think I know where everything is."

"Oh, you do, you do," she said, leaning down to kiss his mouth.

That's when the phone rang on the bedside table and Emmett's beeper rang in his pants on the floor.

"Shit, it's the office," she said, rolling off of him. "Turn your beeper off so they can't hear it, then you can call them back on this phone." She picked up the phone and said, "Bodine." She listened for a moment, then said, "Yeah, yeah, okay, Henry, I'm on my way," and hung up.

"What's up?" Emmett asked.

"All hell's breaking loose," she answered.

SECOND THURSDAY ♦ LAS VEGAS

It was a little before six in the evening when we got to the hospital; at eight I went down to the cafeteria and got as much food and drink as I could carry on one of their trays and brought it upstairs to the waiting room. We weren't supposed to do that, but it was late and nobody around seemed to care much. At 10:30 I went down to the machines and got coffee, using the cafeteria tray to carry 'em all back up. At 1 A.M. I went back to the machines for Cokes and chocolate. At 3:30 A.M. Barbara Jo fell asleep on my shoulder, making it impossible for me to move. At 4 A.M.

Michael came out of his sister's room and took Barbara Jo off my hands. At 6 A.M. the cafeteria opened up and I took the tray down and loaded it up with scrambled eggs, bagels, and coffee. By the time I got back upstairs with my breakfast treats, I could hear the faint sound of a baby's cry coming from Denise's room and all the boys were smiling. At 6:15 A.M. a very tired Maida came out of the room—the first time all night.

"It's a girl," she said.

Her boys crowded around, hugging their mama, while Barbara Jo and I stood back and beamed at 'em. A girl. That was good. A girl was real good.

"What's her name?" I asked when the group hug finally broke up.

"Carol Jean Allen," Maida said with a smile. "You might want to call your wife and tell her, Milt," she said. "The 'Jean' part is definitely after her."

Well, I gotta tell you, that made me swell up like a toad. I was that proud. A little jealous, too. I've helped people a lot in my line of work and never once has anybody named a baby Milton. Well, can't really blame 'em, but still and all . . . I grinned real big and headed for a pay phone. This call couldn't wait.

W ell, I gotta tell you, Jean was tickled pink about the name. She got all professional about it, but I could tell she was tickled, enough so that she wasn't all that mad I woke her up at six-thirty in the morning. I waited until I got back to the hotel to make my other phone call. I'd talked to Emmett, my second in command at the sheriff's office, when we decided we needed to stay in Vegas longer. That had been a few days ago. He'd been just fine about it, said everything was going well, and to do what I had to do. On one hand I was relieved; on the other hand, I figured Emmett would be running for my office come election time. And we'd been such good friends, too.

So it was with some misgiving that I dialed the area code for our part of Oklahoma and the number for the sheriff's office. Gladys picked up on the fourth ring, which was unusual; she usually answered on the first or second.

"Sheriff's department, Gladys speaking," she said, her voice all breathless.

"Hey, Gladys, it's Milt—"

"Gotta put you on hold," she said, and did so.

I musta been stuck there for three or four minutes, listening to the cheap-ass recorded music the county commissioners had barely paid for. Every third song was a Barry Manilow. Finally Gladys came back on the line.

"Milt, where are you?" she said, and she wasn't pleasant about it, either.

"I'm still in Vegas, Gladys, helping out our mutual cousin," I said.

"Well, get your butt back home! You wanna talk to Emmett?" She didn't wait for an answer, just plugged me through.

Emmett picked up pretty quick. "Hey, Milt. When you coming home?"

"Don't have any idea at the moment, Emmett. What's going on there? Sounds like y'all are busy."

"Don't even ask. Dalton's out, broke his ankle, which means paperwork I can't find; we had a break-in last night at the Dairy Queen, stole anything wasn't bolted down; three domestics last night, two out at the trailer park in Bishop and one clear across the county. One of 'em was a propane divorce. Ended up a two-alarmer, guy's in the hospital, second-degree burns. Got another guy in lockup and the one across county hit the road 'fore we could find him. Then we got three drunk and disorderlies out at the Dewdrop Inn, and I can't find that whatjacallit Breathalyzer thing to prove up anything. When are you coming home?"

"What happened to Dalton? How'd he break his ankle?"

"Oh, that was that bank robbery a couple of days ago—"

"Bank robbery?" I almost shouted. We didn't get bank robberies in Prophesy County—that was big-city crime. We got drunk and disorderlies, DUIs, domestics, bar fights, more murders than we should—but not bank robberies!

"Yeah, kid from Tejas County, name of Carl Slydell. Bill Williams knows him—couple of DUIs, a D and D, an attempted B and E, but the judge gave him a suspended sentence. Decided to come over here, I guess, where nobody knew him. Wrote a stick-up note to the teller, but she couldn't read it, and while she was trying to decipher it, Jasmine and Dalton showed up, the kid makes a run for it, Dalton chases him, falls over a security guard, but still grabs the kid, and ends up breaking his ankle. Dalton is a hero, Milt. Can you believe it?"

I grinned. "Well, let the boy shine. Probably won't happen again. Give him my best. But, Emmett, other than that, sounds like a normal day to me. Who set off the trailer?" I asked. A "propane divorce" is what we call it when a wife, often an abuse victim, has had enough, gets her kids and her stuff out of the trailer, locks it up while hubby's asleep, then sets off the propane tank of the trailer. Happens more often than you'd think.

"Lady name of Johannson. Millie Johannson. Common-law husband is Kirk Lawson—"

"Yeah, we've had him on a DUI and a D and D, right?"

"Yeah. Seems Millie's got a twelve-year-old girl from a previous encounter, and old Kirk got drunk and decided to mess with her—"

"So she blew his ass up. Personally, I say good for her, but you've got her in lockup?"

"Yeah, and the social worker lady's got the kids. Two of 'em, the twelve-year-old and a four-year-old that belongs to Lawson."

"Okay, about the other stuff, call up Elberry," I said, naming the former sheriff of Prophesy County, my predecessor. "See if he can come in and relieve you of some paperwork, let you hit the streets. The Breathalyzer's under Gladys's desk, next to her heater. The worker's comp paperwork's in my bottom left-hand drawer, under Johnny Mac's toys, and you might wanna find out what Bubba Dooley was doing last night. Old Jasper at the Dairy Queen fired him couple months back and Bubba was none too happy about it."

"Okay, okay," Emmett said, "wait a minute, I'm writing this down." We sat there silently, except for the scratching of Emmett's pen, then he said, "When'd you say you were coming home?"

"Can't say for sure. But call me on my cell phone if you need me."

"What's that number again?" he asked.

I gave it to him, hung up, and sat back, resting my head on the bed's headboard, grinning like a possum. I had a feeling Emmett wouldn't be wanting my job after all.

SECOND FRIDAY ✦ PROPHESY COUNTY

Oh, that was great, Emmett thought, just great! Next time Milt leaves, if he ever has the balls to do it again, he'll leave Dalton in charge! Call Elberry! Jesus, the man was a crook! Nobody knew it but he and Milt, but if Milt hadn't had so much loyalty to the old fart, he'd be in prison now. So he's supposed to call him and say what? "Hey, Elberry, I'm too stupid to run the sheriff's department, can you come down here and hold my dick for me?"

Shit, he thought, it's Jasmine. All this stuff she's brought up. All the screwing. Jesus, she smells good. Feels good. Damn, stop thinking about it. Get some work done. Where'd he say those worker's comp papers were? Oh, yeah, under the toys.

Emmett found the papers and put them on Milt's desk, got out his reading glasses, and began to scan them. Couldn't understand a damn thing. Couldn't concentrate. It had been too damn long since he'd done this part of the job. And, if the truth be known, he'd loved being back on the street. Those last ten years at the police station, being chief, all he'd done was paperwork, and take meetings. Hell, everybody and his brother wanted a meeting with the chief. And then during the meeting, they'd come up with a committee for this or that, and he'd always get stuck on it. No matter what it was for. And he always thought of that saying, that a camel was a horse designed by a committee. God, that was the truth.

Why in the hell had he volunteered to do this for Milt? Now, wait a minute. He hadn't. Milt had asked him and he'd said yeah. Like it was no big deal, no skin off his nose. Well, his nose was plenty skinned. And it was true, all hell was breaking loose around the county. And he was down to only two deputies, what with Dalton being out, and him being in here doing Milt's job. He *should* call Elberry. Hell, it was an emergency, wasn't it? All this crime going rampant in the county, and only one day deputy and one night deputy to handle it? Maybe he could do a split shift, a little bit days and a little bit nights. That would work.

He picked up the phone and dialed a number he still re-membered. When the man answered, he said, "Hey, Elberry . . ."

SECOND FRIDAY ◆ LAS VEGAS

I slept until about one-thirty in the afternoon, and woke up feeling refreshed and raring to go. I'm not sure which it had most to do with—a few hours' sleep or finding out my county needed me. I called Michael's room, waking him and Barbara Jo up, and asked him to round up his brothers for a meeting at three o'clock. I called room service and found out I could get breakfast if I wanted it, ordered two eggs over easy, hash browns, bacon, pan-cakes, orange juice, and a whole pot of coffee. Then I took my shower. By the time I was out, shaved, and dressed, the food had shown up and I watched *Oprah* while I ate. She was doing makeovers and it was nice to see plain Janes being turned into supermodels.

At close to three, I turned off the TV and brushed my teeth, then headed to Michael's room. I met Barbara Jo coming out of their suite. "Hey, Sheriff Milt," she said, smiling prettily at me.

"How's it going there, Barbara Jo?" I asked.

She reached up and gave me a kiss on the cheek. "That's for all your help with that . . . thing the other day," she said.

"I take it you and Michael figured a way around all this," I said.

She nodded her head. "I'm gonna work overtime for the next couple of months, then buy my own ring!" she said and giggled. "I'm gonna pick it out and everything, then give it to Michael, then he's gonna get down on one knee and propose all over again, and offer up the ring! Isn't that a hoot?"

I grinned at her. "Sounds like a plan," I said.

She hugged me and said, "I'm off to the hospital to see my soon-to-be niece!" She waved and headed to the elevator.

I knocked on the door as I opened it. Three of the boys, Michael, Jason, and Taylor, were already in the room, arguing about politics, when I came in.

"You a Republican or a Democrat, Milt?" Jason asked.

"Yellow-dog Democrat," I said. "Just like my daddy and my daddy's daddy. Why you ask?"

Jason shook his head. "Think it's about time to think for yourself, Milt? The Republican party is the way to go," he said. "Don't you support the president? The troops? The war?"

"I try not to talk about politics much, Jason, being a politician my own self, but, yeah, I support the troops. I'd like to support 'em all the way back home. I got a son at home, ya know, and I surely don't want to see him going off to fight the new Vietnam."

Which I should not have said, 'cause that just started Jason up and he went on and on saying things I coulda fought but decided not to. Michael was rolling his eyes, arguing every once in a while, and Taylor was agreeing with both. Finally the door opened without a knock and John Bob came in, followed by David Lee.

"Well," I said, standing up, "now that we're all here, can we dispense with the politics and talk about the issues at hand?"

Jason, who was counting on his fingers all the people Bill Clinton had supposedly killed while in office, finally shut up.

I got a soda out of the minifridge and we all took our seats. "First I wanna say congratulations to all y'all on your new niece."

David Lee held up his Coke and said, "To Carol Jean and her mama."

We all raised our sodas and said, "To Carol Jean and Denise."

"I know you guys are gonna rally 'round now, take up the slack on Carol Jean needing a father figure," I said.

"Well, I'm in Oklahoma City, Milt, and so's Jason. But we'll try to get down there," John Bob said.

"And we all have our own kids," Jason said.

"I don't know how much I'm gonna be able to help," Michael said, "living in Houston and all. And trying to get ready for a wedding."

"That's okay," David Lee said. "I already talked to Mama and Denise. I'm gonna be moving back home for a while. I'll be working at the insurance agency until Daddy gets all this mess straightened out."

The room was quiet while all four boys stared at their brother. "Well," John Bob finally said, "I think that's a real good idea, Dave."

"Yeah," Michael said, grinning from ear to ear, "I think it's great!"

The other two nodded and smiled at their brother. David Lee turned kinda pink around the edges but just smiled back.

"Well, back to work," I said. "John Bob, you and Michael went to UNLV yesterday, right? What did you find out?"

"It took a while, but we got to the right dean. He didn't want to talk about it at first, but when he found out I was representing the child in the matter, he opened up some."

I looked at him, surprised. "You can do that?"

"Well, I did it. I don't think the Oklahoma bar is gonna find out, do you?"

"Not from me," I said, grinning.

"Anyway, the girl, Belinda Norwalk, reported the date rape the next day. She was pretty bruised up and the campus hospital did a rape exam, which they shouldn't have done—she should have gone to a city hospital—and it was positive. She said it was Larry Allen, her two roommates saw Larry Allen go in their room with Belinda, found her after it happened, testified that she was hysterical and bleeding—from scrapes and scratches on her arms and face, and from . . . well, you know. The dean said they had enough evidence to give it to the city police, but then Walter Allen showed up, gave the school a new wing or something, tried to pay the girl off, and the whole thing got blown over. The girl's family, however, when they found out, they took it to the city police, but by then Walter Allen had gotten to the two roommates and, somehow," he said, raising an eyebrow, "the rape exam results at the campus hospital disappeared. So the girl just left school. That's all he knew about it. Said he'd heard something about a paternity suit like a year later, but never heard any results."

"Did you find out where Belinda Norwalk was from?" I asked.

John Bob gave me a look. "Couldn't very well ask that, Milt, since I said I was representing her kid, now could I?"

I had to agree.

"But I called Betty and she said she'd hack into the university's computer and find out."

"Betty's a hacker?" I said and laughed. "Where'd you find her? The local high school?"

John Bob grinned. "Nope. Betty's sixty-five years old. She's just one of those rare people who took to the computer like nobody's business. Didn't start working until she divorced her husband when she was fifty. Had seven grown kids. Wanted to do something. Went back to school for her associate's degree as a paralegal, found out she liked computers, came to work for me. I'm hoping she keeps on working into her eighties."

"When are you supposed to hear back from her?" I asked.

"Soon as she gets the goods. Won't be too long." He held up his cell phone. "She's gonna call me on this number."

I nodded. "Okay, then. David Lee, you and Taylor checked out that old address on Mickey Barber?"

"Yeah," David Lee said. "John Bob checked with Betty and got the actual street address on Piedmont. It's a resident hotel—or, in the vernacular, a flophouse. The guy minding the front desk is from the Middle East, been in the country about a week, didn't know from nothing. We talked to some of the residents. Taylor, you wanna take it from here?"

Taylor cleared his throat. "Sure, Dave. Ah, well, I found this one old guy that had been living there for over twenty years. I would venture a guess that he was an alcoholic. Smelled like a brewery and he wasn't too sober when we spoke—"

David Lee was shaking his head. "An alcoholic is somebody who makes over fifty grand a year, bro. That old guy was a drunk."

Taylor nodded. "Point taken," he said. "Anyway, he said he remembered Mickey Barber. Said the guy had big hands and feet?"

I nodded. "That's him," I said. "Scary looking almost."

"Well, this old guy—"

"You get a name?" I asked.

"Ah," Taylor reached in his back pocket for his small spiral notebook, riffled the pages and said, "Yes. Ah, Thombody. Garrett Thombody."

"John Bob—" I started, and he grinned.

"I'll get Betty on him," he said.

I nodded at Taylor to continue. "Well, scary-*looking* isn't all," he said. "Seems Mickey used those great big hands to collect for some loan shark. Mr. Thombody said Mickey would grab somebody, choke them half to death, then let up, maybe do it two or three times to get his message across. He said hardly anybody didn't pay up, even if they had to rob a convenience store to get the gig."

"Vig," David Lee corrected. "It's the interest on the loan. Short for *vigorish*; that's Russian, or something like that."

"Huh," I said. "So now we know what old Mickey was doing for those five years. Wonder why he quit?" I asked. It was basically one of those rhetorical questions. I didn't expect an answer.

"Mr. Thombody said somebody, and he thinks more than one somebody, broke into Mickey's room one night and beat him with a baseball bat. He was in a coma for a while, the old man said. He thought maybe he died because he never saw him again."

"Decided to go legit," David Lee said. "Rehabilitation by baseball bat."

"Which leads me to the fact that Mickey Barber has violence in him," I said. "Enough so he'd shoot somebody to get a better job?" Again, a rhetorical question. I guess Taylor never heard of those.

"It's certainly as plausible as thinking Daddy did it for revenge," he said.

"Well, I think Mickey needs more looking into. Problem is, you guys can't go to the Lonestar, and now I'm barred from there for life. How are we gonna do it?"

Michael raised his hand, like he was in class or something. "I got an idea. Barbara Jo's been anxious to get involved with this. What if we sent her in?"

Me and the other boys looked at each other. "Not a good idea," I finally said. "It could be dangerous. What if he *is* the guy?"

"Yeah, but she's really been on me, Milt. You know, she gets bored. . . ." He started and looked at me.

I knew. Anything to keep her out of the shops. But the Lonestar had shops, and she wasn't barred from them like she was at the Bellagio. Neither of us said anything out loud; I didn't think he'd shared Barbara Jo's adventures with his brothers, and if he hadn't, I wasn't about to.

"Maybe we can try a dry run," I said. "See how it goes."

"Yeah," Michael said, "You and me can be waiting outside."

I grinned. "Better yet, there's a side door we can go in during the day—it's not guarded or anything. No car attendants with our wanted posters in front of them."

"Whatever," Jason said. "Is it ever going to be my turn?"

We all turned and stared at him. So far, except for watching from the sidewalk as John Bob got arrested, Jason hadn't done much. "You got something?" I asked.

"Yes!" he said, all indignant. "I told you I was going to question the rest of my foursome at the club yesterday."

"And?" John Bob encouraged, not so graciously.

"*And,*" Jason said, shooting his brother a look, "I got some gossip on the Allens—Walter mostly. The talk around town is that the late Mrs. Walter Allen had help with her car accident. And it wasn't just because she was going to press assault charges. Seems

Andrea Allen used to do Walter's books, and she knew things she might be willing to divulge, what with being pissed off about the battery and all."

"Something crooked going on at the Lonestar?" I asked. "I thought all these new casinos were legit now."

"Most of them are," he said. "My source thinks Walter Allen had some help with his start-up."

"Bent noses?" David Lee asked.

"No, nothing quite so foreign," Jason said. "Seems like Walter Allen used to be involved with that group in Texas who tried to take over the state and secede. Remember them?"

"Yeah, ten, twenty years ago?" I asked. "Some crazy white supremacist?"

"That's what my source says."

David Lee laughed. "You changing your name to Bernstein? Your *source*, Jesus!"

Jason shot him a look.

"I thought that whole thing got broken up years ago," I said. "Didn't the bigwigs go to jail?"

"Yeah, but some of the others joined up with other white supremacist groups. And those guys have a lot of money."

"And they invested in a casino?" I asked, skeptical.

"Casinos are a blank check, Milt," Jason said. "My *source*—" he said and glared at David Lee, "thinks that killing Mrs. Allen was a warning to Walter, and that maybe they followed up with killing Larry."

"Does your source drink a lot?" John Bob asked.

Jason stood up. "Hey, it's as legitimate as any of the crap you guys are coming up with! You just think it's crap because I got it playing golf! I don't have a family anymore, John Bob! I don't have a pretty fiancé, Michael! And as for you, David Lee, just go to hell!" And with that he was out the door.

"Oops," David Lee said.

"Should I go after him?" Taylor asked.

IT WAS CLEAR and bright and in the mid-eighties when Michael and I headed over to the hospital to see Denise and little Carol Jean. I gotta say, she was cute as a button. She didn't have any hair to mention, and her eyes were the blue of most babies, but she looked a lot like Denise had when I'd first seen her, twenty-some-odd years ago. She had Denise's button nose and high forehead, her little pointy chin. And Denise was in love. You could tell it took a real effort for her to let anyone else hold the baby. And Grandma Maida was in her element. She might have been sleeping on a hospital foldout chair again, but she seemed mighty happy to do it.

After we'd ooh'd and ah'd the appropriate amount, we dragged Barbara Jo out of the room and down to the cafeteria. "Let's get pregnant!" she declared to Michael the minute we were on the elevator. Since we weren't alone in the car, there were a few muffled giggles. "Let's have a shotgun wedding!" This elicited a couple of coughs and a downright guffaw.

Michael tried shushing her, but it didn't do much good. "I want a baby right away, Michael! Did you see her little nose? And those tiny hands? Oh, God, you didn't see her feet! They are *so* cute! Little bitty toes! I told Denise we should paint her toenails! Pink! Don't you think pink toenails would be adorable?"

"Honey—" Michael tried.

Sorry, but I was with the rest of the elevator crowd, laughing my ass off, as quietly as possible.

"And I've already picked out names! Lorraine! And we'll call her Sweet Lorraine. Like that song you like? Or maybe Katherine. It's so classy! And there are so many nicknames you can do with Katherine. Kathy, Katy, Kate, Kat, Kay. Or Margaret! You know how many nicknames come from Margaret? Even Peggy! Can you believe it? How, I don't know, but it's true!"

All that in a four-floor ride. We got out of the car and headed to the cafeteria. Barbara Jo didn't stop for breath. "Maggie, Meg, Margie, Marge, Peggy, Peg, Marg—like that pretty redhead on *CSI*? Oh, and Elizabeth! Don't get me started on the nicknames for Elizabeth!"

We didn't but she did. "Liz and Beth and Lisa and Liza, and Betty! Did you know Betty was a nickname for Elizabeth? I didn't, but Denise has this book—"

We finally got to the cafeteria and, luckily for Michael and me, Barbara Jo was starving. The only time she shut up was when she was shoveling food in her mouth.

That's when we gave her our idea. And I gotta say she was as enthusiastic about that as she was about having a baby.

"Ooo, I can go in costume!" she said. "Real slutty! Get his attention right away!"

"Actually, Barbara Jo," I said, "I think refined might make him pay more attention. Slutty is all over the place at that casino."

"Oh, you mean Audrey Hepburn not Madonna, huh?" She was actually silent for a moment while she thought about it. Looking at Michael, she said, "You know, honey, my craziness might come in handy now. I've got a very elegant suit I bought at a shop in the Bellagio. I won't even say how much, because that would just make us both sick, but it looks great. And I have the shoes to go with it." She stopped for a moment, then practically jumped up and down in her seat. "And your mother's got that Kate Spade Denise bought her last year. I saw she had it with her! That would go great!"

"What's a Kate Spade?" I asked Michael.

He shrugged.

"It's a purse!" Barbara Jo said and laughed. "You *men*!" And then she was jumping up and down again. "A French twist! Very classy! And your mother has those clip-on diamonds—"

"What's she talking about, Michael?" I asked.

"Ah, clip-on diamonds I think are earrings," he said.

"A French twist is a hairstyle, dummies." She demonstrated, using her hands to twist her long dark hair up on the back of her head. She turned so we could see what she was doing. "See? With pins and stuff it'll look great. Just a touch of makeup. Elegant is never overdone. As they say, less is more."

I'm not sure who says it or what it means, but personally I thought I'd just let it go.

Before we could leave for the hotel, Barbara Jo had to go back up to the room to see if she could borrow "Miss Maida's Kate Spade and diamond clip-ons," and, with Maida's blessing on the borrowing, but admonitions on the adventure before us, we headed back to the Bellagio to get Barbara Jo all dolled up.

Michael and I were sitting in the living room of their suite when Barbara Jo finally came out. She was wearing a cream-colored raw silk skirt that reached just to her knees, with tiny little pleats at each side with a tiny slit in between. The jacket matched and had a long, soft collar (shawl I think they call it) that buttoned just at the center of her breasts, with a little peek of lace covering her cleavage. The shoes were pinkish-creamish brocade sling-backs, I think I've heard Jean call 'em, with a three-inch heel, and her calves were kinda shiny—either she had on shimmery stockings, or she'd put something on her legs. The Kate Spade (the handbag, for you uninitiated) was kinda tan or beige or something with a gold latch.

Barbara Jo had done her hair in the French twist she'd demonstrated at the cafeteria, much neater though, with one long tendril of hair hanging down the right side of her face, and one long tendril hanging down the back on the left. Her makeup was subtle, just a little color on her lips and cheeks, and a little on her eyes. She had on Maida's clip-on diamond earrings, about a karat each (I know diamonds—I had to buy Jean an engagement ring, and believe me, you learn all sorts of stuff at those jewelry stores), and was wearing a dainty-looking gold chain around her neck with three smaller diamonds (about three-quarter karats total) hanging off it.

I thought Barbara Jo was a pretty girl, but the woman who walked out of that room was Audrey Hepburn in 1968. She was beautiful. Take-your-breath-away gorgeous. Neither Michael nor I said a word for a good two, three minutes. Finally, Barbara Jo said, "Well? Is it okay?"

"Okay?" Michael breathed. "Jesus Christ on a bicycle! You're . . . you're . . . fuckin' gorgeous!"

"Sheriff Milt?" she asked, hand on hip, grin on her face.

"Miss Barbara Jo, you're the prettiest girl in Las Vegas," I said.

"Now that Dr. Jean's left, you mean?"

"Of course," I said. I cleared my throat, and said, "If this doesn't do in Mickey Barber, then the man is gay, that's all I'm saying."

She held out one shapely calf and dangled a foot. "Jimmy Choo's," she said.

I finally figured out she was talking about the shoe. I didn't know they made fancy shoes in China—I thought all the good ones came from Italy.

"Very nice," I said.

"Don't even ask how much," she said. She looked at Michael. "Sorry, baby."

"Honey, it was worth it," he said.

Well, us two guys finally got through gawking and the three

of us headed out. We decided taking a taxi was a bit iffy if we needed to make a quick getaway, so we went to David Lee's room to borrow the keys to his Z. He was a little groggy (I think we woke him up), but his eyes got big when he got a gander at Barbara Jo. He never said a word, just handed us the keys, not taking his eyes off his brother's girlfriend.

Michael glared at him and said, "Get it out of your head, bro."

We left the hotel and, let me tell you, even in the Bellagio, Barbara Jo turned some heads.

It didn't take long to get to the Lonestar; we coulda walked it, but, like I said, if we needed to make a quick getaway . . .

"Remember," I told Barbara Jo as we sat in the car, "this is a dry run. Just see if he pays attention to you. Don't get into anything. We'll make a decision later about whether to go forward with this or not. You got that, Barbara Jo? This is a dry run."

"Gotcha, Sheriff Milt," Barbara Jo said. "Dry run. Just see if he likes me."

"I don't think we need to worry about that," Michael said.

We dropped Barbara Jo off a city block from the Lonestar's front entrance, then drove around to the side, found a parking spot, and went in the side door. The mostly empty hallway led to the lobby, where we had a good view of the main bar area and the casino. We stood behind a smaller replica of Big Tex, which was still big enough to hide Michael.

Barbara Jo came in the front door, turning heads right and left. She walked like a princess, slow and confident, never bothering to make eye contact with the riffraff. She glanced around the casino, as if waiting for someone, then headed for the bar, taking a seat on one of the stupid saddle-looking barstools.

Shit, I thought, I couldn't see Mickey Barber. Was this his day off? Was he not tending bar anymore, now that he was the high muckidy-muck?

Then Michael nudged me with his elbow. Here came Mickey, wearing a suit. He'd surely taken over Larry Allen's job all right, but he was still headed behind the bar, and zeroing in on Barbara Jo. We were too far away to hear anything, so I nudged Michael back and indicated we move in a little. There was an alcove close to the bar that led to the restrooms and phones, and we went behind the Big Tex and some shrubbery to get there. We needn't have worried; Mickey Barber wasn't taking his eyes off Barbara Jo.

"Champagne cocktail," we heard Barbara Jo say.

Mickey glanced at one of the bartenders to make sure he got the order, then leaned in on Barbara Jo. "You let me know if your drink's not to your liking, Miss," he said, a real smarmy smile on his face. "I run this place so I'll make sure it's right."

"Oh?" Barbara Jo said, smiling at him. "You run the hotel?"

Mickey turned a little red. "The bar," he said.

"Oh," she said, sounding just slightly disappointed.

He held out his hand. "Mickey Barber," he said.

Barbara Jo put her hand in his and he held it like he was getting ready to kiss it, and she said, "Audrey," giving no last name. I suppressed a giggle, but Michael nudged me in the ribs anyway.

"I don't think I've seen you here before," Mickey said. "Are you a guest of the hotel?"

She smiled as if the thought amused her. "No, I'm at the Bellagio," she said. "I'm supposed to be meeting someone here, but I don't see him."

"Oh, who's that?"

"Larry Allen?" she said.

"Oh, shit," I whispered to Michael. "What's she doing?"

He shook his head.

Mickey backed away a little. "How do you know Larry Allen?" he asked.

"I don't, actually," she said. "I knew his wife in college," she said. "Vassar?" as if wondering if he'd ever heard of it. "Denise was only there for a little while, but we became great friends. She wrote me that she was having a baby, and I just had to fly out! Denise said it would be easier to find this hotel than their house." She smiled. "So here I am. Doesn't Larry's father own this hotel?"

"This is supposed to be a dry run!" I whispered to Michael.

"Yeah, well, Barbara Jo has a mind of her own," he whispered back.

"Ah, yes, he does." Mickey seemed stumped for a moment, then said, "Audrey, why don't we find a table. I have some very sad news."

"Oh!" she said, placing one beautifully manicured hand to her lips. "Is Denise all right?"

Mickey came around the bar and offered his hand to Barbara Jo, saying, "Denise is just fine."

He started to move her toward a table farther away from us, but Barbara Jo had seen where we were and finagled him toward the table closest to the alcove.

"What is it, Mickey?" she asked after they sat down, placing her hand on his. I think the guy probably got wood, but I wouldn't say that in front of Michael.

"Larry Allen's no longer with us," he said.

"He left the hotel?" she asked, cocking her head prettily. Oh, yeah, girl, I thought, make him spell it out. Okay, so I was getting into it. I was still going to give the girl some shit later. I said "dry run." How many times? A hundred?

Mickey shook his head. "No. What I meant to say is, ah, Larry is deceased. He was murdered."

Barbara Jo gasped. "Oh, my! Oh, goodness! Poor Denise!"

"Well," he said, taking Barbara Jo's hand in his, "it was probably best for Denise."

Again, Barbara Jo cocked her head.

"Larry wasn't a very nice man, Audrey. He actually hit Denise. A lot, as I understand it."

"Oh, this is just awful! Please," she said, actually squeezing Mickey's hand, "where can I find Denise? Can you give me directions to her house? Take me there?"

Whoa shit, I thought. What the hell is the girl doing? There was no way she was going anywhere with Mickey Barber. Even Michael stiffened at that. I was afraid he was going to go charging out there. I put a hand on his arm. "Just wait," I said.

"She's not at her house anymore, Audrey," Mickey said, one hand still clasped in hers, the other moving up her arm, rubbing the silk suit. "Her family's here in town and she's with them. I believe in the same hotel as you. The Bellagio."

"Oh!" she said, and leaned against the back of her chair, which nimbly removed both of Mickey Barber's hands. She shook her head. "I just can't believe this! Denise never said a word!"

"That's a hard thing for a woman to talk about, even to a close friend," Mickey said, moving in with his hands again.

"Was Larry a friend of yours?" Barbara Jo asked, moving toward him.

"Oh hell no," Mickey Barber said. "Larry Allen was a real son-of-a-bitch," he said, moving his head closer to Barbara Jo's and keeping his voice so low Michael and I could barely hear it. "He was a womanizer, and I just can't tolerate a man like that."

I rolled my eyes, but noticed Michael didn't see the irony in the statement; his eyes were glued to Barbara Jo and Mickey Barber and if this didn't break up pretty quick, I was afraid Michael was going to do something. And by "do something," I don't mean yawn or pick his nose. Barbara Jo's entire demeanor seemed to indicate she was buying into everything Mickey was saying, and the boy thought he had a live one for sure.

"You'd think, being the daughter-in-law of the owner," Barbara Jo said, looking confused, "that Denise and her family would be staying here, not at the Bellagio."

"Ah, well, that's the other thing, Audrey," Mickey said, shaking his head sadly, "the police and Larry's father, and everybody else for that matter, think Denise's father killed Larry."

Again Barbara Jo recoiled from the very thought. The kid should give up the oil business and go to Hollywood, I thought. She's that good. "Why ever would they think that? I've met Mr. Upshank and he's a teddy bear, Mickey! I swear he wouldn't hurt a fly!"

"People will do things normally against their nature to protect their young," Mickey said.

Yeah, I thought, and maybe Mickey should join Barbara Jo in Hollywood.

I saw Rita McReynolds walking toward Mickey and Barbara Jo. You remember, the older waitress with the real boobs and the used-to-be-natural-and-now-it's-not-so-natural red hair.

"Hey, boss," she said, leaning an arm on Mickey's shoulder. He glared at her and said, "Not now."

"Oh, I just wanted to say hello to Barbara Jo, Michael Upshank's girlfriend," she said.

Mickey jerked his head from Rita to Barbara Jo. But Barbara Jo, being the trooper that she is, placed her hand on Mickey's arm and said, "Mickey, what is she talking about?"

Mickey wasn't having any. He grabbed Barbara Jo's wrist in one of those big, big paws of his, and that's when Michael went ballistic. He charged out of our hidey-hole and didn't stop when he got to Mickey. He just hit him, knocking him off the bar stool and onto the floor. That's when Rita called for Butch, that big African-American gentleman without the gentle smile or the mouse. Butch picked Michael up by the scruff of his pants, which just goes to show how big Butch was. Meanwhile, Barbara Jo was squealing, I was yelling, and Rita McReynolds was laughing. Finally righted, Barber started yelling about pressing charges. I mentioned Piedmont Street and some outstanding charges we could level against him, which seemed to interest Rita, at which point Mickey dismissed Rita and Butch, who left without much regard to Mickey's bloody nose or scuffed suit jacket.

"What do you people want?" Mickey demanded, staring at us. Then he laughed. "What? You think I killed Larry? Are you out of your minds? Why? Over one of these bimbos?" he said, his hand waving behind him at his waitstaff. "Or over a fucking job?" he demanded. He laughed again. "Jeez, you people need to get a life!" He called one of the bartenders over and asked for some ice. In an aside to us, he said, "Get out of here, and take that skank with you."

Michael seemed to think he meant Barbara Jo, which I guess he did, and grabbed for him, but between us, Barbara Jo and I managed to manhandle Michael out of the casino. All in all, I figured, the whole ordeal had been a big bust.

WE MET BACK in Michael and Barbara Jo's suite at five o'clock, as scheduled. Everybody was there, except Jason. Nobody had seen or heard from him since he'd stormed out earlier.

"I got some info from Betty," John Bob started. "Belinda Norwalk was from Santa Fe. She checked and there are no Norwalks listed there now. Family must have moved. She's working on that. She did a run on Taylor's Mr. Thombody, and what we have here, gentlemen, is a real live war hero. Vietnam vet. Three purple hearts and a bronze star. Which goes well with his fifteen drunk and disorderlies, his four DUI's, and his attempted assault on a police officer," John Bob said, shaking his head. "They used to make a big deal about Vietnam vet burnouts, but I thought maybe that was just a fad, you know?" he said, looking at me. Slapping at the paper in his hand, he said, "But this guy seems like the real thing. Your garden variety bum. As good a witness as one could hope to have."

"Well, ah, he seemed . . . a little, well, unreliable," Taylor admitted.

"I wouldn't go so far as to say that. Betty hacked into the hospital records here, found out which hospital Mickey Barber was in back then, and confirmed the coma. Barber was out of it for like six weeks, in rehab for almost a year. So it looks like your Mr. Thombody's info was partially true. Nothing in the police records about Barber's muscle jobs, but if he never got caught, there wouldn't be."

"Okay," I said, getting a little tired and frustrated. "What do we have? Mickey Barber didn't like Larry Allen, he took Mickey's job, and Mickey has a violent past. Not enough to go to the police. Walter Allen may have killed his second (or was she his third?) wife. May have been associated with white supremacists. But I can't think of any reason in hell why he would harm his son—he seemed devoted to the little asshole." I shook my head in frustration.

"Well, according to Jason," John Bob said, "the scenario is that these white supremacists are after Walter, for whatever reason, and they killed both the third Mrs. Allen *and* Larry as an example to Walter."

Everybody laughed, just as the door opened and Jason came in. We sobered up.

"Hey, Jase," Michael finally said, sounding guilty as hell.

"Yeah, hey, Jase," everybody echoed.

Jason didn't take a seat. Instead, he stood there looking down at his brothers—and me. Finally, he said, "While y'all were out chasing your wild geese, I had a phone call." He was silent for a moment, letting the suspense build.

Finally, John Bob said, "Can the crap, Jason. Who called? Those Texan white supremacists?"

There were a few snickers but mostly the room was silent.

"No," Jason said. "Daddy called."

Well, now the room was deadly quiet. "Seems the operator was dialing every room in the hotel with an Upshank in it, but I was the only one home."

I stood up. I hate to crane my neck to see somebody; 'sides, there's that whole psychological thing going on there. "Where's your father?" I asked. Okay, demanded.

Jason shrugged. "He didn't say. Just wanted to know what was going on. He was quite excited about Denise's baby."

John Bob stood up and came to stand next to me. "Again, Jason, cut the crap. What did he say?"

Jason smiled in a mean sorta way. "I'm sure you won't believe this, John Bob, but our father said he didn't do this."

"He still got the gun?" I asked.

Jason shrugged. "I didn't ask him."

I glared at Jason. "What *did* you ask him?"

Jason crossed his arms in front of his chest and glared right back at me. "I didn't have a lot of time to ask anything. He said he'd seen a couple of us boys—and no, he didn't say which ones—out and about in Vegas, thought we might be looking for him. He said he was okay, he was in hiding, and that he didn't do it. He said to tell Mama he loved her, and to tell Denise he was real proud of her. And he said thank you to me. I guess he meant it for all of you, too," Jason said grudgingly.

"And you just let him go?" Michael said, almost screaming, as he jumped up and confronted Jason. "How the hell could you do that?"

"I didn't 'just let him go,' Mike. He hung up."

"Did you question the hotel operator, to see where the call originated?" I asked.

"No," he said, face flushing slightly.

"Did you tell him the best thing he could do right now is give himself up?" I almost roared.

Well, that brought five pairs of eyes on me real quick, and I can't say they were friendly.

"Give himself up?" Michael said. "What the hell are you talking about, Milt? The police aren't looking for anybody else! Daddy gives himself up, they're gonna bury him!"

"Yeah, Milt," David Lee said. "Daddy can't just give himself up. You think they'll look for anybody else once they have him?"

"They're not looking for anybody else now, Dave," I said. "We're the only ones doing that, and as far as I can see, we're just spinning our wheels."

"So you think Daddy turning himself in is gonna help that?" Michael demanded.

"Look, guys, I'm a law enforcement officer. It's my sworn duty not to harbor a suspected felon. And that's what Burl is. Everything would have been fine if he hadn't run off, but he did. I can't look the other way on this, guys. I just can't."

Strangely enough, John Bob was the one to come to my rescue. "Milt's right. It is his job—mine, too, if it comes to that. I'm an officer of the court—"

"In Oklahoma!" Michael yelled.

"Anywhere, Mike. But the point's moot, anyway. We still don't know where he is. We're as close to finding Daddy since that phone call as we were before the phone call." And John Bob said that with a lot of relief in his voice.

"Well, I'll tell you what, John Bob, Milt," Jason said, "if Daddy calls back, I'll send him your regards, but I sure as hell won't mention to either of you that he called." With that, Jason left the room, with David Lee and Taylor not far behind. If it hadn't been his suite, I think Michael would have left, too.

"Why don't y'all just leave?" Michael said to John Bob and me.

Out in the hall, John Bob and I walked to our respective rooms, which were catty-corner across from each other. "Milt, I had to say it in front of the boys, but I gotta tell you, I'd never give up my daddy, officer of the court or not. And, man, you're family! Could you do it? Would you do it?"

I shook my head. "Hell if I know, John Bob," I said, and used the card key to open my room door and get the hell out of Dodge.

SECOND FRIDAY ◆ PROPHESY COUNTY

He found her parked in her favorite hideyhole, behind the KFC billboard on Highway 5. He pulled up his squad car and got out, getting in the shotgun side of hers.

"Hey," she said, grinning, "what are you doing out here?"

"Got too much going on with Dalton out. Called Elberry to do the paperwork, let me get out on the streets."

"That was a good idea," Jasmine said.

He didn't tell her it wasn't his. "Anything going on?" he asked.

"Had a red Camaro a few minutes ago, going at least ninety. Got him good."

"Passing through or a citizen?"

"Passing through. From Tulsa. Probably play hell getting the money out of him."

"Yeah, I hate these out-of-town speeders," he said.

"Out-of-staters are the worst," she said.

"Oh, yeah. By far."

Her hand was on his trouser leg. He grabbed the cardboard sun screen she kept between the bucket seats, hurriedly threw it up on the windshield, and pulled her into his lap.

"What time do you get off?" she asked between kisses.

"Doing a split shift," he gasped, sucking on her neck.

"If it's quiet, come over," she said, her hands working his belt.

"Oh, yeah," he said, not knowing if he was answering her or just remarking on the wonderfulness of her touch.

Second Friday ✦ Las Vegas

Well, I knew if I wanted to eat dinner that night, I'd be doing it without an Upshank for company. I also knew that I had to tell Jimmy Broderick that we'd heard from Burl. So I called him and invited him to dinner. Thought I could kill two birds with one stone. It was his idea that we go to that all-you-can-eat seafood buffet, but I'll admit I didn't argue any.

After we'd filled our plates with every fried object in the place—including fried corn on the cob (which I'd never tried, but I figured, corn on the cob's good, fried's good, why not put the two together?), we found a fairly quiet corner and sat down to do some serious consumption.

"One of the Upshank boys got a call today," I started out.

"Oh, yeah?" Broderick said, stuffing fried shrimp in his mouth three at a time. "Who from, Sheriff?"

"His daddy," I said, going for a hush puppy.

Broderick looked up, his eyes big, his mouth stuffed. "Ut ee ay?" he managed to get out.

"Not much. Wouldn't give a location, needless to say. Only that he was in hiding, he was safe, and that he didn't do it."

Broderick swallowed in one gulp what a supermodel would consume in a year, and said, "Well, he would say that, Sheriff, wouldn't he? I mean, they all say they didn't do it."

I nodded. "I can see your point, Detective, but my point is, you don't know Burl Upshank. He didn't have to tell me he didn't do this, I *know* he didn't."

"Uh huh," Broderick said, obviously being polite. He didn't believe me. Oh, maybe he believed that I believed, but I could tell by the look on his face, he was as convinced as his lieutenant that Burl had killed Larry Allen.

I just looked at him. "Well, I did my duty. I told you about the phone call, but I want you to know that I don't believe Burl did this. I believe somebody else did, and I'm gonna find out who. I know the LVPD isn't going to do shit to find the real killer, so I'm gonna do it myself. With the help of Burl's sons."

"Now, Sheriff," he said, his voice kinda whiny, "my lieutenant is gonna be real unhappy when he finds out you and those Upshank boys are going all around Las Vegas, sticking your noses in where they don't belong. Y'all could get 'em chopped off, you know."

"Is that a threat?" I asked, feeling all that fried backing up on me.

"No, sir, absolutely not!" Broderick said, shaking his head. "It's a warning. Las Vegas is like any big city, Sheriff. There are a lot of people out there doing things they're not supposed to do, and if you go messing around, you might trip over something that could get you or one of those boys hurt. Now how would you feel if one of those boys got hurt? How you gonna explain that to Mr. or Mrs. Upshank?"

"I call 'em boys, Detective, but they're all grown men. Their mother's as anxious for them to do this as they are. All of them want to clear Burl's name. All of 'em wanna go home to Oklahoma and never think about Vegas again."

I drank some iced tea to calm my stomach. "Oh, by the way," I said, "Denise had her baby. A little girl."

Broderick smiled. "Everybody okay?" he asked.

"Just fine," I answered.

"That's real good," he said.

We finished up and said our good-byes, me thinking it would be a while before I had to look at that face again; you know, when I'm wrong, I'm really wrong.

SECOND FRIDAY ✦ PROPHESY COUNTY

It was quiet. Emmett called Anthony on the radio. "Got anything?" he asked.

"Naw. Just checked the stores downtown, everything's ship-shape."

"I'm going ten-eight now. Cruise by the highway once while I'm down, 'k?"

"Got it. Out."

He wasn't all that hungry. He drove by Jasmine's house. The lights were on in the living room. He pulled the squad car up to the curb and got out, and went and knocked on the door. She opened it quickly, her arms wide. He walked into them, kicking the door shut with his shoe.

She wrapped her arms around his neck, her legs around his waist, and he carried her to the bedroom, their mouths locked together.

Twenty minutes later, lying in Jasmine's arms, he said, "Jeez, I'm hungry."

Jasmine giggled. "Really makes you work up an appetite, huh?"

"Hell, woman," he said, turning and nuzzling her neck. "You mostly just wear me plumb out."

"You want me to fix you something to eat?" she said, nibbling on his ear.

"Yeah, and I want you to stop what you're doing with your hands. I gotta get back on duty. *And* I gotta eat."

"Come back here after shift?" she asked, her voice soft as she breathed her words into his ear.

"Oh, yeah," he said.

She bit his earlobe until he said "ouch," then jumped out of bed. "Eggs okay? Don't have anything defrosted."

"Eggs are fine," he said, watching her fine ass as she moved to her closet and pulled on a robe. "And do me a favor," he said as she walked out the bedroom door. "Don't get dressed while I'm gone." He smiled at her. "I think I'd like to think about you here in that bathrobe, naked as a jaybird. As a matter of fact, I like thinking about it right now."

She slid the bathrobe off her shoulders and let it fall to the floor. "Why don't you remember me like this?" she said, and left the room for the kitchen.

Jeez, Emmett thought, I hope she doesn't burn anything important.

A WHILE AFTER Emmett got back to Jasmine's house after shift, they lay in bed in postcoital bliss. She was resting her head on his shoulder, and he was thinking about maybe getting some shut-eye, when she said, "I think it's time."

He looked down at her. "Time for what?"

"Time for you to talk about J.R."

Emmett was silent for a long moment. What she said made him feel guilty; he hadn't thought about J.R. all day. It was the first time since his birth that the boy hadn't been in his mind most of the time.

"What do you want to know?" he asked, staring at the ceiling.

"Everything, I guess. As much as you want to tell. What did he look like?"

"Blond hair, blue eyes, a crooked front tooth."

"Just like his daddy, huh?"

Emmett smiled at the ceiling. "Spitting image."

"Was he serious, funny, athletic?"

"Funny." He laughed. "Jeez, the kid was hysterical. Almost from the start. And he was athletic. Started out in T-ball, played Little League. I had to fight Shirley Beth for both of those. She wouldn't even discuss peewee football."

"She was protective?"

"Oh, yeah. J.R. was her life. Mine, too, but I had my job."

"How old was he . . ."

"When he died? Ten. Nine when we found out he had leukemia. He lost almost half his weight in that one year it took him to die. We had him on chemo and radiation, and anything they came up with Shirley Beth wanted to do."

"You didn't agree with her? On the chemo and stuff?"

Emmett was silent a moment. Finally he said, "By the time we got to the specialist, J. R. was ate up with it. The doctor told us he had less than a twenty percent chance of survival. He gave us our options, the chemo and stuff, or just taking him home and letting him be. Said it would be easier on the boy. Said he'd have a few decent months, then a couple of bad ones. But Shirley Beth was adamant. She wanted to save him." Emmett shook his head. "I shoulda stood my ground, but I always let her lead the way with J.R. It always seemed so important to her. It was like she was the real parent, and I was just this backup guy. There in case I was ever needed." He laughed bitterly. "Funniest thing, I never was."

"Oh, baby," Jasmine said, moving her body closer to his, kissing his chest. "I'm so sorry."

Emmett shook his head. "It wasn't her fault; I let her do it. But I wish . . . ah, hell, no reason to dwell on it."

They lay there quietly together, neither saying anything for a while. Finally, Emmett said, "I remember one time, he couldn'ta been more than six or seven, the two of us had been to the ballpark, watching the big kids playing Little League, and he said, 'Daddy, when I grow up can I play Little League?'" He laughed. "When I grow up."

Jasmine squeezed his arm, and he could feel dampness where her face touched his chest.

"In the hospital, the last time, his mama had gone home for a minute—Shirley Beth didn't do that much, but she did it this one time. And he said, 'Daddy, it hurts. Why does it have to hurt so much?' And I told him it was the medicine they were giving him to make him better, and he said, 'I'm not getting better, Daddy. Jesus is gonna take me home with him.'"

Emmett stopped talking. His chest was heaving and he didn't understand why. When the tears came, followed by sobs, he felt Jasmine's arms around him, felt her tears on his back, and held onto her for dear life.

SECOND SATURDAY   ✦   LAS VEGAS

The bedside clock said 6 A.M. when the banging started. I got out of bed and peeked through the door to find Mac Grayson and Jimmy Broderick standing outside. I pulled on a T-shirt and a pair of pants and opened the door. Last time I'd entertained the two in a hotel room I'd been in my underwear—I didn't want a repeat of that.

"What now?" I asked.

"May we come in, Sheriff?" Grayson said.

I shook my head, but opened the door anyway. I was tired. "What's going on?"

"Where were you last night, from midnight until approximately four A.M.?" Grayson asked.

"Well, I know this is Las Vegas and all, and you might not believe it, but I was asleep. Why?"

"Can you account for the whereabouts of any or all of Burl Upshank's sons?" he asked.

"No!" I said. "I just told you, I was asleep, and I'm not in the habit of sleeping with any of those boys—or any other boys for that matter! Now, you gonna tell me what's going on?"

"Are you, at this time, aware of Burl Upshank's whereabouts?"

"No! Jesus! What is this?" I asked, about ready to kick 'em both out.

"We're very interested in any alibi you or any of the Upshanks might have for the hours of midnight last night to four A.M. this morning," Grayson said.

"Why?" I demanded.

"Because that's the ME's window for when Walter Allen was murdered," he said.

SECOND SATURDAY ✦ LAS VEGAS

I sat, or fell, down on the bed. Walter Allen murdered. Larry Allen murdered. What did it mean? How did this affect what I already knew? Was Jason right about the white supremacists? Did Mickey Barber have it in for Walter, too? What good would Walter being dead do him, though? But could this be an out for Burl? What reason would he have for killing Walter? Taking an extreme, and wrong, view, you could say Burl killed Larry in the heat of the moment for having hurt Denise and her baby. But why would Burl, after all this time, decide to kill Walter Allen? Answer: he wouldn't.

I stood up and smiled at Lieutenant Grayson. "Well, guess that lets Burl off the hook," I said.

"Why in the cornbread hell would you say that?" Grayson demanded.

"Why would Burl kill Walter? Obviously, whoever killed

Larry killed Walter, right? And if Burl didn't kill Walter, then he didn't kill Larry," I said.

"How many times has your county elected you sheriff? Do they just not know how stupid you are, or are they that stupid, too?" Grayson said.

"You know, Grayson, insult me all you want, but don't you go calling the people of Prophesy County, Oklahoma, stupid! When push comes to shove, I haven't noticed any Einsteins in this burg!"

Grayson jabbed his finger at my chest. "Hey! This is Las Vegas, man! There's no place on earth like this town, and don't you forget it!"

"All I can say to that, *Lieutenant,*'" I said, real sarcastic-like, "is thank God. One hellhole like this is plenty!"

"Ah, excuse me, guys. Lieutenant, Sheriff, ah, we got another murder here?" Broderick said, like he wasn't quite sure if we did or not—have a murder here, that is.

Me and Grayson both pulled back, with me, anyway, trying to calm down a little. I knew all about buttons, and Mac Grayson wasn't pushing mine, he was jabbing at 'em with his index finger.

"Detective Broderick is right, Sheriff," Grayson said, straightening his jacket. "Will you please round up all the Upshanks and have them meet me downstairs."

"I got a better idea, Lieutenant," I said. "Mrs. Upshank's at the hospital with her daughter who just had a baby, so her suite is empty right now. I have a key. Why don't you and Detective Broderick wait there while I round up the boys?"

"Thank you," Grayson said. "That would be fine."

Lord, the two of us were being so polite, I'm surprised one of us didn't just blow to little bits.

I got them settled in Maida's suite and went to round up the boys. I told 'em all to meet me in the hall quick so I could tell them what had happened before we went in to see Grayson and Broderick.

Once I had 'em all in the hall, I said softly, "The police are in your mother's suite, waiting to interview all of us. Seems somebody murdered Walter Allen last night."

There were various reactions to this news—from Michael's extreme shock to David Lee's yawn. John Bob, being a lawyer and all, got straight to the point. "Do they suspect Daddy or one of us?"

"Any and/or all," I said. "Take your pick. If you've got an alibi for midnight to four A.M., that would be a good thing."

All the boys looked at each other. Only Michael raised his hand. He blushed. "Ah, I've got one. Um, Barbara Jo and I were . . . um, up late?" he said.

Sex, I thought, is always a pleasant alibi, but hard to substantiate because, usually, there's only two of you. Nobody around, hopefully, to confirm.

"Well, let's go get this over with," I said, leading the parade to Maida's suite.

Everybody nodded at each other, but there was no shaking of hands. The boys found places to sit, and I pulled up a chair from the dining room table, turned it backward, and sat on it that way. That's not a habit of mine, but I've seen it done on *NYPD Blue*, and I always thought it looked cool.

"I'm sure Sheriff Kovak has explained the situation," Grayson started, giving me a look like I wasn't supposed to tell 'em what happened. Hell, he never said not to. "Right now, I'd like to know your whereabouts between midnight last night and approximately four A.M. this morning."

John Bob said, "Asleep—alone."

Jason said, "Me, too."

Taylor said, "Ah, yes, I was asleep—alone."

Michael said, "Ah, I was with my girlfriend. We were up until about two, I guess. Then we went to sleep."

David Lee said, "I was downtown, hitting some casinos until around two, then I met a lady, went back to her place, and got back here to the hotel around five."

All eyes went to David Lee. I gotta say, the boy had stamina. "Can you substantiate any of that?" Grayson asked him.

"Yeah, I guess. I was at Johnny Dee's at some point in the evening, ran into an old friend and we talked for a while. Couple of people there know me. I don't know what time that was. I wasn't exactly looking at my watch."

"What about this woman?" Grayson asked.

David Lee shrugged. "Afraid I didn't catch her name. Met her at . . ." He seemed lost in thought a moment. "I think it was at Fredo's on Lee Street. She was staying at a motel over off Lee and the Boulevard. The El Camino Real? I think that was it," he said. As usual, David Lee seemed pretty bored by the whole thing.

Grayson glanced at Jimmy Broderick to make sure he was writing all this down, then he changed tactics. "Which one of you got the phone call from your father?" he asked.

Jason raised his hand. "I did," he said, then glared at me for telling.

"Where was he when he called?" Grayson asked.

"He didn't say," Jason answered.

"What exactly did he say?"

Jason repeated the conversation, verbatim as I had given it to Broderick the night before. Finally, Grayson stood up. "We'll be checking with the Bellagio personnel to see if there are any discrepancies in your stories," he said. Looking at David Lee, he said, "And we'll see what we can do with this alibi of yours."

He headed for the door, Broderick a few steps behind. Doing a Columbo, Grayson stopped and turned back to the boys.

Unfortunately, Broderick was right on his heels and they bumped as Grayson turned. "Move the hell out of the way!" Grayson grumbled. Taking a breath, he said, "If anybody else hears from your dad, please let him know I'd like to talk to him."

It would have been a great exit line, except going for the door, Broderick was in his way again, and Grayson had to shove him to get out. If it had been on *Columbo,* somebody woulda yelled, "Cut!"

As soon as they'd left, John Bob looked at his brother, David Lee. "What the hell were you doing out carousing last night?"

"Well, bro, I didn't take into consideration that Walter Allen was gonna get himself murdered. You know, it just never crossed my mind. I go out every night. No reason why last night should be any different."

"You go out every night?" John Bob demanded. "Jesus, and I thought you were going to turn over a new leaf! What in the hell are you gonna do in Longbranch, you idiot? There's not exactly a thriving nightlife in Prophesy County!"

David Lee smiled lazily. "Thought I'd get it out of my system while I was here," he said. "That way I'll be all ready to settle down at Mama and Daddy's."

John Bob shook his head. "That's going to be a disaster," he said. "Hell, this is a disaster." He looked around at his brothers, stopping at each in turn. "As an attorney," he said, "anything said to me by a client is privileged. If any of you need to talk to me in private, please let me know."

"How much are you gonna charge?" David Lee asked.

"Fuck you, David Lee!" John Bob said, which only made David Lee laugh.

"Jeez, John Bob," Michael said, "you actually think one of us killed Walter Allen? Why would we?" He shook his head. "I thought you knew us better than that!"

"Yeah," Jason agreed. "I don't even know what the old fart looked like. But thanks for the vote of confidence, John Bob!"

"John Bob was only saying—" Taylor started, but everybody said in unison, "Shut up, Taylor."

"I don't think any of you killed Walter Allen," John Bob said. "But if anyone else has heard from Daddy, we need to know. I need to know. I need to start making some contingency plans."

"You mean making a cover-up?" David Lee asked. He shook his head. "Hell, John Bob, you still think Daddy did it, don't you?"

"I have no idea," John Bob said, "and if Daddy were here in front of me right now, I wouldn't ask. The only thing I want to do is get him out of this mess."

"Jesus!" Michael said, standing up and heading for the door. "First Milt tells the cops about Daddy, wants to turn him in, and now you! I've never said this, John Bob, but I've been thinking it for a long time, and you just confirmed it: you're an asshole!" And with that, he was out the door.

SINCE I WAS still on the outs with the boys, I didn't think it would hurt to spend part of my Saturday checking out the roulette wheels at the various casinos. First I called home, talked to Jean then Johnny Mac, heard all about his new dinosaur his mama had bought him, heard what a dinosaur sounded like about four jillion times, then talked to Jean again.

"Any progress?" she asked.

"Only if you call having none of the Upshank boys speaking to me progress. Which I suppose it is, in a way."

"How did you accomplish that?" she asked with a smile in her voice.

"They think I'm gonna turn their daddy in." I explained about Burl's phone call, and told her about Walter Allen.

"Oh, my God," she said. "Milt, who is doing this?"

"I take it that was one of those rhetorical questions, honey. 'Cause if I knew, I'd be home now."

"I wish you were home," she said, her voice soft. "I miss you."

"All of me?" I asked grinning.

"Well, some parts more than others," she said.

"I love it when you talk dirty," I said.

She laughed. "Tell you what," she said. "You find this psycho who's doing this, and meanwhile I'll read some romance novels, and when you get back I'll have all sorts of things to teach you."

"Wicked woman," I said.

"Let me count the ways," she said and giggled. Pretty soon afterward we hung up, and I sat on the bed missing my wife, missing my boy, missing my job, missing my life. I finally decided I could sit there all day and feel sorry for myself, or I could get my butt up and go check out the casinos. I knew it wouldn't do any good, but at least I'd be doing something.

The Bellagio's slot machine bells were ringing, smoke was heavy in the air, even at nine in the morning, but the gaming tables were empty, not even any dealers present. I went in search of breakfast, then headed out on the strip. It was too early for the gaming tables at all the casinos I went in, and when I ended up at NewYorkNewYork, I decided what I really needed was a roller-coaster ride. I did that about three times, got the adrenaline pumping, then took a taxi to the hospital.

When I got to the room, Denise was asleep, the baby asleep in a bassinet next to her. Maida was sitting in a chair by the window, reading a mystery novel.

"Getting some ideas for me?" I asked her quietly. She shushed me anyway and motioned for me to go outside to the hall. Once we were both out there, I asked, "Wanna go to the cafeteria for some coffee?"

We took the elevator down to the first floor and walked together in companionable silence to the cafeteria. At least the coffee was strong, I thought as I took a sip of the murky brew.

I told her about Walter Allen. Maida sighed. "What's going on, Milt? Who's doing this?"

"The police think Burl did it," I said.

"I assumed as much," she said and sighed again. Then she looked me in the eye. "I hope you know that Burl didn't do this—neither Walter nor Larry. It's not in his makeup. I'm not saying he wouldn't kill somebody in the heat of the moment, if somebody was threatening me or one of the kids, but that's not what happened here, Milt. Whoever did this was opportunistic. They saw a way to kill Larry and pin it on Burl because he'd just beaten up Larry. Now, Walter, I don't know. I guess he saw his opportunity again, and again thought he could pin it on Burl."

"Maybe not a 'he,' Maida," I said. "Could be a woman."

"Sure. A gun. Easy." Then she laughed. "Remember that time your mama took a shot at you?"

I laughed, too. "Thank God the woman couldn't hit the broad side of a barn."

"That's what you get for sneaking in at three o'clock in the morning! She thought you were sound asleep in the bed."

"I've always been thankful she couldn't wake Daddy up. He was a damn good shot."

Maida sighed. "I miss her," she said. "We were always good friends. Cousins, sure, but friends, too. She was a lot older than me, but as we both got older, that didn't matter so much." She laughed. "Looking at little Carol Jean reminds me of when your mama found out she was pregnant with Jewel Anne. You know, she had two miscarriages before you."

"I didn't know that," I said, thinking of my mother, that

funny lady who always had a switch handy. She hardly ever used it, but the threat was always there.

"She had trouble having you, almost lost you twice, then after you were born, the doctors said she wouldn't be able to have another. Then thirteen years after you came along, here comes Jewel Anne."

"Oh, yeah, that embarrassed the crap out of me, I can tell you that," I said, laughing. "Thirteen and your mother's pregnant. That meant every guy in the locker room knew my mama and daddy were 'doing it.'"

Maida hit me on the arm. "God, you boys. You're all alike. John Bob was the same way when I had Denise. Anyway, Lucy calls me one day, crying, says she's going through the change early. All upset. I tell her to go see the doctor, but she won't, she doesn't want to know for sure. Couple of days later she calls me and says it's bad enough she's going through the change early, now she's got the flu on top of it. Throwing up. I say go see the doctor. Make a long story short, she's in her second trimester before she realizes the early change, the flu, and the weight gain might be something else."

"I remember her being all upset around that time, but of course, I didn't know what was going on. I remember knocking my friend Linn flat when he said something about my mama getting fat."

Maida laughed, then sobered. "I sure could use Lucy's guidance right about now," she said, a tear in her eye. "She always had a way of making things better."

I remembered that about my mama. The scraped knees that merited another piece of pecan pie, not making first string my freshman year and the trip to the Dairy Queen, the first girl to break my heart and, even with a new baby in tow, a day trip to Tulsa to see the sights.

"Better get back upstairs," Maida said, finishing her coffee in one gulp. "Denise or the baby could be waking up."

I stood up and walked around the table and hugged her. "Thanks," I said.

She patted her hair. "Whatever for?" she said, and headed out of the cafeteria.

SECOND SATURDAY ✦ PROPHESY COUNTY

"Emmett, you gotta talk to Jasmine," Anthony said. He'd just left the house to go to his squad car. Wasn't gone two minutes before he was back, knocking on Emmett's door. Since things had calmed down in the county, Elberry had taken to coming in in the mornings only. Emmett was back in charge in the afternoon.

"What about, Anthony?" Emmett asked.

"The squad car! This is the third time this week I've found fast-food crap all over the passenger-side floor! She just throws that crap down there and doesn't clean it out!"

Emmett got up from Milt's chair and went to the door. As he passed Anthony, he patted him on the arm and said, "Sit down a minute and cool your heels. I'll be right back."

He went into the bull pen where Jasmine and Gladys were having their daily girl talk. He excused himself and asked to speak to Jasmine. They walked a distance away from Gladys, and Jasmine whispered, "You think we should be doing this in the office?"

"Had a complaint, Jasmine," he said quietly.

Her whole body stiffened. Jasmine was well known in the sheriff's department for not taking constructive criticism well. Emmett was beginning to sweat. "What about?" she asked.

"Anthony said you've been leaving fast-food wrappers in the squad car. You really shouldn't do that. Leave the car like you find it, Jasmine, that's the rule."

"Well, you can just tell him that he should stop smoking in the car then! Every morning when I get in it smells like an ashtray!"

Emmett shook his head. "Nobody's supposed to smoke in the squad cars," he said with a sigh.

"Well, you can just tell that to Anthony!" With that, Jasmine whirled around and went out the front door, which meant she didn't have to pass Anthony, but she would have to walk around the building to get to her Mazda.

Emmett stood in the bull pen for a minute and collected his thoughts. He'd wanted her to go clean out the squad car, but she'd gotten away from him before he had a chance to tell her that. Should he just go clean it himself, let Anthony think Jasmine had done it? Or brace Anthony about smoking in the squad car, and let him worry about picking up the fast-food wrappers? Damn, he'd be glad when Milt got back.

He went back to Milt's office to find Anthony sitting in the visitor's chair with his feet on Milt's desk.

"Take your feet down, Anthony," he said.

Anthony did and stood up. "You talk to her?" he demanded.

"Yeah, and she says you smoke in the squad car. That true, Anthony?"

"Jesus Christ, that bit—Excuse me, Emmett. But she has some nerve! No, I don't smoke in the squad car!" he said adamantly. Then added, "Not really."

"Jasmine says the squad car smells like an ashtray," Emmett said.

"She's lying! It does not! The only reason she thinks I smoke in the squad car is 'cause she saw me! And I wasn't really smoking in the car! I was sitting in the car, but I was hanging out the window so's no smoke would get in the car!"

Emmett sighed. "The rule is no smoking in the squad cars,

Anthony. And that means no sitting in the squad car and hanging your head out the window to smoke. Get out of the car and smoke on the street, okay?"

Anthony's fists were clenched. Finally, they loosened and he said, "Okay. Fine. I won't sit in the car when I smoke. But what has that got to do with her leaving fast-food crap all over? Is she cleaning it out?"

Emmett sighed, "Probably not," he said softly. Then to Anthony he said, "Let's go outside and look at the car."

He followed Anthony out and around the car to the passenger-side door, which Anthony opened with a flourish, pointing to the floor. There was a McDonald's quarter pounder box, a hopefully empty Coke cup, a bag they'd all come in, and some wrappers from Taco Heaven. Emmett saw Jasmine's Mazda pulling out of the parking lot, coming their way, the only way she could go. He stepped in front of her, making her slam on the brakes.

Moving to her driver's side window, he motioned for her to open it; when she finally did, he said, "You need to get out here and clean out the squad car."

She stared at him for a full minute, but Emmett refused to break eye contact. Finally, she slammed the car into park and shoved open the door, attempting to hit Emmett with it obviously, but he sidestepped it easily.

Jasmine marched over to where Anthony was standing by the passenger-side door and, glaring at him, leaned in and scraped all the fast-food litter onto the asphalt parking lot. She marched back to her car, got in, put it back in gear, and drove off, leaving a very small space between her car and Emmett as she did so.

"Did you see what she did?" Anthony yelled. "She just threw it on the ground! I'm gonna arrest that bitch for littering! That's what I'm gonna do! I'm gonna arrest her ass!"

Emmett walked over to the squad car and said, "Anthony, get in and start your tour. You're late."

"But look at this shit!" he said, pointing at the ground.

"Just don't run over it, okay? Just get to work."

Anthony slammed the passenger-side door a lot harder than necessary, and glared at Emmett as he got in the driver's side.

"Emmett, you gotta do something about her!" he said, starting the car.

Emmett sighed. "Go to work," he said. "Please."

After Anthony drove out of the lot, Emmett picked up the litter and put it in the Dumpster at the back of the lot and decided maybe tonight would be a good night to stay home and watch a ball game on TV.

SECOND SUNDAY ♦ LAS VEGAS

I woke up at three o'clock in the morning with a powerful thirst. One a glass of water wouldn't quench. I needed a Diet Coke. Nothing else would do. There was a Coke machine on our floor, so I put on my pants and a T-shirt, grabbed some ones and some change (sometimes those machines can be finicky), and headed for the door.

I'd barely opened it when I saw John Bob's door open cattycorner across from mine. A blond head peeked out and I pulled mine back, watching through a crack in the door. Thinking it was all clear, the owner of the body came through the doorway—and what a body it was. Even in the severe business suit she was still wearing at three o'clock in the morning, those long legs shone. I'd forgotten all about my gut feeling that there was something going on between John Bob and Melissa Greevey; now here she was, sneaking out of his hotel room at 3 A.M. I watched until I saw her enter the elevator, then I went across the hall and knocked on John Bob's door.

"What now?" he said, ripping the door open. When he saw me, he turned red.

"We gotta talk," I said, pushing my way into his room.

"Hey!" John Bob squeaked. "Get the hell out of my room! It's three in the morning!"

"Not a good time for guests, huh? What about Melissa?"

John Bob was in one of the Bellagio robes, partially covering his hairy chest, with the purple pajama bottoms peeking out at the legs. He rubbed his face with both hands, sighed real heavy, and sat down hard on the bed. "Just leave it alone, Milt," he said, sounding and looking like death warmed over.

I took one of the chairs at the desk and sat down. "I need to know what that was about, John Bob. Especially if it could affect what's been going on here."

"It has nothing to do with either Larry's or Walter's deaths. I promise you that. My word as an officer of the court."

"Well, seeing how fast and loose we've both been playing it around here, I'm afraid your word as an officer of the court doesn't hold water. Talk to me or talk to Maida."

"Oh for Christ sake! I'm getting sick and tired of everybody threatening each other with Mama's wrath! What are you gonna tell my mother, Milt? That I had a late-night call from a lady? It'll disappoint her, that's for sure, but she won't be taking me over her lap!"

"What about your wife? Can I threaten you with telling your wife?" I asked, just curious, really. I wouldn't tell his wife. Probably.

John Bob laughed. "Oh, that's good, Milt!" He touched his chest. "Dead man walking," he said. "You tell my wife and she'll take the kids, the house, both cars, and my 401k. She's a better lawyer than I am."

I shook my head. "I won't tell your wife," I said.

He sighed. "Might as well tell you, get you off my ass." He sighed again. "Denise came here to college—UNLV. Her freshman year. She roomed with Melissa. Melissa's the one who introduced Denise and Larry." He shook his head. "She didn't mean to, though. She'd been sleeping with Larry since she was in high school, pretty much madly in love with him." He shook his head again. "Women," he said. "As smart as most of 'em are, they can be pretty dumb."

"How did you get involved with her?" I asked.

"Denise told Mama and Daddy about Larry. She was in love and wanted to talk about it. Neither of them were too impressed with their eighteen-year-old daughter seeing a twenty-six-year-old man. Not to mention that his daddy owned a casino. So they sent me out here to deal with it."

John Bob stood up from the bed and went to the window, opening the curtains to the neon jungle below. Las Vegas was glowing, as only it could. Flashes of red and blue, streaks of yellow and green, all dancing off glass and chrome.

"I didn't come on to Melissa—she came on to me. Can you imagine it, Milt? Nerdy old me? And a girl like that? She seduced me, big time. And here I was, alone in Sin City, my first time in Vegas." He turned and looked at me. "I had an affair with Melissa. I actually thought she cared for me, but she was just doing it to try to make Larry jealous. So of course, to make him jealous, he had to know about it, so she told him. He knew why I was there. To break up him and Denise."

He rubbed his face again, shook his head. "I don't think Larry had ever met anyone like Denise before. She was a total innocent. A virgin—until she met that asshole. He didn't love her, he wanted to own her. That was the thing. I can see it now. Back then, I just wanted to believe that he loved her. That he'd be good to her. I had to believe that. He came to me at the hotel where

I was staying, said he knew about me and Melissa, and that he'd write my wife a nice long letter, with details, if I didn't clear him with Mama and Daddy." He looked at me, and in his eyes I could see years of guilt and pain. "So this is basically all my fault. If I'd brought Denise home with me, she would have eventually gotten over him. Married some good old boy from Oklahoma, have a nice little house and a passel of kids. But I was as scared of my wife then as I am now. That was the only time in our marriage that I ever strayed, and believe me, I learned my lesson." He laughed bitterly. "Or I should say Denise learned my lesson for me." He looked me in the eye. "But I got to tell you, Milt, I didn't know he was beating her. I swear to God, until Mama called me when Daddy got in trouble, I didn't know."

"So what was Melissa Greevey doing here now?" I asked.

"She thinks Daddy killed Walter," he said. "Walter was like a father to her, and she's grieving bad. I told her he didn't do it. I know Daddy didn't do it."

"You think Melissa could have killed Larry?" I asked.

"Yeah, she coulda done it. She's got it in her. She's a tough kid. If it hadn't been for Walter, God only knows where she'd be now. She could have killed Larry, but she would never hurt Walter. Not for anything. She owes him her life. Owed him. Whatever."

"What if Walter decided to dump her, too? What if he figured out she killed Larry, and he told her to get out? If he abandoned her?"

John Bob looked up at me. I was glad to see the sharp-eyed Oklahoma lawyer was back in town. "Yeah, it's possible. If he fired her, threw her out. She lives in the hotel. If Walter fired her, she'd be homeless and jobless. Totally on her own." He nodded his head. "Yeah, it's a definite possibility."

"Think maybe you should talk to her some more?"

The lawyer slipped out of his eyes, and the vulnerable nerd took its place. "I don't know about that, Milt. She probably wouldn't see me. And even if she would—I've got no business talking to her." He shook his head.

"You had feelings for her, didn't you, John Bob?"

He laughed. It wasn't a happy sound. "I've thought about her every day since it happened. When I make love to my wife, sometimes I see Melissa's face."

There was enough damage going on around here, I thought. Putting John Bob in that situation was too much. I wasn't going to do it. You've got to have a moral code—lines you won't cross. I'd just found one.

"Tell you what," I said. "You call her and make the date, but I'll show up instead of you."

Jeez, Milt—" he started, then nodded. "Okay. Fine. Yeah. I'll do that."

I patted him on the shoulder. "Get some sleep, John Bob. I'll see you in the morning."

I walked back across the hall to my room, totally forgetting about the Diet Coke.

SECOND SUNDAY ✦ PROPHESY COUNTY

It was Emmett's day off and he and Jasmine had made plans. There was a big swap meet going on outside of Tulsa, and they were going to take his truck and she was going to look for antiques. He thought it sounded boring, but part of him thought it would be fun. Fun to see her having a good time. But he was disturbed about yesterday. About Jasmine's behavior over the squad car incident. Totally uncalled for, he thought. Childish even. He had to call her on it.

He knew that years ago, with Shirley Beth, he'd never have said anything; he never did. But he had to stand up to Jasmine.

He had to learn how to do this now, 'cause he had the rest of his life to live, and he wouldn't do again what he'd done with Shirley Beth. He called Jasmine on the phone.

"Hello?" she said.

"Hi, it's me. I'm coming over," he said.

"You're not invited," she said.

"I rarely am," he said and hung up, got in his pickup, and drove the five miles to her house.

Jasmine was in her Mazda, backing out of the driveway. Emmett used the pickup to block her escape. Standard police procedure for apprehension. He got out of his pickup and walked up to the passenger side of her car, but the door was locked.

He leaned down to the window and said, loud enough for her to hear with the windows closed, "You wanna do this out here or in the house?"

Jasmine slammed the car into park, jerked the keys out, opened the door, and stomped up her front porch, slamming the door on her way in.

Emmett opened it and followed her inside. She whirled on him. "How dare you do that to me yesterday? How dare you!"

"Do what to you? You are overreacting like a son-of-a-bitch, Jasmine!"

"You sided with Anthony Dobbins against me!"

Emmett shook his head and sat down on the sofa. "There were no sides there, honey. There was you being a total reactionary. You made a mess in the squad car, you needed to clean it. Anthony said it was the third time that week—"

"Well, he's a goddamn liar!" Jasmine shouted.

"Yeah, well, he said you lied about the car smelling like an ashtray. But I told him he can't sit in the car and smoke, even if he holds his head out the window, which he claimed he did. I told him he has to get out of the car and smoke on the street. And I'll tell you, for the next week, you'll bring the squad car to me for in-spection before you give it to Anthony, and if it's got a mess in it, you'll clean it, and you'll get a suspension just as soon as I can spare you."

"You are out of your ever-loving mind!"

"Just 'cause we're sleeping together, Jasmine, doesn't mean I'm not still in charge while Milt's gone. We don't know how long he's gonna be in Vegas, so I gotta have everybody's cooperation until he's back. Especially with Dalton out with his ankle. I've only got you and Anthony. And if you two are sniping at each other about stupid shit like this, we're not gonna get anything done."

"You cannot order me around!" she screamed.

Emmett stood up. "Oh, yes, I can. I'm in charge. I can't or-der you around and I won't when it comes to our private life, but at the department, I'm in charge. And don't you forget it."

Emmett headed out the door and was gone, missing the day they could have had together.

SECOND SUNDAY ◆ LAS VEGAS

John Bob had made a brunch date with Melissa Greevey at a small café off the strip for eleven o'clock that morning. She was sitting at a back booth, her short blond hair spiky and stiff, wear-ing too much makeup and another power suit, this one a cran-berry red, the skirt as short as the other. Lovely legs were crossed in the aisle, as she sat sideways in the booth. I sat down across from her and she said, "I'm waiting for someone, and I'm not in the mood."

"John Bob's not coming," I said. "I'm a friend of his. Milt Kovak." I held out my hand to shake, but instead she reached into her purse and pulled out a leather cigarette case, took a menthol out, and lit up.

"You're that Oklahoma sheriff, right?" she said.

I nodded my head.

Melissa laughed. "Rita's told me a few things about you. I can see why you didn't want to meet at the hotel."

"I wanted to tell you how sorry I am about your loss," I said.

She glared at me and deliberately blew smoke in my face. "What do you want? I know this isn't a condolence call."

"There are things I know and things I don't know. I'll tell you the things I know—you tell me the things I don't know," I said.

"Sheriff, we could be here the rest of our lives with me telling you the things you don't know," she said, smoke billowing toward me again. "And why should I tell you anything?"

"Well, there's no reason why you should," I said, "but is there a reason why you shouldn't?"

"What does that mean?" she asked, glaring at me.

"I just meant, if you haven't got anything to hide, why not answer my questions?"

"Oh, let's see: one, because it's none of your business; two, because you're representing the man who killed my boss; and three, because I don't like you."

"Burl Upshank didn't kill Walter, and he didn't kill Larry," I said. "I'm trying to find out who did. I think you can help me there."

"And how could I do that? If I were inclined to do so," she said, sarcastically.

"Tell me about Walter's enemies," I said.

She snuffed out her cigarette and said, "Walter didn't have any enemies. He was a businessman. He had rivals."

"What about those white supremacists?" I asked.

She looked blank for a minute then laughed out loud. "That whole Texas secession business? Is that rumor still floating around?"

She shook her head. "I have no idea if Walter knew any of those people, but I will tell you this: Walter made billions in oil. Billions. He didn't need seed money from any white supremacists. He spent a lot of his own money building the Lonestar, but he's more than quadrupled it in the last fifteen years."

"What about Mickey Barber?" I asked, mentally checking the white supremacists off my list.

"Mickey Barber?" she said, surprised. "That skeezoid bartender who's taking Larry's job? What about him?"

"He wouldn't have Larry's job if Larry was alive. As I understand it, he had that job before Larry came to work at the Lonestar, and got demoted so Walter could give it to Larry."

She shrugged. "So what? You've never heard of nepotism? A quarter of the employees there have a son or daughter or niece or nephew working." She laughed. "You think Mickey Barber killed Larry over a *job*?" She shook her head. "And what about Walter? Why would he kill him?"

Well, she had me there. I had no idea. Actually, I had no idea about anything. And I was getting more confused by the minute.

"What about Walter's wife? Did she have relatives who would have been pissed that Walter . . . well, killed her?"

"Andrea? You think Walter killed Andrea?" She shook her head. "Andrea was dead drunk when she drove her car off the road. She was drunk a lot, Sheriff. Andrea Allen was an alcoholic and anyone could tell you that."

I sighed.

She cocked her head and looked at me. "Am I punching holes in all your half-cocked theories, Sheriff?" she asked. "You think it might be because your friend Burl Upshank got upset because Larry hit his little girl, and, after beating Larry up, he went back to his house and shot him? And then, because he's gone a little nuts being on the lam like he is, he decided it was all Walter Allen's fault, so he snuck into the Lonestar and killed him, too?"

"How?" I asked. "How did Burl sneak into the Lonestar? All your security staff is looking for him—hell, even your valets and doormen are looking for him. How would he get in the hotel?"

She shrugged. "I don't know. But it's a better theory than any of yours." She got up. "Look, tell John it was just great seeing him again, and the next time he's in Vegas . . ." She grinned. "Well, you know."

With that, she dropped some bills on the table and left the café.

WHEN I GOT back to my hotel room, the light was flashing on the telephone. I checked the message. "Milt, come on to my room the minute you get in," said Michael's voice. "John Bob got some stuff from Betty that he said is interesting, but he won't tell us until you get here."

I washed my face and hands, took a deep breath, and headed to Michael's suite. All the boys were there, and Barbara Jo, who now considered herself part of the war party, and a room service table was sitting in the middle of the room, heaped with food. Everybody had plates they were filling and all turned to look at me when I walked in.

"Help yourself, Milt," John Bob said. "I thought we all needed some sustenance."

Since I hadn't eaten at the "brunch" with Melissa Greevey, I helped myself to sandwich fixings, potato salad, and coleslaw, and found a beer and a seat. "So, what's up, John Bob?" I asked.

He held up a finger, swallowed, then said, "Got some info from Betty." Took another bite, chewed, swallowed, and said, "She found out where Belinda Norwalk is."

"Great!" I said through a mouthful of sandwich. Sorry, I don't have John Bob's manners. "Where?"

"Flagstaff, Arizona. Unfortunately, that's where she's buried."

"She's dead?" I said, shocked.

"Um hum," he said, chewing. He swallowed and said, "She committed suicide over four years ago."

"Ah, jeez," I said. "That's awful. What about the kid?"

"Betty said the obit said she left behind a daughter, mother, father, and brother. I would assume either the parents are raising the kid or the brother is."

"Are the parents still in Flagstaff?" I asked.

He shook his head. "No. She did find them, though, back here in Nevada. About forty miles from here, place called Ketchum, Nevada."

"Anybody for a road trip?" I asked.

Jasmine was in the parking lot of Emmett's apartment building before he got there. He'd stopped off at the grocery store for some chips and beer for watching the game. He got out of the pickup with his bag of groceries and she got out of her Mazda.

"I'm sorry," she said. "You're right—I overreacted."

"I cleaned up the mess you left in the parking lot. Do that again and you'll be looking for a new job—understaffed or not."

"Don't push it, Emmett."

"You're the one who pushed it, Jasmine. You acted like a child. I was embarrassed for you."

"Okay," she said, looking away from him. Quietly, her head turned so that he could barely hear, she said, "I do that sometimes. My therapist said it was because I didn't get enough attention as a child. I was the middle child."

"Well, you're a grown woman now. Get over it. Understand

that your behavior affects others. Especially on the job. The little things can mess up the big things, Jasmine. What if you need Anthony for backup someday, and he's still mad at you for messing up the squad car? What if Anthony needs you for backup and you're still mad at him for turning you in to me? I'm not saying either one of you would hesitate to protect the other on purpose, but the subconscious does strange things."

She nodded her head. "That's true." She sighed. "I'll apologize to Anthony when he gets back on Tuesday."

"Okay, you do that. I'm gonna go watch a ball game on TV," Emmett said, heading for the stairs.

"Unless you want to go to that swap meet like we talked about?" she said. "We've still got time. It doesn't close until six."

He looked at her for a long moment. "This over?" he asked.

"Yes, and I won't do it again," she said, then grinned. "Unless I'm having PMS."

Emmett shook his head and wrapped an arm around her neck, pulling her toward him. He kissed her on the lips. "Jeez, you're a pistol," he said.

SECOND SUNDAY ◆ LAS VEGAS

Let me tell you something about Nevada, in case you didn't already know. It's a great big old desert. The only thing green that I could see was some neon in Las Vegas; once you got outside of the city, it was just sand and rocks and scrubby cacti. And some mountains. We had to cross over one to get to Ketchum.

But the sky: now that was something. The fall's the rainy season in this part of the West, and there were banks of black clouds to the east and you could see the rain falling on some far-off land. To the south were white fluffy clouds, and I knew if I stared at 'em long enough, I could make out a bunny or bird or something neat to see, if Johnny Mac were here. To the north, the way we were going, it was blue skies, and to the west, a mixture of clouds and blue. It was as if you were on the top of the world and the whole sky was right there before you. I guess that's the way it is when there are no pesky trees in your way.

Now, there are those coming from a big city who would say Longbranch was a small town. But at least we got churches with steeples, a hotel and a motel, two whole streets of stores, two banks, four or five fast-food places, three bars and a pool hall, and a real pretty county courthouse. We got streets with big old houses built before statehood, nice neighborhoods and rough neighborhoods, and middle of the road neighborhoods. We even have a trailer park on the land that used to be the drive-in theater.

But if you wanna talk small towns, then we should be discussing Ketchum, Nevada. There was a general store/post office/ video rental/pool hall/bar and grill/casino in the middle of town. One building, one room, all those things. There were three or four houses and about fourteen trailers. There wasn't a tree, flower, or bush to be seen.

Thinking that all of us barging in on Belinda Norwalk's family would be unseemly, the boys had drawn straws to see who would go with me. David Lee had won, which meant we had to take his Z. We didn't talk much on the ride since it was hard to do over the noise of the open windows (his A/C was broken) and the sound from the rear of the car (his muffler was nonexistent).

When we got to the city limits sign, it was only about another hundred or so feet to Maverick's, the all-in-one establishment I mentioned earlier. Inside on the right was a bar with five stools and a man standing behind the counter drying glasses. Immediately to the left was a slot machine, with three tables falling in line the length of the store, with a pool table bringing up the rear. On the other side of the tables was a row of videos, the newest one I could see was an old Sylvester Stallone movie, and beyond that rows of foodstuffs. The post office was straight across from the front door at the very back. We were the only patrons in the place, and the man behind the bar appeared to be the only employee.

"Excuse me," I said, walking up to the bar.

"What would you gentlemen like?" he asked.

"Coors Light for me," I said. "Dave?"

"Same," David Lee said.

The bartender brought out a couple of longnecks, opened them, and asked, "Glasses?"

Seeing the condition of the glass he was cleaning, I shook my head no. Dave did the same, and the man handed over the longnecks and we handed over some cash.

"We're looking for some friends who moved out this way," I said. "Norwalk?"

"Ben and Emily? Yeah. Moved here four or five years ago."

"Can you tell us where we might find them?" I asked, smiling.

"Sure," he said, coming out from behind the bar. I followed him to the front door and he pointed. "See that yella trailer there on the left? Behind the water tower?"

"Yeah," I said.

"Well, turn at that yella trailer, go past Smitty's place—he's the one with all the geegaws in the front yard—come back this away two trailers, and on the other side, across the ditch, that's the Norwalks' place."

I looked at David Lee to see if he got all that, but he appeared to be concentrating on his beer. I finished mine, put the bottle on the bar, and thanked the bartender.

"You ain't bringing 'em any trouble, are you?" he asked.

"Oh, no, sir," I said. "Just wanted to stop by and say hey."

"Well, give 'em a hidey from me," he said, and went back to polishing his dirty glasses.

So David Lee and I got back in the car, turned right down a small narrow street to the yellow trailer, took a left—the only way to go—at the trailer, found Smitty's place with no problem—there were pink flamingos, bobble-headed ducks, miniature windmills, and every other front yard ornament you or anybody else could dream up—turned left, passed two trailers, saw the ditch, and drove over a flimsy rail bridge into the yard of what I hoped was the Norwalks' place.

They must have been the rich folks in town; this trailer was a double-wide, well kept, with a smidgen of grass in the front yard and a window box full of well-blooming flowers by the front door. When we got close though, I discovered the flowers were plastic. I guess you do what you gotta do. We walked up the steps of the wooden front porch and rang the bell. It was a minute or two before it opened, the blast from the air-conditioning enough to almost knock us over.

A tall thin man opened the door. He had wavy gray hair, a little long in the back, and a long nose. His dark brown eyes were as friendly as a cocker spaniel's, but I doubted they'd stay that way long, not with what we had to say to him. I almost regretted the pain we were bringing. "Yes?" he said.

"Mr. Norwalk?" I asked.

"Yes, sir, and who might you be?" he asked.

"Sir, my name is Milt Kovak, and I have no jurisdiction here, but I'm the sheriff of Prophesy County, Oklahoma."

Ben Norwalk laughed. "Sir, I've never been in the state of Oklahoma, so whatever it is, I didn't do it."

"This is about your daughter, Mr. Norwalk. Can we come in a minute?"

Well, I gotta say, the laugh dried up when I mentioned his daughter. The eyes pooled with water and his shoulders slumped, but he opened the door wide enough to admit David Lee and me.

"Come in," he said, and walked in front of us into the living room.

"Emily," he called, as he showed us to seats on the couch. "Honey, can you come in here?"

The woman who came out of the kitchen, drying her hands on a dish towel, was dressed in blue jeans and a green top. Her long silver hair was pulled back in a ponytail. She was a slender woman, several inches shorter than her husband, but still tall for a woman. A pretty woman with a smile on her face, but I knew I'd be ripping that smile right off in just a minute, and I was sorry that I'd be doing that. These people seemed nice, and I was bringing them probably unnecessary grief. I wanted to turn around and leave, but the fat was in the fire, nothing to it but to do it.

"Honey, could you sit down a minute?" Ben Norwalk asked his wife.

She looked a question at him, but sat down. "These gentlemen are from Oklahoma. Sir, could you tell my wife your credentials again?"

"Yes, sir," I said, and did so. Then I introduced David Lee. "I'm sorry to be bringing this up, ma'am," I said, "but it's about your daughter."

Just call me Nostradamus, 'cause I sure as hell predicted what happened. Emily Norwalk's smile disappeared and was replaced with palpable pain.

"My daughter's dead," she said.

"Yes, ma'am," I said. "And I'm real sorry about that." It was about then I noticed that there were no toys laying around, no small-sized chairs or beanbags, nothing to indicate a five-year-old child lived in this home. Probably the brother and his wife were raising the little girl, I decided. "We have news that probably won't be all that bad for y'all," I said. "Larry Allen got murdered a couple of days back."

"Good," Emily Norwalk said.

"Honey," Ben said, taking her hand in his. "Don't."

"Unfortunately," David Lee said, "my sister was married to him. He beat her up a lot. We didn't know until recently."

"He's that kind of man," Ben Norwalk said. "Real filth."

"Yes, sir," David Lee said. "Unfortunately, my daddy was in town and saw him do it, knocked him around a little, then later he got shot, so the police think my dad did it."

"More power to him if he did," Mrs. Norwalk said.

"That's just it, ma'am," I said. "He didn't do it. And yesterday, Walter Allen was also killed."

The smile came back to Emily Norwalk's face. "Good," she said. "That man was pure evil."

Ben Norwalk just shook his head.

Not knowing what else to say, I said, "Your granddaughter lives with your son?"

Both faces clouded up again. "Our granddaughter," Mr. Norwalk said, "is about twenty miles from here, in a private facility."

"You see, Sheriff," Emily Norwalk said, her voice getting strident, "when we had the paternity hearing, the old man came up to Belinda and said he wanted to talk to her privately. Then he offered her money. She declined. Then the young one said he wanted to talk to her privately. She never told us what he said, but she took the money. That night she went into the garage of our house with the baby. She shut the door and turned on the car. When we found them in the morning, Belinda was dead, but Selena, the baby, had fallen to the floor of the car and had escaped most of the carbon monoxide. Just enough to cause irreparable brain damage. She's five years old now, but she has the mental capacity of a one-year-old. And she always will. That's why I'm glad both those bastards are dead. I just hope they suffered."

I didn't know what to say. How do you respond to such

a horror? I wanted real bad to tell this woman that both the Allens had suffered, but they hadn't. They'd gone out of this world fairly easily, at least Larry had. Maybe the old man had seen what was coming, had begged for his life, had cried, whimpered, drooled a little. I could only hope that was so, and knew it was an evil thing to wish on someone, but hearing this made me think that justice could only be served if my wishes were true.

"Ma'am," I finally said, "I'm so truly sorry. And I'm sorry we came here and brought all this back up. But an innocent man is being hunted for something he didn't do, and we're just hitting all the bases we can to try to find out who *did* do it."

Emily Norwalk stood up. "I didn't kill those bastards, and neither did my husband. And my son James had nothing to do with this, either. Part of me wishes we could claim this, but we can't. Now if you gentlemen don't mind, I'd like you to leave my home."

I was glad for the broken air conditioner and nonexistent muffler on the way back to Las Vegas. I couldn't talk about what we'd just witnessed. There was no discussion for this, no way to hash it out. No one would ever know what Larry Allen said to Belinda Norwalk that day, but I could imagine. He raped her, impregnated her, then, just as surely as if he'd stuck a gun to her temple and fired, he'd killed her. And for all intents and purposes killed the baby, too.

All I knew for certain was that once we got back to the hotel, I was calling my son. I needed to talk to him. Real bad.

SECOND SUNDAY ✦ PROPHESY COUNTY

"Now my grandma called that a chiffarobe," Emmett said, as Jasmine examined an antique oak wardrobe.

"It's a wardrobe, or an armoire. Maybe 'chiffarobe' is a bastardized version of the French," she suggested.

"Well, all I can say is my grandma could barely speak English, and I know she didn't speak French."

"I need another closet in the guest bedroom, and this would beat the hell out of remodeling."

"How much they asking?"

Jasmine glanced at the tag and smiled. "Two hundred."

Emmett said, "Dollars? They want two hundred dollars for that old thing? Coulda got it from my grandma for free."

"Do you have your grandma's chiffarobe?" Jasmine asked with her hands on her hips.

Emmett shook his head. "My dad's sister got all her stuff when she passed."

"You think she'd give it to you?"

Again, he shook his head. "Naw, she passed, too, a while back, and I think my cousin's probably got it or sold it by now."

"Then shut up and let me think about buying this thing, okay?"

"Still seems like a lot of money to me," he said, pulling at the drawer under the closet part and finding that it stuck.

"You know nothing about antiques," she said, sticking her head inside the closet part and sniffing.

"Well, I know a real antique isn't mill made," Emmett said. "Look here. See this?" he said, pointing at the drawer. "This was made in a mill, probably in the twenties or thirties."

"Like I said, Emmett, you know nothing about antiques. I couldn't afford anything that wasn't mill manufactured. The handmade stuff is going for thousands, and not at swap meets, my friend. You've got to go to Tulsa or Oklahoma City, to one of those fancy antique shops."

"Two hundred dollars, jeez," he said.

"I'm not paying two hundred for it," Jasmine said. "Just stand back and keep quiet."

She walked up to the woman whose stand they were at and said, "That armoire over there?" The woman nodded. "The drawer sticks."

"Probably work out if you rub some soap on it," the woman said.

"Maybe," Jasmine said, frowning. "Maybe not. I'd hate to pay that much for it, get it home, and find out I couldn't use the drawer."

"Hunnard and fifty," the woman said.

Jasmine frowned some more. "I could see going *maybe* seventy-five, but I don't know . . ."

"One twenty-five and that's final."

"I'll give you a hundred cash for it," Jasmine said.

The woman stuck out her hand.

The woman's husband helped Emmett haul the thing to his pickup. When the man walked off, Emmett looked at Jasmine and laughed. "Hey, let's go to Mexico one weekend," he said. "You'd be killer down there."

She grinned at him. "Where do you think I got that suede sofa and my dining chairs?"

He pulled her to him and kissed her long and hard on the mouth. "Every day you surprise me more," he said.

"Is that a good thing?" she asked, smiling.

"Mostly," he said. "Mostly."

SECOND SUNDAY ✦ LAS VEGAS

Later that evening, John Bob, David Lee, and I were standing in the elevator alcove of the hospital, waiting for an elevator to take us up to the labor-and-delivery floor to visit with Maida, Denise, and little Carol Jean. The door opened and who should pop out of it but Melissa Greevey.

Everybody just stood there for a minute, long enough for

the doors to close and the elevator to go someplace else. Finally, David Lee said, "Well, fancy meeting you here, Melissa." You could tell he was a little shook—not a real good line for David Lee.

"Excuse me," she said, and started to pass us.

"Excuse *me*, Miss Greevey," I said. "You here visiting a sick friend?"

She turned and glared at me. "No. I was here visiting a friend and her baby."

"You've got some goddamn nerve—" John Bob started, but I placed a hand on his arm to shut him up.

"And how did you find Miss Denise and her baby?" I asked.

She straightened her spine and smiled—not what you'd call a friendly smile—and said, "We'd been hoping for a boy."

"We?" I asked.

"Walter and I, and Larry, of course. Someone to carry on the Allen tradition."

"What tradition is that?" David Lee asked. "Smacking women around and sleeping with anything in skirts?"

She took her time to glare at each of us in turn, then pivoted neatly and walked toward the outer door.

"What a piece of work," David Lee said. "I'd like about twenty minutes alone in a hotel room with that one—calm her down a bit."

Not knowing the history between his brother and Melissa Greevey, I doubt David Lee noticed the look on John Bob's face when he said that—he was too busy watching those great legs go out the door. But I saw it—pain. Lots of pain. John Bob had it bad, and since it had been four years since his time with her, I was worried he might not ever get over it. I knew the feeling, and I felt for the guy.

I pushed the button for the elevator and it came immediately, like it had been sitting there waiting for us the entire time. We got in and went up to the labor-and-delivery floor.

I'd only been here yesterday, but it seemed little Carol Jean had changed already. Babies are like that. She was a spunky little thing. I washed my hands real good so I could hold her. She was strong, trying to lift her head up already. And nothing got by that one, let me tell you. She was checking out everything that went on around her. I only got to hold her a minute or two before her uncle David Lee took over.

I watched him with her. David Lee was enchanted, and that was a good thing to see. He was so un-David-Lee-like, I almost thought he was channeling someone else. He cooed and baby-talked, tickled her tummy and told her how things were gonna be. Maida beamed and Denise smiled.

John Bob, though, hardly noticed. He was real quiet, lost in his own thoughts, I guess.

I couldn't help but think of another baby girl, this one's half-sister, wasting away in a "private facility." At least one good thing came later from Larry Allen, and I silently thanked God for little Carol Jean.

I said to Denise, "We met Melissa Greevey leaving."

She took her eyes away from her baby and her brother for a second and smiled at me. "You know Melissa?" she asked, making me remember that Denise was out of the loop when it came to the whole investigation.

"We met while we were staying at the Lonestar," I said.

"We were roommates in college," Denise said. "She introduced me to Larry." A cloud passed over her face, then she looked back at her baby and the cloud disappeared.

I motioned for Maida to follow me outside. Once in the hall, I asked, "What did she want? Melissa Greevey?"

Maida made an unpleasant face, then said, "To see the baby,

I guess. She didn't stay long." She sighed, then said, "That woman's a bitch."

I was a little taken aback, hearing Maida say that. She was of the old school where women didn't curse. I think that was the first time I'd heard her say such a word.

I smiled. "Gotta agree with that, cousin." Then I told her what Greevey had said about wanting a boy.

Maida shook her head. "That gives me two horrible thoughts, Milt. If the baby had been a boy, and if Walter Allen hadn't been murdered, can you image the legal battles we'd have had?"

I shook my head. "Don't say that to anybody else, Maida."

Again she sighed. "Yes, even with it being a girl, that old bastard might have wanted her. Gives Burl another motive, huh?"

"Something like that," I said.

Maida shook her head and went back to Denise's room. I followed.

We'd barely gotten back into the room when there was a loud knock on the door, it opened, and a woman's voice said, "Yoo-hoo!" And in she walked. Her hands said she was at least in her sixties, but her face was stretched so tight there wasn't a wrinkle on it and she had a perpetual surprised look. Her hair was a platinum blond I hadn't seen since Jean Harlow, and her skin was so brown her ethnicity was in question. The unwrinkled face was painted with so much makeup it was hard to tell what she might really look like, and she was wearing a short zebra-print skirt, see-through acrylic three-inch heels, and a black see-through top with a red bra underneath, about three inches of brown-specked cleavage showing above.

"I've come to see my niece!" she declared to one and all.

Me and the boys just looked at each other.

"Hello, Nadine," Maida said, disgust in her voice.

"Hi, Mrs. Jeffries," Denise said with a resigned sigh.

"I'm calling her my niece because I'm much too young to be a grandmother!" the woman declared, batting her eyes at me and the boys.

"Guys," Denise said, "this is my mother-in-law, the first Mrs. Allen. Nadine Jeffries."

"The Jeffries is from my third husband. He died so I kept the name, even after I dumped my fourth!" she said and giggled. "Let me look at her!" She wiggled her way over to Denise's bed and bent down over the baby. I could smell the booze from where I stood and knew Denise didn't want the woman anywhere near the child.

I walked over to the bed and stuck out my hand. "Mrs. Jeffries, so nice to meet you. I'm Maida's cousin, Milt," I said.

She straightened up, getting her boozy breath away from the baby, and took my hand, smiling and doing that batting thing with her eyes again. "Call me Nadine. Any cousin of Maida's is a cousin of mine," she said. "The kissing kind, though." The giggle again.

"So sorry about your son," I said.

The woman stiffened. "Right." She turned to Maida. "Now I don't mind your husband killing Walter, God knows he had it coming." She teared up. "But why did he have to go and shoot my little boy?" Then she walked up and slapped Maida in the face.

None of us saw it coming, but me, John Bob and David Lee were on her like a snake on a june bug. John Bob grabbed his mother, and me and David Lee hustled Nadine Jeffries out of the hospital room.

Then she started crying in earnest, big heaping sobs, saying, "Why'd he go and kill my baby?" She hit David Lee on the arm. "Why'd your daddy do that?"

"He didn't, Mrs. Jeffries," David Lee said.

Misunderstanding, Nadine said, "He's alive? My baby's alive?"

I sighed. "No, ma'am," I said, "he just means that Burl Up-shank didn't kill Larry. Or Walter."

She burst into tears again and threw her arms around my neck. I patted her on the back and then noticed her body getting real close to mine. Before I knew it, she was rubbing her personal parts against mine. I tried to gently move her, but there was nothing to it but to push her away.

"David Lee," I said, "could you walk Mrs. Jeffries downstairs and get her a cab?"

"Do I have to?" David Lee asked.

I gave him a look, and he took her by the arm and led her to the elevator. I feared for David Lee's manhood if they were alone together in the elevator.

The door to Denise's hospital room opened and Maida stuck her head out. "Is she gone?" she asked.

"Yeah, thank God," I breathed.

"She try to hump your leg?" Maida asked and giggled.

The woman was shocking me more and more. "I refuse to answer that on the grounds that it might humiliate me," I said.

She came out of the room and said, "I forgot to tell you, they're letting Denise and the baby out tomorrow. I don't know what to do. We can't keep a newborn in a hotel suite, but we can't go back to Denise's house—there are probably bloodstains everywhere."

I thought about it for a minute. "Look, get the key from Denise. Me and the boys will go by the house, see how bad it is, either clean it up ourselves or get some service to do it. She's got a nursery set up already, right?" Maida nodded. "The best place for y'all then would be at her house," I said. I patted her on the shoulder. "Don't worry about it, Maida," I said. "I'll take care of it." I said that like I knew what I was doing, that I was a take-charge kinda guy. Like I'd done something for her up to now. Yeah, that's right. A big zip is what I'd done.

The thought of walking in on days-old blood and gore didn't sit well with me, but I'd done it before. I'd done worse before. The boys might get a lesson they didn't want to learn, but you did what had to be done. And, finally, this was something I could *do.* Something I could accomplish. And maybe Burl was hiding out in the back bedroom. And maybe pigs could fly.

WE USED JOHN Bob's cell phone to call the rest of the boys (and Barbara Jo, of course) and asked them to meet us at Denise's house. I figured the more people we had, the quicker we could get it done.

I'd never been to Denise's, but wasn't surprised much when I saw the house. Knowing Larry Allen had bought the place before he and Denise got married, the modern, split-level, stucco-and-glass house was expected. Inside was all chrome and glass. The smell was bad, not just blood, but the other smells you get when a house has been shut up for a week unexpectedly. Rotted food, must and dust, and that just plain empty smell a house gets.

We walked up six steps to get in the front door; straight ahead were stairs leading to the second floor, to our immediate right were opened french doors leading into what could only be Larry's study. All chrome and glass. To the left, three steps led down into the living room. Black leather sofa and black sling-back chairs centered around a chrome and glass-topped coffee table. A huge black entertainment center covered one wall, with a big-screen TV taking front and center stage. All this was on a pristine white carpet. Pristine except for the area around the sofa where the blood had pooled. There was blood on the black leather sofa, too, but that would wipe off. The white carpet, however, was another story. No way was that coming out.

The one thing I noticed right off was that this was the most baby-unfriendly house I'd ever seen. With all the steps and stairs, white carpet, glass, and sharp edges, nobody in their right mind would want to raise a baby here. After a quick tour of the house I noticed one thing for certain: the only rooms Denise had had anything to do with decorating were the kitchen and the nursery.

The master suite had a black platform bed with a black satin coverlet, black Chinese lacquered furniture, and weight equipment. The only sign of Denise was in part of the walk-in closet—a small part. What color Larry lacked in his home furnishings he made up for in his wardrobe. The clothes hanging in the closet would have looked proper on a pimp in a 1970's police show.

The spare bedroom had a round bed covered in black faux fur, and a disco ball hung from the ceiling. I shuddered to think it, but the thought crossed my mind that this might be where Larry brought his lady friends. I cringed for the life Denise must have led with Larry Allen.

But the nursery was all Denise. Knowing she was having a girl, the curtains were pink-and-white checked, the baby bed white wood with a pink-and-white-gingham-checked nursery set with yellow teddy bears and baby dolls in white dresses. A pink-and-white-striped platform rocker sat near the bed, and a white eyelet ruffled basinet was next to the rocker. A fluffy pink rug covered part of the white carpet, and pictures of yellow duckies, teddy bears, and baby dolls covered the walls. This would be a good place for Carol Jean to come home to, and it would all be easy to get back to Oklahoma.

Downstairs, the kitchen yelled Denise. Although the floor was covered in black-and-white-checked tile, and the breakfast table was a new old-fashioned dinette set of black Formica and chrome, and all the appliances were stainless steel, she'd dressed it up with bright red canisters, and glass jars filled with pastas and colored dried beans, with a black cat wall clock, whose tongue marked the time, and pictures of her nieces and nephews held on the refrigerator door with colorful and comical magnets.

"First the kitchen," Barbara Jo said with authority. "The trash needs to be taken out, and the refrigerator cleaned," she said, pointing at Jason. "The floor needs to be mopped and the counters wiped down," Michael this time, "and then we start on the living room." She opened the cabinet below the sink and started handing out cleaning supplies. "Check that door over there," she said to anyone listening, "it should be the pantry. Find a broom and a mop and anything else that we need." David Lee looked at me, I ignored him, and he went to the pantry and did as he was told.

"Milt, start calling carpet companies. We need to replace the living room carpet. Tell them a medium beige Berber. Find someone who can do it first thing in the morning. John Bob," she said, handing him some orange cleaner and a sponge, "go after that sofa. And be sure to lift up the cushions. There's probably blood down there, too."

"Why can't I call the carpet companies?" John Bob whined.

Barbara Jo gave him a look and he hustled out to the living room, sponge and orange cleaner in hand. Even John Bob knew you didn't argue with a woman in a cleaning frenzy.

By the time I'd made arrangements with the third carpet company I'd called (John Bob's cell phone was a picture phone, and the guy at the carpet company had one, too, so Barbara Jo was able to pick out just the color she wanted), Michael, Jason, and David Lee had finished (to Barbara Jo's approval—took three tries) in the kitchen, John Bob had finished with the couch (the stains on the white lining under the cushions wouldn't come out, but you couldn't see it with the cushions in place), and Taylor had mopped the entry hall and vacuumed the stairs. So we were ordered upstairs. Barbara Jo wouldn't trust the nursery to anyone but herself, but instructed us to take the round bed and disco ball out of the spare bedroom and move the platform bed and dresser in there. "She won't want to sleep in their room," she said. I didn't mention that she might not want to sleep in their bed, either. Seems we had the choice of their bed or the bed Larry had his trysts in. We also moved Denise's clothes into the spare bedroom closet. Taylor, who had decided the vacuum was his personal property, did the hall, the nursery, and both other bedrooms, while Jason cleaned the hall bath and Michael and David Lee cleaned the master bath. John Bob and I carried the round bed down to the garage, where we found a futon stuffed into a corner. We brought that up and put it in the master bedroom for Maida. Barbara Jo beamed at our initiative.

It was 1 A.M. by the time we were finished. Having seen Denise's brand new minivan in the garage, we found keys for it in a cabinet and I drove it and everybody except David Lee, who was in his Z, back to the hotel.

I didn't manage to take a shower before bed; hell, I didn't even get my clothes all the way off before I was sound asleep. I was that tired.

SECOND SUNDAY ✦ PROPHESY COUNTY

They'd spent most of the evening setting up the new armoire in the guest bedroom, cleaning it, and moving Jasmine's winter clothes in there. They had been stuffed haphazardly in the small guest room closet, along with her luggage, her tennis racket, a Ping-Pong table, and some golf clubs.

"Didn't know you played golf," Emmett said.

Jasmine grinned. "I don't. I hate golf. These were Lester's.

When we were dividing up the house, I demanded either them or the dog. He took the dog. Which was good. I hated him, too." She picked up the clubs in their bag. "You want them?" she asked.

He shook his head. "Who was it? Winston Churchill? Said that 'golf consists of chasing a small, white sphere about a pasture with implements ill suited to the purpose.'"

"That's putting it nicely," she said.

Emmett tugged at the drawer in the bottom of the armoire. It wouldn't budge. "What did that woman say who sold you this? Something about soap?"

"Um hum," Jasmine said, sorting through her winter accessories she'd heaped on the bed. Emmett couldn't help thinking that for a woman who wore a uniform every day, she sure had a lot of clothes. "I've heard that before but never tried it. You're supposed to rub the sides of the drawers and the thingies they slide on. The soap's supposed to make 'em slide better."

"Yeah, well that's fine and good, but what if you can't get the drawer open enough to use the soap?" He sat on the floor, put his legs against the sides of the armoire, using them as leverage to pull on the drawer. It still didn't open. "You got any tools around here?" he asked.

"If you take a hammer to this thing I'll break your neck. I just spent a hundred dollars on this!"

"I'm not gonna use a hammer! Jeez!" he said. "You got a crowbar?"

Jasmine plopped down on his lap, straddling him, her hands around his neck in a mock choke hold. "You are not going to use a crowbar on my wardrobe!"

Emmett rolled her over on the floor, laughing, grabbed her T-shirt, and lifted it, exposing her stomach. "You know, you never told me," he said, his fingers finding her ribs, "whether or not you're ticklish." She was squirming and laughing, trying to get away from his hands. "Are you ticklish, Jasmine? No, you're not?" he asked, as she tried to catch her breath. "That's a shame," he said, grabbing a bare foot and tickling the arch. "I'd have a real good time if you were ticklish!"

"Stop!" she shouted.

"On one condition," he said, back to her ribs, "tell me where the crowbar is!"

"Never!" Jasmine kicked out with her legs, hitting Emmett in the stomach. He fell back and she jumped on him.

Gasping for breath, Emmett got out, "Lord, woman, I can't breathe!"

She rolled off of him. "Okay, no crowbar," she said, trying to catch her breath, but still laughing. "Together, okay? You grab one handle, I'll grab the other, we'll use our feet for leverage like you did, see what happens."

"The handles will come off," Emmett said, sitting back up and getting in position.

"If the handles come off you'll fix 'em," she said.

"Like hell I will," he said. "Okay, you ready?"

"One," Jasmine counted, "two, three!"

They yanked as hard as they could and the drawer opened. Opened so much that it came shooting out of the wardrobe and landed on the two of them, knocking them over.

They were both laughing when they pushed the drawer off of them and sat up.

"Hey, look," Emmett said. "There's something in here."

Inside the drawer was something wrapped in what looked like old sheeting material. "What is it?" Jasmine asked, grabbing for it.

"Wait now," Emmett said. He leaned in and cocked his ear to the package.

"Boom!" Jasmine said, giggling.

"Oh, you're funny!" Emmett said, his hands going for her ribs.

"You do and I swear I'll hurt you!" Jasmine screamed, backing away. "I mean it, Emmett!"

"Okay, settle down before the neighbors call the police. Oops, we're the police, right?"

"Let me have it!" she said, pointing at the package.

He handed it to her. Gingerly, Jasmine unwrapped what turned out to be an old pillowcase. She opened the case and slid out the contents on the bed. Inside was a Seth Adams clock.

"If it had been running, you probably would have thrown it out the door!" Jasmine said.

"Yeah, probably. Man, that's a beauty."

It was a schoolhouse clock, beautiful in its simplicity. "It's gorgeous. This is mahogany, Emmett!"

"Might be," he said.

Jasmine sighed.

"What's the matter?" he asked.

"I have to take it back to that woman. I paid for the armoire, not for this."

"Whoa, now, girl. Did you see the signs all over her stand? 'All sales are final,' 'no refunds,' and my favorite, and the one most appropriate to your position at the moment, 'as is.'"

"Which means that if we opened this drawer and it was full of rat feces, then I'd have to deal with that, right?" she said, brightening.

"Exactly. And if it was filled with diamonds, they'd be yours. As it is, honey, you got you a new clock."

Emmett followed her into the living room and they spent the next hour trying to decide the best place to hang the clock.

Second Monday ✦ Las Vegas

At 3 a.m. I was awake again—this time because the phone was ringing off the hook. Still groggy, I shakily lifted the receiver.

"What?" I said.

"Hey, cousin-in-law," Burl Upshank said.

That woke me up big time. I shot up in bed, throwing my feet on the floor. "Where the hell are you?" I demanded.

"Now, Milt, don't go getting your bowels in an uproar," he said, and chuckled, damn his eyes.

"I swear to God, Burl, when I find you I'm gonna beat the ever-lovin' shit out of you!"

"Yeah, you and what army?"

"Where are you?" I demanded again.

Burl sighed. "Milt, I'm not gonna tell you that! You think I'm an idiot? I just talked to Jason and he told me how you wanted to turn my ass in! Thanks a lot, cuz."

"I don't want to turn you in, Burl, but you'd be in better shape in jail than out running the streets like you are. Me and your boys are trying to find out who did this, but having you out and about isn't helping."

"Yeah, so how you doing on finding the perp? That's what you call it, isn't it? Perp? Perpetrator, right?"

"You need to come in, Burl. You heard about Walter Allen?"

"Yeah, Jason told me. Too bad. My heart's bleeding for the S.O.B."

"The police think you did that one, too."

"Sure they do. Why wouldn't they? Have they decided to pin Jimmy Hoffa on me? What about Amelia Earhart?" He sighed again. "You never answered about how you're doing finding out who really did this."

"We're nowhere, Burl. We've had a lot of leads, then they just fizzled out."

"Think it's about time I left the country, Milt."

"Jesus, Burl. Don't be an idiot! Tell me where you are. I have Denise's car. I'll come get you, bring you back here, get you some room service, let you take a shower and clean up. Then we'll talk. How does that sound?"

"You gonna have the *po*-lice there waiting for me, Milt? Old cousin, pal of mine? Sounds like you *do* think I'm an idiot! See you 'round the monkey bars, cuz," he said, and hung up.

I still had my pants on, so I ran downstairs, but there was no operator; the call had been direct. No way to trace it.

I went back upstairs and crawled back into bed.

SECOND MONDAY ◆ LAS VEGAS

I drove Denise's minivan to the hospital to pick up her, the baby, and Maida. Everybody had to go with us. It was a snug fit: me driving, Maida riding shotgun, Denise and Barbara Jo in one seat in the second row, the baby in a car seat across the short aisle from Denise, and all five boys smashed together on the not-long-enough back bench. There was a lot of grousing, bitching, and complaining, until Denise whirled around in her seat and said, in a very mean whisper, "If you wake this baby up, I'll beat the crap out of all of you!"

The boys straightened up fast. Looked like Mama wasn't the only female Upshank to be afraid of.

When I pulled onto Denise's street, we could see a long red Cadillac in her driveway.

"Oh, shit!" Denise said and burst out crying.

"Who is it?" I said, pulling in next to the red car.

Teeth gritted, Maida said, "Nadine."

Remembering Denise's mother-in-law, I almost put the car in reverse, but this was Denise's house.

I stopped the car and got out, then went around to help the ladies and the baby. I figured the boys could fend for themselves.

The front door of the house was standing open. I put my

hand up in a gesture to Maida and Denise to wait, and walked over the threshold. "Hello?" I called. "Anybody here?"

"Why, hi there, cousin!" sang Nadine Jefferies, coming out of the kitchen. "Just thought I'd clean up a little for the baby! What happened to Larry's beautiful white carpet? It's turned all beige," she said.

She was wearing skintight wet-looking black capris, a shimmery leopard-skin-printed top—showing even more cleavage than the night before—and red faux high-top sneakers with three-inch heels. Her ankles wobbled as she crossed the thick carpet.

Behind me, Maida asked, "Any way we can pin this on her?" Then she moved around me and faced Nadine. "What are you doing here, Nadine?" she asked.

Nadine bristled. "This is my son's home, Maida Upshank! And don't you forget it! I've got as much right, maybe more right, to be here than she does!" she said, pointing a claw-long red fingernail at Denise.

"Mrs. Jeffries, if you wake this baby up, I'll have to hurt you," Denise said.

"Well, you Upshanks are real good at that, aren't you? Like you didn't hurt me enough not even inviting me to the wedding—"

"That was Larry, not me!" Denise said, her voice rising. Barbara Jo snuck up and lifted Carol Jean from Denise's arms.

"I'll just take her upstairs," she said. I'm not sure Denise noticed as Barbara Jo and the baby headed up to the nursery.

"How dare you say that when my son can't defend himself! He'd never do that to his mother!"

"He had his choice, Mrs. Jeffries," Denise said, her face turning red with fury, "either you or his father, but not both. And who had the money, Mrs. Jeffries? Certainly not you!"

"You say these things about my boy! These awful things! I bet you told your daddy to shoot my baby! I know you were behind it! You never deserved my baby—"

David Lee was on her in a heartbeat. "Listen, Mrs. Jeffries. I don't know if you know this, but that *baby boy* of yours beat my sister almost every day they were together! And the night this all happened, he kicked her in the stomach! He kicked his own child! What have you got to say to that?"

Nadine Jeffries straightened. Even this early in the morning, I could smell booze on her breath from where I stood. She said, "Then the baby must not have been his." This made her indignant. She put her hands on her hips and said, "No wonder he beat her, the cheating whore!"

Very quietly, Maida asked me, "Milt, do you have your service revolver?"

I moved into the living room, Upshanks flanking me on all sides. "Mrs. Jeffries, this is Denise's home until the courts tell us different. You should leave."

The crazy woman folded her arms across her ample chest and said, "I'm not moving an inch!"

"Okay," David Lee said, still the closest to Nadine, "I've got a new theory." He held up his hand. "Hear me out, guys. Walter left everything to Larry, and Nadine thought that if Larry died, she'd get it all, so she killed them both."

John Bob shook his head. "Remember, Dave, Larry died first. She'd have to kill Walter first, *then* Larry for that to work."

"Oh," said David Lee, crestfallen.

"But," John Bob said, "it's obvious the lady is mentally impaired. I think, as an attorney, I could build a case that she just got confused and killed them in the wrong order. Or," he said, brightening, "this is even better. You notice how she's made a pass at anything in pants, right?"

We all agreed that she had. "Well, maybe she got so drunk she made a pass at her son, which of course repulsed him, on so many levels, and she shot him out of embarrassment? Then killed Walter for the hell of it?"

"That's good," I said. "I like that one."

Nadine Jeffries was holding herself with both arms, her eyes wide, her mouth hanging open. "You people are crazy!" she said. "That's just sick, what you said! Sick!"

"And we just got started," I said. "Want to know a theory I just came up with? It's got animals in it."

Nadine grabbed her red purse off the sofa and used it to push her way to the front door. "You people are out of your minds! I'm going to the police!"

Calling after her, I said, "Be sure to ask for Lt. Mac Grayson!"

I grinned at John Bob, who grinned back. "I'd almost like to see that," he said.

"You think this is funny?" Denise screamed. "This is my goddamn life! This isn't funny!"

She fell into her mother's arms, crying. Maida pointed at the door and made shooing motions. Barbara Jo came back downstairs as this was going on, and we all went out to the minivan, suitably ashamed of ourselves.

When I got back to my hotel room, and having no leads and no real thoughts on the subject of who killed either or both of the Allens, although I still would have loved to pin it on Nadine Jeffries, I decided to call my office. Gladys picked up on the first ring.

"Prophesy County Sheriff's Department," she said, a smile in her voice. Since Gladys didn't smile, I was a little confused.

"Hey, Gladys, things going better now?" I asked.

"Oh, Milt! Hi! Yes, everything's under control. The sheriff is back."

I was the sheriff, but I knew she meant Elberry Blankenship. "He around?" I asked. "If he's not busy, I'd like to talk to him."

"Well, Milt, of course he's busy, but I'm sure he can spare some time for you."

She put me on hold and I thought, okay, fine, I didn't lose my job to Emmett Hopkins; instead I lost it to the old codger I replaced. Great. Just fine.

"Milt, you old dog. That you?" came Elberry's good ol' boy voice.

I'd worked for the man for fifteen years, mostly as his senior deputy, so even after three years as sheriff myself, it was still hard to call him by his given name. But this time I tried real hard. I'd be damned if I'd give him *my* title. "Hey, Elberry," I said. "How's it going?"

"Couldn't be better. Thanks for giving this old workhorse something to do. Emmett's just not up to the paperwork, know what I mean? Don't know how he ever ran the police force."

I bristled. "He did a real good job on the force," I said.

"I know that! I know that! Hell, the boy's a winner. Good thinking on your part hiring him here. He's almost as good as my old second-in-command."

Now I guess I could have taken that as a compliment, but in my frame of mind, all I thought was that he was reminding me of my place.

"Anything going on I need to know?" I asked.

"Just the usual. Wrecks on the highway, fisticuffs in the bars, a domestic out at the trailer park. Ruth Sanchez?"

"Yeah?" I said.

"Beat Ray bloody with a baseball bat. Caught him with her sister."

"Little Isabel?" I said, remembering a pretty little girl in a ponytail and braces.

"You haven't seen Isabel in a while, have you, Milt? Ain't so little anymore." He laughed, then asked, "So how's it coming with Burl?"

For some reason, maybe because I'd brainstormed cases with him for so many years, I ended up telling Elberry everything. It took a while, but I just ignored the long-distance charges I knew would be coming.

"Hum," he said when I'd brought him up to date. "You got a bad one, boy, but I gotta agree with you. I've known Burl Upshank all his life, used to go hunting with his daddy. No way did Burl do this. Jean called it: Burl woulda beat his ass blue, given the chance, but I can't see him shooting an unarmed man, much less a sleeping one."

"I got too many people who had it in for both these assholes, Sher—Elberry, but no real motive. Not one as good as Burl's anyway."

"Well, seems to me the ones with the best motive are the Norwalks. You say they got a son?"

"Yeah, James, I think the lady said."

"You done any checking on him?"

"Ah, no," I said, sheepishly. Shoulda done that. Shoulda done that the minute I got back from Ketchum.

"So have John Bob's girl check that out," he said.

"I'll do that, Elberry. Right now. Thanks. Good talking to you," I said, and hung up, adding out loud, "and don't run for sheriff, okay?"

I called John Bob's room and he actually answered. "Mornin'," I said. "Call Betty. Have her check out James Norwalk. That's Belinda's brother. Find out where he is, see if he has a sheet, the usual."

"Morning to you, too. Thanks for asking, but no, I didn't

sleep well," John Bob said. "I can barely move after all that manual labor last night."

"Yeah, and they call women the weaker sex. You know, a lot of 'em do that every day?"

"No wonder my wife's always in a bad mood," John Bob said. He sighed. "Let me call Betty. I'll get back to you."

I called room service and ordered breakfast, then went in the bathroom and took a shower, shaved, and got dressed. I was pulling on my last sock when room service knocked at the door. My breakfast was hot and steamy, the eggs sunny-side up, just like I like 'em, the bacon nice and fatty, and it came with a fancy croissant with strawberry butter. There weren't any hash browns or grits, but a nice little fruit cup. Jean woulda been proud.

I was thinking about licking the plate when a knock came at the door. "It's me, Milt," came John Bob's voice.

"It's open," I called back.

He came in, looking hangdog. "Betty couldn't find anything on James Norwalk. Not even a birth certificate that matched the mother as Emily Norwalk. She found a Beatrice Norwalk who gave birth to a James in 1947 in Philadelphia, and a Candace Norwalk who gave birth to a James four years ago in Little Rock, but no Emily Norwalk."

I pushed away the room service tray and stood up. "Hell, I coulda sworn she said James." I went to the phone. "Let me call David Lee. See if I got the name wrong."

"Hell, Milt," John Bob said as I moved to the phone, "the only birth record Betty could find for Emily Norwalk was Belinda."

I was confused. I picked up the phone and dialed David Lee's room. After I woke him up sufficiently enough to speak and think, I asked, "Remember when we went to the Norwalks? Mrs. Norwalk said something about her son. What was his name?"

"James," David Lee said without much thought.

"Well, hell, that's what I said. But Betty can't find any record of James Norwalk, and nothing showing Emily Norwalk ever gave birth to anybody but Belinda."

"Hum," he said, yawning. "That's real interesting. Can I go back to bed?"

I hung up the phone. "So she lied? She doesn't have a son?" I asked John Bob.

He shrugged, just as the phone rang. I picked it up to hear David Lee say, "She said 'my' son. Not 'our' son. Right?"

"I don't know," I said. "Did she?"

"Yeah, she did. So maybe it's her son by a previous marriage. Different last name."

I hit my head like I coulda had a V8, and said, "You're brilliant, David Lee."

"I've been telling y'all that, but you just haven't been listening," he said, then hung up.

"Call Betty," I said. "Have her trace Emily and Ben Norwalk's marriage license. See what name the missus used, then meet me in Michael's suite."

After John Bob was out the door, I called Michael and asked him to gather the troops.

"Everybody's here except you, John Bob, and David Lee. When I called Dave, he said he'd already contributed his two cents' worth and hung up on me."

"Be there in a minute. John Bob's on the phone with Betty, he'll be there soon." I hung up and dialed David Lee's room. "Get your ass over to Michael's," I said, and hung up.

I went to Michael's suite. There was another room service tray heaped with breakfast goodies. Remembering I'd already had breakfast didn't stop me from grabbing a bear claw. I dropped into an armchair and said, "I don't even wanna see the hotel bill when we finally get out of here."

"I think we should charge everything to Walter Allen's estate," Jason said. "Seems only fair."

I thought about it for a minute. "You know, you're right."

"How much of that estate do you think will go to Denise?" Michael asked.

We all perked up at the thought, then John Bob walked in, having heard the tail end. "None," he said. "I found out Larry Allen didn't buy that house Denise is living in, Walter did. So she has no claim to that. If Walter had a will, and he didn't say anything in there about Larry predeceasing him, then maybe Denise and/or Carol Jean will get some, but if he did, I doubt he left anything to Denise or the baby, if he knew it was a girl. I'm trying to locate Walter's attorney now, see what we can find out. For Denise's sake."

"Betty come up with anything yet?" I asked.

John Bob gave me a look. "I just called her, Milt. The computer is a wonderful thing, but it *will* take a few minutes."

"Just asking," I said and reached for a cake donut. Cake donuts have a lot fewer calories than the glazed kind. David Lee dragged himself through the door, blue jeans unbuttoned at the top, shirt undone, hair mussed. Strangely enough, he looked less like a guy who just got out of bed and more like a male model.

John Bob, David Lee, and myself filled the others in on the possibility that Emily Norwalk had been married before, and that we might be able to trace her son James that way.

The bedroom door opened and Barbara Jo came into the room. Tears were streaming down her face and we all stood up, thinking something was wrong with Denise or the baby. At least that's what I was thinking.

Seeing Michael, she ran to him and threw her arms around his neck and her legs around his waist. "I just lost my job!" she wailed. The rest of us sat back down.

"Ah, honey," he said, patting her back. He sat down on the couch with her in his lap. She was sobbing now.

"How am I going to pay you back now? Oh, God!" she wailed, and sobbed some more.

"Pay him back for what?" Taylor asked.

"Shut up, Taylor," I said. I stood up. "Why don't we go downstairs and see what's happening in the casino?" I suggested.

David Lee and John Bob stood up immediately to follow me, but Taylor and Jason seemed glued to the drama on the couch. David Lee popped Jason on the back of the head, which got both their attentions. "Get!" he said.

Once downstairs it took me and John Bob both to keep David Lee away from the gaming tables. "I thought y'all said we were going to check out the casino!" he whined, his male model image withering.

"Let's go get some coffee," I said.

David Lee yawned. "Make it an Irish and I'm with you, bro," he said.

I shook my head, wondering myself about the wisdom of David Lee moving back home. But then I thought every child needed one no-good uncle to look up to. I'd had my daddy's brother Bart, always referred to as "Black Bart" around the dinner table, who'd been married three times, drank too much, and told me stories nobody but me believed. I'd cried my eyes out when he'd driven his car into a bridge abutment while drunk when I was eleven.

We went into one of the coffee shops and drank coffee and shot the shit for about an hour, then I found a phone and called up to Michael's suite to see if everything was okay.

"Yeah, we're fine," he said. "Can you believe they fired her just because her vacation was up a couple of days ago and she's not back yet? I mean, this is a family emergency, for God's sake! But it's not all bad. She had a pretty good 401k plan, and she should be eligible for unemployment. Barbara Jo's always wanted to write, and seeing little Carol Jean has inspired some children's stories. She's already written a couple. So she's gonna take some time off and try that," he said. "But y'all need to get back up here. John Bob left his cell phone up here and Betty called. Said she had some information."

We all hightailed it back up to Michael's suite, and John Bob called Betty back.

"Yeah, it's me," he said into the phone. Then, "Uh huh, okay. You're sure? No, shit. Okay. Betty, remind me to give you a raise," he finally said and hung up.

He looked at each of us in turn. Finally he said, "Betty found out Emily Norwalk's name before she married Ben Norwalk."

"Okay," I said. "What was it?"

He said the name and we all just stared at each other. Suddenly the pieces all fell into place. But Michael put it best, I think, when he said, "Shit fire, what do we do now?"

It was early morning and they were lying in Jasmine's bed, talking softly, when her cramps started.

"Ooo," Jasmine said, moving her hand to her stomach.

"What's the matter?" Emmett asked.

"Guess I'm going to start my period," she said. "Cramps."

He had never known about Shirley Beth's time of the month. The only mention of it had been when she was pregnant with J.R. She'd kept what she called her "womanly business" totally away from him. So this was new to him. If Shirley Beth had had cramps, she'd kept those from him, too.

"You okay?" he asked when she sat up in bed, hunched over at the waist.

"They're just really bad this month, that's all," she said, breathing heavy. She turned her head and grinned at him, saying, "My body's not used to all this sex, I guess."

He put his hand on her bare shoulder and he could feel her body shudder. "Are they supposed to be this bad?" he asked her.

"I don't know," she breathed. "They never have been. And I shouldn't be having my period until next week—" She doubled over, almost falling off the bed.

Emmett jumped up and ran around to her side of the bed, holding her body. "Jasmine, jeez, are you okay?"

"I don't think so," she said. Even in the pale light barely coming through the closed blinds of the bedroom, he could tell her face was ghostly white.

He looked around for something for her to put on. He had to get her to the emergency room. The only thing on the floor was her uniform. He ran to the closet, opened the door, and pulled out the first thing he found.

Jasmine laughed weakly. "Not that, Emmett. It's a cocktail dress."

He dropped it on the floor and looked in the closet. "That denim dress hanging there," she said. "It's loose. I don't think I can wear anything around my stomach."

He grabbed the dress in question and took it to her, helping her get it over her head, helping her stand and pulling it down over the rest of her body. "Some panties," she said. "I'm not going to the hospital with no underwear." She pointed to her dresser and he opened it, finding all sorts of wonderful panties. He pulled out some pink ones with lace and helped her step into them, realizing that *this*, more than the sex, was the most intimate thing he'd ever done with a woman.

It was barely 6 A.M. and the streets of Longbranch were mostly empty. It was misting heavily and the roads were slick with it. The town was shining in the streetlights, sparkling with the damp. He drove as fast as he could to Longbranch Memorial, not caring if the city cops caught him, just anxious to get Jasmine some help. He pulled the pickup in front of the ER entrance, and helped Jasmine get out, letting her lean on him as he walked her into the hospital.

He could see that she was biting her lip to keep from crying out, one arm around his shoulder, the other around her middle, trying to hold back the pain.

At the counter, he said, "This is an emergency. Got a sheriff's deputy here in real pain."

A nurse came running out with a wheelchair that Jasmine dropped into with a sigh. "She been shot?" asked the nurse.

"No, nothing like that. Non-duty related. It's her stomach."

"Feels like the worst cramps I've ever had," Jasmine told the woman.

The nurse took her behind the counter to a small closed-off room where she took her vitals, then got someone to roll her back to a room.

"Can I go with her?" Emmett asked.

"Are you family?" the nurse asked.

"Yes," Emmett said. "I am."

SECOND MONDAY ✦ LAS VEGAS

What we did now, I decided, was tread real carefully. The name Betty had given us, Emily Norwalk's name before she married Ben Norwalk, was one we couldn't just walk into the police station and say, "Look who did it!" We had to tread very carefully. We had to get all our ducks in a row. Somehow I didn't think Lieutenant Grayson would take real kindly to me saying, "Oh, Mac, by the way, your detective Jimmy Broderick is a stone-cold killer."

"I can't say I blame him," David Lee said. "After what Larry Allen did to his sister, he needed killing."

"If he'd killed the S.O.B. and then turned himself in, most juries woulda found some way to let him go," I said. "But he didn't do that. Jimmy Broderick premeditatedly killed Larry in his sleep, then framed your father for the murder. When I told him we were trying to find out who really did it, that's when he killed Walter, to up the pressure on finding your dad." I sighed and shook my head. "And here I was giving him a laundry list of everything we were doing, every step of the way."

"Hell, Milt, it's not your fault," Michael said. "He's a police-man. He's on this case. You were doing what you were supposed to do."

"But I liked him!" Barbara Jo said. "He was such a nice guy!"

"He probably is a nice guy," I said. "When he's not murder-ing people and framing others." I shook my head. "What hap-pened to his sister, and his little niece, that could drive anybody over the edge. But I can't forgive him for framing Burl."

"So what are we gonna do?" Taylor asked.

I thought a minute, then said, "I've got an idea. Jason, we need to talk to your daddy."

Second Monday ✦ Prophesy County

It seemed like they were there for hours, and when Emmett looked at his watch, he realized they had been. It was already 8 A.M., and he hadn't called Gladys, letting her know what was go-ing on. Jasmine was still lying in the fetal position on the gurney in the little ER cubical. He sat beside her, stroking her shoulder, her back to him.

"Rub my back," she whispered. Then added, "Please."

To hell with Gladys, he thought. Elberry's there. Let him handle it.

He rubbed her back, softly, so as not to jar her, so as not to cause more pain. He'd never seen anything like this. Her face was so white, her hands clinched in fists, her body rigid. He hadn't been in the delivery room with Shirley Beth, hadn't witnessed any of her labor or her delivery, so this was the worst pain he'd experienced with someone he cared about. Oh, he'd held people's hands at car wrecks when part of them was lying a few feet away, sat with a guy once whose innards were spread across the parking lot of the Dew Drop Inn. And of course, there'd been J.R. He'd worked through most of J.R.'s pain and agony. Shirley Beth had stayed by their son's side at home and at the hospital, telling Emmett to go on to work. She'd handle it. And so he had. He hadn't even been there when his boy had passed. He found out hours later when he got to the hospital after his shift.

He'd always resented that, he realized now. Resented that Shirley Beth hadn't shared that with him. That he hadn't been there with his boy, holding his hand, rubbing his back like he was rubbing Jasmine's back right now. That he hadn't been there to say good-bye. It hit him all of a sudden like a ton of bricks: he'd never said good-bye to his boy.

"Oh, God, I can't stand this," Jasmine said, the first tears starting in her voice. He moved his chair to the other side of the gurney so he could see her face.

"Hold on, honey," he said, taking one of her hands in his. "Squeeze just as hard as you can."

And she did, almost crippling him. Damn, the woman had strong hands, he thought. He almost smiled, remembering what those hands could do.

They'd taken blood and urine earlier, taken an EKG and an EEG. He wondered why they hadn't taken an X-ray. Maybe she had an ulcer, or some obstruction. Couldn't an X-ray find that?

The ER doctor came in with a smile on his face, patted Jasmine on the butt. Emmett's first reaction was to push his hand away, but thought that might not be the right thing to do.

"Well, Jasmine, looks like you had an ovarian cyst and it ruptured," he said.

"When is the pain going to stop?" she gasped.

"Pretty soon. Sorry we can't give you any pain medication, but you're pregnant."

SECOND MONDAY ◆ LAS VEGAS

I was right in thinking Jason had known where Burl was from his first phone call. Unfortunately he'd been hiding out in Denise's house, and he'd had to move when we all traipsed over there to clean things up.

"I've got him stashed in a motel," Jason said, "but I won't tell you which one until you tell me your plan. And if I don't think it'll work, I'm not telling."

All his brothers looked at him, and he said, "Beat the crap out of me, guys, I don't care. I ain't talking."

So I told him my plan. After due consideration, he said, "It might work." Then he told me where to find Burl.

We still had Denise's minivan, so we all piled in and drove to the motel. It was a seedy one, in the downtown area; half the neon letters were out or blinking, and all the cars in front of the units hadn't been new in the eighties. We parked the minivan a block away and took turns, two at a time, walking to the motel. Jason went first with Michael, then I followed with David Lee, then Taylor and John Bob pulled up the rear. We thought it might be too obvious with six guys barging in on a motel room. Someone would notice. There was a lot of hugging going on when I got there, then more when Taylor and John Bob showed up. I sat in front of the TV where Burl had been watching a ball game, and waited for the reunion to be over.

"Milt's got a plan, Daddy," John Bob said.

"Well, it's about goddamn time," Burl said. He looked at me. "Finally figure out who done it?" he asked.

I told him. "Jesus H.," he said. "Don't that beat all. And him a cop." He sat down on the bed, surrounded by his sons. "Okay, so tell me," he said, and I did.

"Broderick," Burl said into the phone. "This is Burl Upshank." He listened for a moment, then said, "Yeah, the one and only. I'm ready to turn myself in. I'm getting indigestion from all the bad food I've been eating." He told him where he was—well, not actually, he said he was at Denise's house. Broderick said he'd be there in twenty minutes.

Taylor had already taken a taxi to the house to move Denise and Maida and the baby out of there and back to the hotel. The rest of us climbed into Denise's minivan and hightailed it over to the house.

Burl was sitting in the living room when Broderick let himself in the front door. He was alone—no Mac Grayson, no uniformed backup. If I needed confirmation of his guilt, that did it. His gun was in his hand.

Burl put down the magazine he'd been perusing, and said, "Well, hey, Jimmy, how you doing?"

"Mr. Upshank, you have the right to remain silent—"

"Oh, hell, never been silent in my whole life," Burl said. "Matter of fact, I got a story to tell you."

"Mr. Upshank, we need to get you downtown. Got a lot to do," Broderick said.

"Oh, sit yourself down. You'll find this story real interesting. It's all about Larry Allen. You remember him, right? The guy I supposedly shot? Except I didn't do it, Jimmy, and you know that. Okay, here's the story. Seems when old Larry was in college, he was as big a shit then as he was the day he died. Hell, he was probably that big a shit the day he was born. Anyway, he meets this girl, real innocent type. He liked those, the innocent ones. That's why he went after my girl Denise. 'Cept he was more impatient in those days, didn't take the time to woo the girl like he did my Denise. No, he just forced himself on this one, what they call date rape. That's when the girl knows the asshole who's raping her—"

Broderick waved his gun at Burl. "Stop it. Stand up. Let's go."

Burl shook his head. "Haven't even got to the tear-jerker part yet, boy." He looked real hard at Broderick. "Sit down!" he said. Broderick sat.

"Now this sweet little girl cries rape, just like she should, got witnesses and everything, but Larry's got his old man and all his old man's clout and money, and the witnesses just go away. The girl's left hanging out to dry, everybody thinking she's just some floozy out to get poor Larry's money."

"Stop it," Broderick said quietly.

"Anytime you wanna jump in to correct a wrong assumption, Jimmy, you just do that, okay? Anyway, the girl quits school, goes home to Mama and Daddy—oh, and her big brother. Big half-brother, anyway. Lo and behold, a couple months later, the poor girl finds out she's with child. That musta been real rough. You try to talk her into aborting it? I probably woulda, and I don't even believe in abortion—vote Republican mainly 'cause of that— but this was rape, right? No way should she carry a child of rape. Bet you thought that, didn't you?"

"Shut up," Broderick said, his voice quiet.

"But she has the baby. Who talked her into the paternity suit? You? Hell, you knew all about the Allens, living here in Las Vegas; you knew the old man owned the Lonestar, that he was richer than God, and why shouldn't Belinda and little Selena have some of that? Hell, they were entitled! But it backfired on you, didn't it, Jimmy? That sweet little girl just didn't have the gonads to stand up to those two assholes. Were you there in the courtroom? Did you see Larry pull her aside? Bet you wanted to know what he said to her, huh? How much did they finally pay out? Couple of thousand? Maybe a low five figures?"

"A hundred thousand," Broderick said. "A measly hundred grand. Mom and Ben ran out of the money Selena's second year in the home. I went to Walter, told him about Selena, asked for more money to keep her in a good place. The asshole just laughed at me. Said we'd already settled all that in court. He didn't owe her a dime. No, that's not what he said. His exact words were: 'I don't owe that little retard a dime.'"

"Is that when you shot him?" Burl asked, his voice low.

"Yes," Broderick said.

Burl shook his head. "Hell, Jimmy, I don't blame you, boy. He had it coming three times over. But why'd you frame me, boy? What'd I ever do to you?"

Broderick stood up, his gun pointing at Burl's chest. "I'm sorry, Mr. Upshank. I didn't mean to do that. It just sorta happened. I'd been watching Larry all these years, since Belinda died, saw him get married, saw he was having a baby. I thought maybe he'd changed. That he had turned over a new leaf. Then you got arrested, and I found out he hit your daughter, while she was pregnant. Kicked her in the stomach! Jesus, the guy was below scum. He was—he was evil!"

"So you got in here and you killed him," Burl said. It was a statement. No question to it.

"Yeah. Then my boss decided it had to be you, and everything just snowballed. I'm really sorry, Mr. Upshank."

"You gonna shoot me now, boy?" Burl asked, his voice even.

"Yes, sir. I don't see any other way out of this. I'm really sorry," Broderick said.

I stepped out of the kitchen, Burl's Colt .45 in my hand. "Drop it, Broderick," I said. "It's all over."

He looked at me, turned and flew out the front door.

The word just sat there in the room like a three-hundred-pound gorilla. Slowly, Jasmine let go of Emmett's hand and turned to the doctor. "What?" she said.

"Pregnant," he said, grinning from ear to ear. "You could have had that cyst there for a long time, but your body's getting ready for the growth of the fetus, so it had to get rid of it. That's why it ruptured."

"I can't be pregnant," she said. "How—how far along can I be?" she said, looking at Emmett.

"Not far," the doctor said. "I'd say about four to five days. One of those home pregnancy pee tests wouldn't have shown it, but the blood never lies." He patted Emmett on the back. "Congratulations you two," the doctor said. "You can take some Tylenol, but nothing stronger than that. I'm going to do the paperwork then you two can go home."

They sat in silence until the nurse came in and gave Jasmine two Tylenol and a paper cup of water. She took them, thanked the nurse who then left, and they sat there in silence some more, both staring off into space, neither facing the other.

Finally the doctor came in with her discharge instructions, wished them well again, and they left.

Emmett had left his pickup in front of the ER entrance. It had been moved and ticketed. He found it and drove it back up to the door to pick up Jasmine. They rode to her house in silence.

He stopped the truck in her driveway. He could tell the Advil was taking effect, or the pain was lessening on its own. Her color was back and her fists weren't clenched.

"I need to get on home. Get dressed, get on to work," he said.

With her hand on the door handle, Jasmine said, "I won't be coming in to work this morning. I think I need to rest."

"Ah, well, sure. That's fine. That's a good idea. I'll call you," he said as she slipped out of the pickup. She didn't say good-bye and she didn't look back.

Now, if I'd been thinking, I'da had somebody out front to catch Broderick when he bolted, but at least part of my plan had worked. David Lee came up behind me, grabbed Burl's .45 and ran for the front door.

"Don't shoot him!" Burl called. "We need his confession!"

David Lee gave his father an exasperated look. "I won't shoot anything vital!" he said as he ran out the door.

I was on David Lee's heels. Broderick had a two-front-yard advantage, but I gotta say, David Lee could run. Broderick had the bulk, but David Lee was lean and his long legs covered the ground like Michael Johnson at the Olympics. I was a front-yard back when David Lee tackled him. Broderick hit the ground like a ton of bricks, the service revolver flying out of his hand. David Lee straddled him, the gun pointed at the back of Broderick's head, and when I got close enough I could see the grin on his face and hear David Lee saying, "You have the right to remain silent . . ."

Emmett drove home in a fog. This couldn't be happening, he kept telling himself. No way was this happening. A baby. God no. He couldn't go through that again.

He got to his apartment and fell down on the faux Scandinavian sofa. He stared at the ceiling, his mind reeling. He totally forgot about going to work. His mind was in chaos.

Loving was losing, as far as Emmett's experiences went. You bring a baby into the world, you love it, put all your hopes and dreams on its small shoulders, then God hiccups and it's all gone. He couldn't stand the pain. Not again. Not ever. It was bad enough letting Jasmine in. What if something happened to her in childbirth? It still does, he knew. But a child? After J.R., he knew he could never go through that again. That mind-crushing, stomach-tearing pain. That pain that just keeps on giving.

Did he love Jasmine? he asked himself. Yeah, maybe. If he let himself, he knew he could. She wasn't Shirley Beth, not anything like her. Jasmine was a strong woman. A cop, for God's sake. But a child? A baby? He was fifty-five years old. What right did he have fathering a child at his age? But the good thing about that, he realized, was that chances were real good he would die before the child did.

He leaned forward on the sofa. Jeez, what a horrible thought, he said to himself. Finding good news in leaving a poor child fatherless! You're a sick bastard, Emmett Hopkins, you know that? he asked himself.

He fell back down, resuming his job of staring at the ceiling. Jasmine would be a good mother. And if he was with her, he'd have more of a say in the rearing of the child than he had with Shirley Beth. Hell, Jasmine was a cop, and he doubted she'd give up her job. So they'd share the child rearing. And, if it was a boy, it would only be like three or four years younger than Johnny Mac, Milt's boy. Maybe him and Jasmine could move up to Fall's Mountain, couple of houses up there been for sale for years. He knew Jean and Milt weren't having any more kids, and Johnny Mac could have a surrogate little brother, and his boy could have a big brother.

And, hell, what if it was a girl? He smiled, thinking about it. All pink and fluffy, with freckles like her mother. And her and Johnny Mac would have just the right years between them to someday get married. He liked that thought. He and Milt, fathers-in-law, and if they worked real hard at it and both of 'em lived long enough, they could be grandpas together.

He fell asleep with these thoughts on his mind, and woke up hours later to pounding on his front door.

He got up, rubbing the sleep from his eyes, yelling, "Hold it a minute! I'm coming!"

He opened the door to Jasmine. "Hey—" he started, but she held up a hand to quiet him.

She pushed past him and stood in the middle of the living room floor. It was her first time in his apartment, but she didn't even look around. "Don't talk," she ordered. "Just listen."

"Okay—"

"I said don't talk. I've made up my mind. I'm raising this baby on my own. You don't have to have anything to do with it. I've wanted a baby my entire life, and now I'm going to have one. I don't need you. Your money or anything. As far as the rest of the world will know, I'll say I went to an artificial insemination clinic." She took a deep breath. "That's it. I've said my piece. Good-bye, Emmett." And with that she headed for the door.

He caught her arm before she could get out. "My turn?" he asked.

"You don't have anything to say that would interest me," Jasmine said.

"Well, whether it interests you or not, I'm gonna say it." He took a breath. "When they said that this morning, I gotta admit I was scared shitless. All I could think of was J.R., and losing him. The thought of bringing another baby into the world, and maybe losing it, too, was just too much for me. But then I got to thinking, and chances are real good it won't happen to me twice. And I also got to thinking that losing you was something I didn't want to do. I got to thinking that maybe I love you. And maybe you love me.

I think maybe this has been more than sex. And I got to thinking that maybe we should get married, and have this baby together, and maybe buy a house on Mountain Falls Road—"

"Up there where Milt lives? Why?"

"Because he's my best friend, and Johnny Mac could be like a big brother to our little guy or gal—"

"Jean doesn't like me."

Well, that stopped his forward momentum. "What do you mean Jean doesn't like you?"

Jasmine sat down on the faux Scandinavian sofa. "She's always cold to me."

He sat down next to her. "Honey, I think you're imagining that."

"Oh, no I'm not! Don't tell me I'm imagining something! That's what Lester always said when I smelled perfume on him!"

He took her hands and got down painfully on his knees. "I'm not Lester and you're not Shirley Beth. And I don't care where we live as long as we live there together. Jasmine, will you marry me?"

She took his head in both her hands. "Oh, Emmett, this is gonna be rough on you, isn't it?"

"I'm tough. I can stand it. And it won't happen again."

She smiled. "No, it won't. This will be a happy, healthy, beautiful baby." She kissed him on the mouth. "Yes, Emmett, I'll marry you."

Second Tuesday ◆ Las Vegas

We were in Denise's dining room, eating take-out egg McMuffins, biscuits and eggs, hash browns, and anything else McDonald's had to offer.

We'd spent most of the previous night at the police station. The recording that Taylor had made of his father's conversation with Jimmy Broderick had helped seal Broderick's fate, and made it easier for him to confess it all to Mac Grayson. I told Grayson I needed to ask Broderick one question.

"What is it?" Grayson asked me.

"Personal. Just between me and Jimmy."

"You've got no right asking—"

I glared at Grayson. "Yeah I do. You had the wrong man, or don't you remember that?"

Grayson sighed. "Go," he said. "Ask. I don't care."

I went into the interrogation room and turned off the intercom. I knew Grayson and his henchmen were watching, but they wouldn't hear my question. Or Jimmy's answer.

"What do you want, Sheriff?" Broderick asked, his shoulders slumped, a picture of defeat.

"Just one question. One your mama asked me. I'd like to know for myself and for her. And for Denise. Did Walter Allen suffer?" I asked.

He frowned at me. "I didn't torture the man, Sheriff. I just shot him."

"Yeah, I know. But did he know it was coming?"

Broderick thought about it for a moment. "Well, he saw the gun. His eyes did sorta get big right before I shot him."

I thanked him and left, wondering at myself for asking. But in the end, I guess he did suffer a little bit, maybe not enough for Emily Norwalk, but at least he'd seen it coming. Knew he was going to hell.

Outside in the bull pen, Lieutenant Grayson tried to shake Burl's hand in apology, but Burl wasn't having any of it.

He said, "Since Larry Allen's no longer alive, I'm hoping the charges against me for beating the crap out of him are going to be dropped."

"Already done," Grayson said.

"What about the charges against my brother?" David Lee asked.

Gray sighed. "They're dropped."

"So, okay, what about that bail money?"

"Come on, son," Burl said, wrapping an arm around David Lee's shoulders, "we're going home."

"But—" David Lee started, then realized he was already outside.

After that, we'd gone to the hotel to see a startled but happy Maida, then Maida and Burl had taken Denise and the baby back to her house. We all agreed to meet up at Denise's in the morning.

Before I left the hotel, I made three calls: one to my wife, one to my office, and one to the airline for my reservation back home. The earliest I could get was the next morning. One more night at the Bellagio.

"I feel sorry for Detective Broderick," Denise said. "I wish I'd known about Belinda before I married Larry." She looked down at Carol Jean, sleeping peacefully in her baby carrier at Denise's feet. "Maybe not," she mused.

"I don't know what I'da done in his shoes," I said, "but the thing is, once you do one wrong, other wrongs get easier. I think that's what happened to Broderick. He took a man's life. How much easier is framing another man?" I shook my head. "I wish I knew what Larry said to Belinda Norwalk."

"Oh, I know," Denise said. Everybody at the table stopped eating and looked at her. With her eyes on her baby, she said, " 'You think I'd ever have anything to do with you and that bastard of yours? Probably isn't even mine,' " she said, her voice low, mimicking her late husband's. " 'But let me know when she gets old enough—I'll come pay her a visit.' "

We were all silent. She looked up at us and said, "At least that's what he said when I found out I was having a girl."

At that point, David Lee got up from the table and walked into the living room. He picked up one of the black leather slingback chairs and threw it through the front of the large-screen TV. "Rot in hell, Larry Allen," he said.

I GOT A taxi back to the Bellagio later that afternoon. I figured the Upshanks needed some family time together, and although I was family, I wasn't of the immediate variety. I thought it best to leave 'em be. Burl tried to go with me, something about a roulette table calling him, but Maida pulled him back inside and shut the door, leaving me on the outside.

I was feeling kinda blue, missing my own family, thinking about the Norwalks and the new pain they'd be going through, thinking about poor Belinda and her baby daughter. If Larry Allen had said those words, the words he'd said to Denise, then Belinda Norwalk must have believed them, believed that he'd come back someday and hurt her daughter. Believed that she wouldn't be able to stop him. So she took the only way out she knew.

I believe God gives us each a clean slate when we come into the world, but those slates can be sullied by paternity. Walter Allen had raised his son to be his spitting image, had taught him that women were the dirt beneath his feet, and told him he was more important than ordinary people. Some people, some really strong people, may have been able to fight those lessons, but I guess Larry wasn't very strong. He'd taken what he was taught and ran with it.

But his daughter had another clean slate, and that one would be written on by Denise and Maida and Burl and David Lee and a hundred other people who would love her and teach her and guide her. There'd be no Allen left in Carol Jean. Her big sister's slate was still clean, and would be forever. No one could write on it, the slate couldn't take it.

I was sitting in my room brooding and simultaneously thinking about dinner when there came a knock on the door. I opened it to find John Bob standing there. He had a big grin on his face.

"What's up?" I asked.

"Talked to Walter Allen's attorney, finally," he said. I ushered him in the room, and he took a seat on the bed. "Found out what's in the will."

"Looks like good news," I said. The grin still hadn't left his face.

"Well, he did have something in his will about Larry predeceasing him. He split his estate three ways: Melissa Greevey and Rita McReynolds—"

"That good-looking older waitress?" I interrupted.

"Yeah. The redhead. They each get a third. And they're supposed to share in the running of the hotel." He grinned again. "Should be some interesting catfights in the next few years."

"And the other third?"

"Goes to, and I quote, 'my grandchildren.'"

"So Carol Jean gets a third?" I said, grinning.

"*Grandchildren*, Milt. I don't think it'll take much for me to prove that Selena Norwalk is his grandchild, too. He paid a hundred grand to the child. I can do this with my eyes closed."

I grinned at him. "You're going to handle the case for the Norwalks?" I asked.

"If they'll let me. Denise won't fight it. Should be a cakewalk."

I stood up and hugged John Bob. He looked a little taken aback, until I said, "You're not as big an asshole as I thought."

He grinned. "Fuck you, Kovak."

AFTER A LEISURELY dinner with John Bob, David Lee, Michael, and Barbara Jo, we moseyed out into the casino and I remembered Emmett's ten-dollar bill. Black fourteen, he'd said. I bought a ten-dollar chip and placed it on black fourteen.

Two hours later I dragged myself to my room, my pockets filled with bills, hoping Emmett would want to keep his job after I paid him the four hundred dollars he'd won. And, thinking of money, I wondered how long I should wait before I hit Burl up for that six hundred dollars' worth of undies.